# WELCOME TO
# HEAVENLY HEIGHTS

# WELCOME TO
# HEAVENLY HEIGHTS

RISA MILLER

ST. MARTIN'S GRIFFIN ☙ NEW YORK

www.stmartins.com

Library of Congress Cataloging-in-Publication Data

Miller, Risa.
    Welcome to heavenly heights / Risa Miller.—1st ed.
       p. cm.
    ISBN 0-312-30180-4 (hc)
    ISBN 0-312-32615-7 (pbk)
    1. Americans—West Bank—Fiction. 2. Political violence—Fiction.
3. Land settlement—Fiction. 4. Jewish families—Fiction. 5. West Bank—
Fiction. I. Title.

PS3613.I5524 W4 2003
813'.6—dc21                                  2002031876

First St. Martin's Griffin Edition: January 2004

10  9  8  7  6  5  4  3  2  1

TO MY PARENTS AND MY HUSBAND

# ACKNOWLEDGMENTS

My deepest thanks to: Elinor Lipman, who beamed her eye on me and made this book happen—her virtues deserve a book of their own; Jill McCorkle, especially for walking me over to Ellie that Friday afternoon; the faculty at Emerson College; Joan Millman and Rosemarie Sultan; my agent, Lisa Bankoff, and my editor, Dori Weintraub, for their care and equilibrium; my parents, Dr. Melvin and Shirley Bulmash, for their resounding encouragement; my husband, Harry, and children, Leah, Saul, Sara, Ari, Miriam, and Eli, who provide the energy for this and all my endeavors.

WE WILL RAISE JERUSALEM
ABOVE OUR CHIEFEST JOY.

—Adapted from Psalm 137,
inscribed on top of traditional
wedding invitations

# PROLOGUE

ONE THOUSAND B.C.E., KING DAVID, SWEET SINGER OF ISRAEL, BOUGHT the heart of Jerusalem from Aravnah the Jebusite. He paid six hundred silver shekels.

Three thousand years later his descendants were still protecting the investment, building settlements, facts on the ground, making demographic rings high and wide as the mountain range. Heavenly Heights was the settlement closest to the stars, the crown of the Judean ridge.

At just that spot where the new two lanes entered the mountain, where the city bus drivers jammed down their accelerators pretending the entry curve was a parapet uphill, Building Number Four emerged. Number Four was the kind of building where, on Friday nights, when the husbands went off to *Shabbos* prayers, the women collected their porch chairs and sat together on the biggest balcony to shake off the weekday world.

Regional war? Not this week.

"This isn't *Shabbos* talk," said Tova, the newest arrival. She'd come, after all, for the religious badinage. If the entire planet was a face, the settlements were the brow and Jerusalem was the eye.

Or, if the entire planet was an eye, the settlements were the lid and Jerusalem was the pupil.

They talked like that until wide-breasted, zebra-striped birds circled the tops of the trees in the forest. The sun dropped into the mountains between glances and the helicopters dipped above the balcony as if they were looking for an invitation to a *Shabbos* meal. Then, in order to get down to real business, the mothers distracted the older girls, sending them off to different apartments for a baby bottle, a sweater, a diaper. Was it also a matter of heavenly decree that certain people found themselves together as neighbors?

"You mean you're wondering if now that we're all *home* we'll be able to stand living on top of each other like this," Debra said. Behind her head radar towers blinked a halo of red dots. Below, a trivet of roads floated in the half-light: to the east, Amman, Jordan; to the west, the Tel Aviv bypass; and to the south—hitching the place to its heart like a pulmonary system—the road to Jerusalem. There, one car toddled, a lonely *Shabbos* desecrater.

"My granny used to have words on that," Debra continued. "She used to say, 'Neighbors are like relatives. You don't choose them but you're sure obligated to figure out how to get along with them.'"

The mothers nodded, even the ones who didn't agree. They forced the children to put on the sweaters because a chill came in after full sunset when the clouds began their night position.

In the morning the clouds would lift off the balconies like heavy steam.

# GOOD, SWEET, MAYBE

TOVA ZISSIE.

The name meant good, sweet good, or good and sweet. Tova had three first cousins with the same name, including today's bride, each—as was the custom—named for their grandma, a third-generation Jerusalemite raised and married in two cavernous rooms carved out of a stone buttress fifteen steps from the Western Wall.

In family legend, sweet meant never complaining: in the siege of 1948, Grandma divided a one-egg omelette for her six young children and smiled. Good meant an instinct for the right counteroffense. In the last hour between surrender and evacuation, Grandma launched Psalms of David, *capitle* after *capitle*, line by line: ". . . if I forget you, O Jerusalem . . . and . . . Bring back the captives . . ." When the family slouched to America, Grandma expired like a fish out of water.

Grown now, the Tova Zissies used the weddings (and bar mitzvahs) to see how they compared to the original. And today, at least on the outside, like the bride and groom with an eye to a glorious future, Tova made a perfect match. One of Grandma's *capitle* Psalms had boomeranged in the Upper World and landed directly on Tova. In ninety days she and Mike were leaving for *Eretz Yisrael*—not as much the state of Israel, but the Land of Israel, the biblical promised portion. They were making aliyah, literally meaning going up, like going up a mountain: returning to the land, fulfilling a dream, reversing the exile. Going home.

Home! One damp, warm day last February Mike walked in from work—stalked in was more like it—and tipped the delicate balance between their Baltimore home of twelve years and the primordial home of three thousand. "It's time to pull up and go," he announced.

Tova didn't respond. She was used to Jerusalem dreams. Like every Orthodox Jew she pledged allegiance in all the prescriptions of daily life, from morning prayers to blessings after a piece of bread. Future aliyah was the hovering operative.

But Mike was serious this time and he dogged her around the kitchen: to the cabinet, the refrigerator, the microwave, back to the cabinet, and then to the table where, finally, they sat across from each other and shared a plateful of Triscuit pizzettes. Once they sold their house—he nudged her—they would have enough to buy a new place in *Eretz Yisrael* and still have their nest egg left over.

He was on fire that day, a visionary. Like a veil had lifted, he said when she asked what was going on: the future and the future-of-the-species were in their hands. And the *YESHA* council, already ten or fifteen years old, always needed virtuous voices like his; detail-focused minds, like his; hewers of ambition and ideology and technology, like him. *YESHA*, the Hebrew acronym for the biblical—and current—Judea, Samaria, Gaza. He could be a part—"What will we tell our children?" he asked. "And our children's children? All it takes is a plane ride and we don't go because of this?" Mike jumped up and toed the compressor vent built into the baseboard of the refrigerator. The compressor vent dislodged, hung off on one side. Couldn't the *YESHA* council live and breathe without them? She rose and toed the compressor vent in the other direction, flush again against the cabinet wall. Like forceps, Mike's little dramatics could pince Tova's nerves in their tender spots.

By the time she reached for another pizzette the Triscuits were stone cold and congealed, circling the plate in a half smile.

Out in the driveway, Tova smoothed the cleaner's plastic over the sleeves of her green bridesmatron's dress, the Tova Zissie dress. She bent into the car and hooked the metal hanger behind the passenger seat. There, in spite of the kids' peanut butter and crumbs, and splatters of apple juice, the car still smelled new and leathery. Tova loved the Camry, sky blue in the middle of the day, silver blue in the fallow light of this wet Baltimore morning. Without a second thought, though, she could give up the Camry for a better car. Why was it that much harder to apply the same principle when giving up one life for what was supposed to be a better one?

It had to be easier for Mike. Not only was he calling her in on the fantasy, he was making the career move he'd been dreaming of for years, turning his back on the whole American trend of onward and upward; Bio Optics and *The Wall Street Journal* had tracked his ascension since graduate school, exalted his promotions, and now interpreted his lateral move out of the company as betrayal. *"Project Managers Just Don't Quit."*

"Yes they do if they want to," Mike answered, snapping down the paper, impatient that they just didn't get it, again. He wasn't entirely quitting anyhow. He just wasn't going to make his job his life anymore. He would pick and choose his projects; there were fax machines and e-mail, even a laboratory or two in Israel if he really needed one. He was going to learn Torah. "And what are we really giving up?"

Tova, who pictured his success like a cresting wave and her Baltimore home like a safe shoreline, could invent a list, right on the spot.

Tova waited inside the Camry for Mike to close up the house. Leaning into the rearview mirror she practiced the Tova Zissie smile. At every family affair the Tova Zissies arranged a photograph together, and several weeks later, a Tova Zissie souvenir came floating through the mail slot.

In the family's eyes, Mike and Tova were heroes, venturing out on the Green line, protecting Jerusalem, spirited keepers of the flame.

But once the decision to go was made, they didn't argue politics or heroics, but their particular material needs. Tova tried an in-town strategy: if she was going to move at all, Tova hankered for sidewalks and a ten-minute walk to the library. Mike set his mind on open air and a mountain view. He wanted two more bedrooms and more savings left over; on the practical level the prices in the center of town reflected the agitated market, how the whole world wanted to live in Jerusalem's ancient borders! So they looked at commuting neighborhoods, a little to the north— settlements if you needed to be technical—and ended up buying in Heavenly Heights where a double apartment (still half the size of their brick colonial) cost a fraction of the same apartment in town. Add to that the government subsidies for the settlements. Then, finally, the mortgages there were underwritten by Someone—a mystery someone. An unidentified do-gooder well-wisher Godfather who wanted Judea settled and settled now. The Godfather and Mike were beckoning; Mike bribed her with every luxury she could ask for. Mike won; so how she designed! Mediterranean arches with Andersen windows. Marble floors, teak wood built-ins in the master bedroom, including wraparound built-in CD speakers. Two dishwashers and an Amana side by side with water and ice in the door.

But the material perks had a flip side. A week ago they'd received a letter that the water pipes in Heavenly Heights had been, as it was gently introduced, *altered*.

"Sabotaged," Mike said out loud. He could read between the lines; the infrastructure was laid ten years earlier by passive-aggressive local day labor trucked in from their little villages, before the contractors began to think twice and before the government abated *those* tensions by easing up visa restrictions and bringing in foreign workers, mostly from Thailand.

The letter continued; Mike had been right on target. Urgent! Now! If they wanted their water and their bathrooms and their kitchens, each home owner was assessed an extra $2,000 to extract the row of concrete bricks wedged into the water main.

Tova had cried. Not because of the money. They had more money than they'd originally figured after they tallied the stock options in Mike's company. She cried because of the vulnerability. The *perceived* vulnerability, Mike argued. Who said where they were safer? A person could get killed walking a street in Baltimore any day. Wasn't the same heavenly plan in force every place in the world? He was asking Tova to suspend the belief in her senses, her rationality; what she preferred to forget was that the parcel of—and around—Heavenly Heights had always been subject to some menace or another. Before 1948, fifty lonely *dunam,* it had been a tent-and-farm settlement with a burgeoning pickle factory. In the War of Independence the settlement was lost to marauders, cucumber plants singed to the roots. Even now, borders redrawn in 1967, Heavenly Heights was close enough to Jordan that a combat tank starting out in Amman when you boiled your water for coffee would have you serving to its corpsmen before you finished your own first cup.

When Mike finally appeared in the driveway, Tova's watch read 9:10. The wedding began in New York at two. Like all Orthodox weddings, from the invitations to the dance music to the rabbi's final blessings, Jerusalem was the theme of the day—its image more joyous than the joy of the bride and groom. Tova's own theme lay on her heavily—leaving home, making a new home. The kids, since breakfast, had been tucked away at Horowitz and Goldman, neighbors on either side. Their three colonials, just like their lives, looked like triplets from the curbside. Were they friends first? Neighbors first? She'd have to remake her whole life to make friends like that again.

Out on the beltway, past Havre de Grace, she wondered that the expression was cold feet. Her chill had begun, headfirst, immovable as an iceberg and just as submerged. Mike accelerated, switched lanes, switched back. In the backseat, next to the Tova Zissie dress, the baby's empty car seat rattled off the belt, all floppy without its ballast.

Mike stared straight ahead. He always had a look of deep concentration in the morning—the same look for prayers, Dear Abby, Orioles scores, tying a kid's shoes. Tova remembered when they'd met; she imagined the inside of his brain in three dimensions like the credits on *Star Wars*: big things, spinning in space, fitting together until a large picture emerged from the chaos. His first spoken ideas in the morning were grand, making him prone to hyperbole. "We're making history," Mike said, switching lanes again with the barest of glances in the sideview mirror.

Tova didn't argue. Instead she found the metal lever on the side of the seat. Feet against the carpet, she released the seat back and pushed herself into a reclining position. More than once it had occurred to her that what she thought was his strength was more like a vision, that all he was doing was matching his thoughts to some cowboy energy, but the depth hadn't been tested, neither for strength nor endurance.

He looked over at her. "Sleep," he said.

Wherever the energy originated from, when she felt depleted and he operated on a full tank she didn't mind his advice, even if it sounded like instructions. What he meant, anyhow, was the kind of sleep she wasn't getting anymore, the kind where consciousness blocked itself out, released, because these days, whenever she closed her eyes, instead of *that,* she rewound her life like a home video, the way the rabbis said—and the irony didn't escape her—it happened the moment you died. But she was just going away; her thoughts whined along and then, oversensitized to real sound even with her eyes closed, she absorbed the thud of the car seat when he braked, slightly, the throb of the wipers, the animal snort of a large truck barreling past her right window.

Eyes closed, a picture of Esther sprung before her, Esther as a baby, eleven years ago, lying in her crib when a sunbeam came across her face and Esther snatched it and broke it apart with her bare fist. Another Mike, she remembered thinking.

Then her camera-eye panned back for the long view: what was surprising was the lack of surprise in how much home they'd created for themselves in such a short time, how natural was the nesting instinct, layering so much emotion on top of the furniture and ambience, their decor of plastic and rubber, crib toys, squeezy noisy things, scallops of kittens, pink and blue bears. In her own parents' house she'd taken the home feeling for granted too.

Then, Tova fast-forwarded to the night before last when a raccoon outside had kept her awake. From where had he entered their lives? From the woods in the county a half mile away? He was homeless, a scavenger—scaring himself away by dropping the trash-can lid he'd pilfered with his own hands. There were no raccoons in Israel, except in the zoo near Tel Aviv. There wasn't even a word for raccoon in Hebrew, Mike told her. When they moved she could only guess what would be the scary things in the night. Tova would trade rodent for rodent, pest for pest.

The cadences aroused her, not soothed her, and she sat up again. The Camry took the tufts of fog easily, cutting through a whole fat quilt of it over the Delaware Memorial Bridge. They drove toward the New Jersey Turnpike. Tova relaxed into a small fit of sleep.

By the James Fenimore Cooper rest stop, her eyes were open for good. Outside the window the crunchy spring-yellow grass was turning industrial site. The fog turned into rain. The wipers couldn't clear the windshield of the pollution, the smut. Mike was more awake now, less thoughtful, more willing to chatter: her parents would arrive an hour early at this wedding hall—wedding mall (lately Mike let go of all his restraint against what he called "gross American materialism"). Her parents would arrive an hour early, wandering lobby to lobby, then greet Tova and Mike with a pushed-back hysteria from all their waiting as if Tova and Mike—by coming on time—had arrived late.

This would be the last visit with her brother. Tova brought the seat back halfway up.

They free-associated, of course, to Mike's parents. His father was sluggish lately, aging quickly, seventy-six to his mother's sixty-six, the ten years suddenly and for the first time cutting a hard wedge between them.

When would Tova tell her students? She'd been teaching English to new Russian immigrants for three years now and they depended on her. The thought, another point of disengagement, made her tired.

Their small talk made a fog of its own on the inside of the Camry. Mike leaned into the windshield and didn't complain. He could dance at this wedding all afternoon, drink a half-dozen *l'chayims*, then drive them back the same night. He would never mind if she just shut herself down and borrowed his energy, like a moon to a sun. He turned and beamed it on her. Tova smiled, the Tova Zissie smile, flipped up the passenger seat straighter-than-straight and looked out the window to study the exit signs.

# TEACHING AT THE GENETIC POOL

TOVA WOULD ANNOUNCE HER DEPARTURE TO HER RUSSIANS AT THE end of the semester, otherwise, in their drive *en rapport* they would finesse their lessons and overfocus on her. Of course, the way they scrutinized her, in fourteen weeks they would notice anyhow the lines on her forehead, which Esther called worry waves and which Sergei would swear, in combination with the under-eye gray, meant she was headed straight for kidney malfunction. In the Soviet Union, Sergei had been a doctor. Now, too old to retrain and too poor to play golf, he learned English.

Tova's Russians were Jewish stragglers, the infirm, old-fashioned kind; they came for economic opportunity and education for their children. They came to be like Tova. But only Tova the American, not the Orthodox Jewish Tova. Bleached of their own Jewish identities, and for all the personal comments they took liberties with, they never once acknowledged that Tova wore a marriage wig, or that her sleeves—even in the summer—always fell to her elbows and usually to the wrists. Tova concluded that it took a certain sensibility to religion to recognize its signs, and since her job was to teach English she never mentioned it. This being hidden behind a curtain, holding a rudder against the howling Diaspora wind, the tension of being the sub-culture (very Jewish) of a subculture (Jewish) was the real reason she'd finally said yes to Mike. Once she arrived in *Eretz Yisrael*, she wouldn't be a sub-sub anymore; in the neighborhood they'd chosen she'd even be one of the normals or dominants—wearing her marriage wig, even a marriage head scarf, as proudly as the black women here wore their braids and cornrows.

Funny, Tova called her students Russians. In Russia they were called the Jews. Here, Tova was an American—and she was venturing out to be a Jew.

Still, the American in Tova couldn't help spot the Russians at a mile in the Giant supermarket line. It wasn't the clothes, though that too—the over-belted slacks, the new leather-look sneakers. She and Mike would be spotted at a mile too.

But Tova envied her Russians the thrust of their decisions, their sparse, unencumbered material lives. How much easier is it to move with a samovar and a set of candlesticks in a sack on your back? Besides, they *had* to leave, the same way Jews had leapfrogged from country to country for thousands of years, though, if you asked Mike, they had to leave also.

Outside, if it was October instead of April, you would call the weather Indian summer. The day was hot and humid, the spring had looped into summer and back twice in several weeks. The cherry trees in D.C. had been lured to blossom early and the following week all that pink was covered in frost; the newspapers turned the blossoms into scandal with a philosophical twist: opportunity lost, hopes that were dashed.

She looked out at the class. The Russians lined up in the same seats they'd chosen the first day, knees together under their desks, raising their hands (when they didn't call out) straight off the elbow—former communists, Young Pioneers. When she first started teaching the Russians she was daily shocked by recognition. Their faces were entirely familiar and not because they were her students. She'd held a theory that there were only a hundred Jewish faces in the world—all the rest were variations on the root types. Sergei's eyes were mean as Uncle Jack's (father of Tova Zissie two). Like Uncle Jack, Sergei was an orthopedic surgeon. But Sergei had three gold teeth in the front of his mouth.

Lyudmilla Rosen looked like her oldest cousin, Tova Zissie one—hairline slightly retracted, smoky eyes that verged on the oriental, as if, after generations, some Khazar blood had asserted itself. On Lyudmilla's face, though, were little mosses of brown hair that jiggled when she laughed. But Lyudmilla—like a lot of these immigrants—didn't laugh often.

Standing at the blackboard Tova smelled a steamy smell that reminded her of the last water from the bottom of a coffeepot. The radiator, confused as the cherry trees but stupider, had turned itself on. Now the radiator hissed at her.

The first fifteen minutes of class loosened the English tongue, like stretching exercises before a morning jog. Tova asked them questions. "What did you eat for dinner? How did you cook it?" The second part of the question, when directed at a man, made him squirm. She had several spouse pairs there and not all of them sat together; others shared notes and turned in homework like one entity. As a teacher she resented the copying and sharing; as a wife she admired the solid couplehood.

Certain days, when they free-associated, the students competed to be the first to tell. Today, three students called out the news: *katyusha* rocket attacks in northern Israel. Tova's stomach danced.

Most Mondays, big news or not, they came into class with questions stored up from over the weekend. In the classroom they exploded, like sappers into a safety zone. Tova was their question woman, their arbiter of culture, their American. Yvegenia raised her hand. In 1961, Yvegenia worked the assembly line in a munitions factory, standing next to a young man named Lee Harvey Oswald. "On TV," Yvegenia said, "I heard this talk about the King. What is the King?"

"Who," Tova corrected. "Who is the King?"

Sergei slid forward to the edge of his chair, rocking his weight on the balls of his feet. This would be Mike in a classroom: all his energy and intelligence concentrated, looking as if he were preparing to launch. Sergei owned cultural trivia. The week before he'd asked a question about Spiro T. Agnew. "There is one king in America," Sergei announced.

The class turned to him. Yvegenia looked hurt. She'd wanted Tova to answer the question. She'd wanted Tova to *kvell* over her budding American culturalism. And when Yvegenia was hurt she became defensive. "Who-o-o?" she snarled at Sergei, the whole time looking at Tova for approval.

Sergei rolled his eyes and unbuttoned his sweater over perfect triangle shoulders and narrow waist that were hard to ignore. Sergei said he swam at the JCC every day, winter and summer. "In America there was one king. Elvis Presley."

"Is," Tova said. "Is one king."

"Was. Is. Excuse me." When Sergei made a mistake he apologized. Then he pushed against it to prove he was right anyhow. "Some people say he was, some people say he is."

"Is what?" Lyudmilla asked. "Is dead? Is alive? People go to his grave, think they see him places. People think all kinds of crazy things." She said the "th" like an "f," a speech defect, not an accent thing, Tova thought. People fink all kinds of fings.

"So who is the Queen?" Lyudmilla asked.

Tova looked around the room. Yvegenia was sulking. Sergei was quiet for a rare moment, stretching his shoulders as if the question meant nothing to him. All these adults reduced to schoolchildren unnerved her.

"Aretha Franklin," Tova said, regretting it the moment she said it. She didn't want to talk any more trivia. The radiator blew, clanged, hiccuped, and sizzled all at once, like a sidewalk entertainer. Tova sneezed.

Three hands shot up like salutes.

Yvegenia was back. "In America, what do you say when someone sneezes?"

In *Eretz Yisrael,* what do you say? Tova thought. She hadn't learned practical, modern Hebrew in her childhood Bible classes. She opened the top desk drawer, rooting for a tissue. There the evening class teacher stashed everything but—pens, sharpened pencils, plastic spoons.

*"Gesundheit!"*

Tova looked up. Who said that?

"Is *gesundheit* American?"

"German."

Yiddish? Tova wasn't sure. It was just Jewish to say *gesundheit.* What business did she have confusing them?

"Bless you. That's what you say in America." Lyudmilla swooped in for the rescue and Tova turned the word and the help into a teaching moment. "Bless you. That's correct. How do you spell 'bless'?"

"B-L-I-S-S," Yvegenia called out.

"Bliss is something else—entirely." Tova smiled to herself because irony in a second language was subtle, acquired. She wrote *bless* on the board and the word, as the words often did when she committed them to print, looked like a foreign language to her too. A sensation of fraud overwhelmed her. Her face burned hot from the neck to the top of her wig: here she was, committing herself to aliyah, the ultimate act of a Jew, and at the same time teaching American culture like an authority; telling her entire family she was going home when her home was right here, going off like a spiritual hero, her spiritual confidence buoyed with a stock portfolio and a nest egg of bio-tech stock options.

"Get out your *Azar*," she said, almost shouting. *Azar*—the grammar text. Last week they worked on present perfect tense. Today's lesson was present perfect continuous: actions or situations that began in the past and are still true in the present. Heaven help all these orphaned, open faces.

# WELCOME TO HEAVENLY HEIGHTS

ONE BALCONY ON NUMBER FOUR WAS EASY TO FIND: TWO FLIGHTS above ground level, a clothesline swung with girls' underwear and blouses. Stiff as plywood from a two-day cycle of dew and sun and the dry sauna heat of late summer, the laundry should have been taken inside after an hour. Here and there a man's sock curled on the balcony floor, a little nylon snake in the mountain dust.

Past the sliding-glass door that trembled a little on its tracks, past a scarred and chipped upright piano decked with a wedding picture in an olive wood frame, one Friday morning, Tova—who had abandoned her marriage wig for a new, blue cotton head scarf—sat with a second woman wearing a green denim head scarf. The two had paused from their *Shabbos* preparations and convened in the kitchen. Six weeks earlier, Tova and Mike and the kids had made their aliyah—returned to the Land, arrived *home*. Officially the jittery thing Tova was going through was called absorption. But was she supposed to absorb into something or was it supposed to absorb into her?

Watching Debra, who had lived in Israel fifteen years and whose apartment this was, Tova wasn't certain she wanted to know the answer. Like a strange country herself, Debra was the most curious blend of elements Tova had ever seen, definitely not one of the one hundred Jewish root faces on her Jewish map but definitely possessed of more Jewish soul than anyone she'd ever met.

Debra pushed her straw-colored bangs into the crown of her head scarf and lifted a pyramid of potato peels off the table. She rose and cast about for the trash can, mysteriously tucked behind the refrigerator. Finally placing the peels onto open newspaper spread on the cooktop, she offered a rejoinder from Old Country culture.

"You know you made a mistake before. 'Respect' was an Otis Redding song. First," Debra said.

"I remember—Aretha Franklin . . ." Tova heard the little quiver she'd developed at the end of everything she said. She was like a political cartoon with her feet in one continent and her head in another and the effort to steady the bridges drained her. Good thing Mike still had plenty of energy; she siphoned him daily, hourly. At the thought of siphoning, Tova found herself fingering the side of a red plastic bowl, full of water and the peeled potatoes. How did it balance on the edge of the table like that? Tova pushed the bowl to the center of the table.

Debra stood up straighter. With only the slightest movement at the hips, her sun-yellow, elastic-waist skirt took life beneath her, swirling like chiffon. "I sang 'Respect.' "

"Where?"

"There."

Tova stretched her neck as if she were looking for something. But this was a knee-jerk politeness (also Old Country culture), and even before Tova retracted her line of vision Debra pointed to her own head, then laughed at Tova's need to be so literal.

"There. You know, on the road I took off from that became the road not taken. Music was my ticket and so I took the left fork. I never guessed where to."

Tova had never heard it from Debra herself, but she knew the scratchy details from the neighbors: born and raised in Appalachia—Cumberland, Kentucky—Debra had set off like a bird in flight—singing, performing, choosing against more of that life, and becoming a Jew along the way. This mixed stew, the way Debra presented it, did she make it happen or did it happen *to* her?

"How about if I sing 'Respect' tomorrow night at the concert?" Debra said.

Would Debra really sing "Respect"? Should Tova believe her or not? "You're kidding me."

"I sure am." Debra laughed. "I can't wait to hear what you think of these concerts."

Debra had described them for Tova so many times that Tova could describe them back: a series of stand-ups, women singing devotional songs, and, in accordance with the customs of modesty, performing for an audience of women only. "You should see the women—some even pregnant—playing the sax, the drums."

"Okay," Tova said, not sure if the picture of the singing women was the okay thing, or if she'd assented, at least verbally, to Debra herself. Not that she was ready for that: Debra was, on one hand, so much raw material, her music the astral high notes. How could Tova figure all the contradictions in one package? Perhaps she wasn't ready for a phenomenon like Debra and it was her failure, or Debra was, well . . . she struggled back the formulations. Didn't the Sages clearly discourage negativity about other people? Tova couldn't sieve one word, anyhow, to clarify her reaction. Debra, meanwhile, bent over her sink, and began scrubbing vigorously at something, her posture humped, strictly charlady. Now her skirt stretched tight across the rear, outlining the back of her legs. Debra's constant transitions from grace to crudeness hurt Tova's eyes. Debra turned back and tossed another potato into the red plastic bowl. The splash wet Tova's lap. She peeked into the bowl. A child's brown fingerprints and bite marks ringed the edge of a couple of potatoes bobbing at the top.

From the moment of her arrival Tova found Debra equally repelling and attractive, equally suspect and superior.

Certainly Tova's perception had been wadded up in fatigue; after the good-byes, the eulogies in Baltimore, the kudos to their heroics, and after all the summing-up from friends and family and the quiescent feeling of having attended her own funeral— then came the next hard part: the plane, the customs, the security interview from the border police, and a mental fitness screening by the bureaucrats. In a holding pen at Lod airport, since she held the valise with all their documents, visas, credit cards, birth certificates, and social security cards, Tova finished the business while Mike took the children for *petel* water and cookies. Esther walked back with a cup of *petel* for Tova and when she handed it over she pointed to the man at the other side of the desk and said, "Why does his skin look like leather?" In her fatigue, Tova smacked her on the shoulder. Where had Esther suddenly gotten this big mouth?—even if the man's face did look like an old wallet—and Esther refused to look Tova in the eye for an hour.

When the cabdriver understood they were going to Judea, he demanded a fifty-shekel surcharge. Turning northeast out of the airport, he touched his fingers to a dashboard picture of the tomb site of Rabbi Shimon Bar Yochai, renowned miracle-worker, and he rolled up his windows.

When they arrived at Number Four, the cabdriver unloaded their suitcases and cartons off the roof rack and scattered them across the curb, the entire width of the Number Four lobby. If Tova understood him correctly, he wanted extra money if he was to stack the cartons. "*Ta-ya-rim?*" he asked. Tourists?

"*Olim,*" she'd snapped, immigrants by choice. Heroes.

He laughed at her.

Debra materialized from the lift door, fluent and facile as if she were walking onstage. But she snarled at the cabdriver till he drove off, and then she said—twanged—to Tova, "I'll take those things if you're nervous."

Nervous had been a generous word.

Esther said too loud, again, "Why does she sound like she's yodeling?"

"Quiet!" Tova said. Esther was right but Tova had also heard something else—that Debra's twang ascended in a scale, like an aria where there was no real end.

Then a cluster of girls in blue skirts and white blouses appeared. They were Debra's, all seven of them, and they dragged the suitcases and boxes into the lift.

Later, Tova noticed the girls made a cardboard fort from the first of her unpacked boxes, by the entrance to the bomb shelter. They huddled, shoulder to shoulder, eating what looked like raw, peeled potatoes. Debra called them up for dinner but they ignored her. Tova remembered thinking it odd they could hear such a voice and nullify it as if it were the voice of any average mother.

Tova couldn't resist one good poke at a potato bobbing in the red bowl. The potato spun, buoyant as a bumper boat, and righted itself, bitten edge up.

"Clara's teething," Debra said, pointing to the potato. "Don't worry."

Why should Tova worry about Clara teething? What she wanted to do was talk about herself, confess: three times that week she'd run to her English-to-Hebrew dictionary to find the translations. And all the words had been stress words: anxiety, confusion, tension. Debra would say, "What was the use? Look them up, say them once, forget them right away." Tova had told her Russians the same thing: you had to acquire the language holistically. Tova squirmed, looked at her watch, almost noon. The boys could be picked up from *gan* in an hour, Esther from camp, and they needed lunch—in their former life a benign activity. Of course Esther didn't like the crust on the bread they baked here. And, sharp-eyed as ever, it had taken Esther only one day to notice that the other kids got chocolate spread in their sandwiches.

"Forget the chocolate spread," Tova had told Esther. "Even though you must change some things, there are some things you can't change." The words had no sooner come out of Tova's mouth when she saw them splatter at her feet. Outside, on one of the constant building sites, a tractor beeped its backward roll. Tova looked over at Debra; another transition: Debra's face was alert like a fine animal, responding to noises a forest away.

# BRED IN THE BONES

1957

DEBRA'S GRANNY WAS A DIVINER. IF A GIRL CAME FROM OUTSIDE THE family, Granny would tell her, in a second, who she was and what would be instead of spending her childhood with a question mark on her brow. But all Granny would tell Debra was what Debra already knew: a dead mother, a long gone, dead Jewish father.

Debra and Granny sat on the porch glider, thigh to thigh. Nine months a year they stared at Pinnacle mountain; Pinnacle mountain staring back at them. Under its high, hooked shadow, generations of backwoods women had gone from cradle to grave in a cycle. This night they were handpicking the pits out of the citrons. The fruit was bone-hard and didn't juice when you handled it. Two citrons made a tongue-turning jelly, and if they got a third fruit off the tree, they brewed liquor so tangy even Uncle Bunt lost his breath from it.

What was outside the citron wasn't inside: the heaven smell and the thick yellow skin could fool you. What was inside was really the essence. The citron tree grew in the kitchen between the stove and the wall and Debra loved the citron tree because it was the only concrete thing she grasped of her father, besides her very self.

After her parents were married, but before she was born, Debra's Jewish father drove up with his fin-tail car and unwrapped this citron tree from cotton wool. He was a botanist, haled from Cincinnati to work for the U.S. Forest Service. Naturally, Granny was the first one to see because she knew every herbaceous plant in the woods. And he knew every medicine name for them. Together they counted 126 plants, and he thought there was money to be made. Granny pronounced Mr. Aaron Levy's name the way it was written, with two flat, long "a" s—ay-ay rone.

If Debra could explain herself to Granny, she would tell her the souls weren't mixing inside her; they were wrestling inside her. If she told Granny she was mistakable as a citron Granny would spoon her ten portions of fenugreek tea from her boiling-up pot, hot, purple-black tea that tasted like fire and mint. But fire couldn't put out fire.

"Had you ever seen a Jew before Mr. Levy came around?" Debra asked. Getting information from Granny was hard as prying open the slats of a packing barrel, but she never knew when Granny would let go a little.

"No. Never," Granny said.

Debra bent to her citron. Her fingers smelled like lemon candy, but she knew not to lick them.

But Granny continued. "I had these pictures from the Bible—dark, crooked, bent. Mr. Levy wasn't far from it, I have to confess, but his singing voice made up for it all. Did I ever tell you Mr. Levy had an opera singing voice and he explained his name meant that his people were the singers when the Israelites had their Temple in Jerusalem? His people were in charge of the worship music there."

The music! The worship music. Debra never heard that before and her chest jumped just to hear it. "Granny, tell me what's to be with me." It was more a whine than a question.

But Granny took it as a serious request and she wouldn't look Debra in the face directly, which always meant that what she was about to say needed some interpretation but she wasn't going to give that too. "Girl, what's bred in the bone can't be beat out of the flesh." Then Granny suddenly slid way back on the porch glider. Debra's feet lifted off the floor and the glider struck against the porch wall, as if the glider were holding its breath.

# UNDER THE HEAD SCARVES

THE ELEVENTH MONDAY MORNING IN *ERETZ YISRAEL* TOVA STUCK HER entire hand into the garbage disposal of the dairy sink. On top of organic slush, pulped to a cream, a layer of onion peels completely befuddled the grinding mechanism. The motor wouldn't turn over.

The plumber—the *installator*—was a Russian immigrant who spoke English. Who had taught him, Tova wondered, to say "you" in that accusatory, haughty fashion? The *installator* could afford to be an independent man; if you asked any Israeli mother what a son should do for a living the potential of the *installator* made a mother's eye gleam. As he bent under the sink, full torso into the cabinet, Tova heard him click the red emergency button. As if the problem—or Tova—were so simple. The red button did nothing. The *installator* crept out of the cabinet, backward and on all fours, like a giant spider. When he stood up he opened his toolbox in disgust. "Why did you install such a thing in the first place?" he asked.

The nerve! Tova thought for the tenth time. Chutzpah, she translated to herself, as she paid him, as she showed him to the door. She ran down to tell Debra.

Debra made her first comment after Tova finished telling the entire story, including the better, imagined rejoinders.

"Forget the customs and the Ministry of Absorption and the *bureaucratzia*. Now you've really arrived," Debra said. "Everyone has an *installator* story." With that, Debra dismissed the whole conflagration and, rising to the kitchen sink, began to wash a stack of paper cups, paper cups with girls' names inked on their sides. Tova understood why she washed the paper cups instead of throwing them away; what she wanted to ask her (but didn't) was how she washed them without washing away the names.

At that moment, Debra's husband, Dave, walked in, cardboard carton on his hip, breaking into a once-over of nervous gestures. He pulled his white shirt at the waist, retucked it, centered his belt, stretched his neck. "Will you be happy, Debra?" He'd been next door at the Burgers' apartment sale. The Burgers were unsteady and taking stock. They spoke about returning to Chicago, giving up, they said, after all their bad *mazel*: three car stonings in a row. In one they were ambushed and knocked off the road. Two hospitalizations for their toddler, eye surgery for the baby. Rumor had it that the Godfather was trying to forestall the Burgers by forgiving three months' mortgage payments. The Burgers might recant, go back anyhow.

Debra wiped her hands on her skirt and smiled. Her skirt did that swirl thing around her knees again. Tova jumped up, curious. She was drinking her third coffee of the day here, getting her third pearl of wisdom for the day here. She knew what a new settler brought. What happened when a settler was reconsidering?

Dave slid the box down on the kitchen table. "I've got some electric curlers. And . . . a karaoke machine. You said you wanted the karaoke." He looked at his new neighbor, "Oh, hello, Tova."

He laughed. He was used to her visits but had a habit of banking hellos as if to make each greeting a surprise. "I also got the indoor grill. You told me to try and I did it!" He pulled out a George Foreman, brown grease-streaked, and held it up—a trophy.

Tova caught her curiosity as it turned to shame: she was a voyeur!

Was it the husband? the wife? Most couples, Tova observed, just like Mike and her, had a *drag-er* and a *drag-ee*.

Debra set the karaoke machine next to the potato bowl and fingered the mike, smiling. Dave finished spreading the entire contents of the box on the kitchen table. A *101 Dalmatians* calculator, Legos—large and small. Nancy Drew books. Harry Potter, which some parents allowed, others didn't because the wizardry threw them. Debra nodded approval—to everything—and as soon as Dave emptied the box he reloaded. When he tried to slip the karaoke in, Debra grabbed it back and centered it on the kitchen table next to the potatoes.

Then, before he picked up the box again to head off, he scratched his head vigorously at the side. "Debra, I'm crawling again," he said, his voice rolling, afraid.

For a minute Tova didn't understand what he was talking about.

Debra exploded. "Darn it. Wouldn't you just figure it. That means I've got 'em too."

Tova was puzzled. Were they talking about the children?

Debra turned to Tova. "Possibly the biggest challenge about living here." She pulled something out of Dave's hair, threw it on the floor, stomped her foot.

Tova looked at the floor and didn't see anything. She bent down. Still nothing. Then she saw Debra working on Dave's head, pinching against something invisible.

Head lice!

They had head lice in the States, a medical problem all the families took care of immediately. No one walked around with them.

"Oh, it's too much," Debra said. "I don't have time for this. Not before my concert." She turned to Tova. "Want me to check your hair?"

"I don't mind leaving while you ladies lift your head scarves," Dave said. He carried the box out to the balcony. After setting it beneath the hanging laundry, he scuttled down the bedroom hallway.

Debra took Tova's hand and pulled Tova onto the living-room sofa. The back of Tova's head cricked where Debra pinned Tova's neck on her lap. Tova smelled the sour starch of old potatoes on Debra's hands and the uric smell of a body that had been at labor since early morning. The way Debra split the back hair of Tova's scalp and walked her fingers on Tova's head reminded Tova of baboon mothers in *National Geographic*.

Maybe they were baboon mothers. Or maybe Debra was but Tova wasn't going to be.

For all Mike's prompting and all his spackling in of her weak spots, she thought she'd achieve spiritual ascension. But—beautiful music made by a woman with head lice? Back in her apartment, Tova began *Shabbos* thinking that if she had to yield to another new and weird thing she'd blow like a manhole in a comic strip or a lid to a pressure cooker.

She could not go to the concert, she told Mike. No, it wasn't a better-than-thou thing, she said, he could say what he wanted. But when he did, and he told her to tough things out, the argument mottled down to a script so obvious she could have written it before they moved: she heard herself complaining that she wanted to be home. Yes, she knew she was home, she answered, yes, she knew better. But the getting there wasn't what she'd call arriving someplace.

You've got to be *somewhere,* Mike said. That's when she answered that Debra was strange and she didn't want to go to Debra's concert, which cartwheeled them back to the opening act. What was the relationship between making a new home and going to Debra's concert? Mike wanted to know.

Tova wondered the same thing; over *Shabbos* the problems squeezed themselves out together at the end of the tube that was her brain; by Saturday night Tova stood at the kitchen sink where the *Shabbos* pots were already stacked and draining, the dishwasher was humming and gusting through a cycle, and the view of what she knew and what she could control steadied her. She filled the kettle and drizzled hot water across the granite. *This is home,* she rhythmed, trying to convince herself, *this is home.* She rubbed down the countertops with a store-bought rag made of mystery shiny material. Who'd thought to pack rags? Who'd thought she'd miss rags? Those repositories of family history: Esther's first Florida T-shirt, Mike's old terry robe he'd thinned at the seat from all those years sitting, sitting in the same place.

Tova wrung the store-bought rag over the sink. When it puckered down to a synthetic walnut she threw it under the cabinet. It landed with a thick thud. Next, Tova washed—no, did *spongia—* on the floor, with a stick that instead of a mophead on the end had what looked like a windshield wiper. For openers she soused the floor, which could have been fun except raking back the dirt and slosh was annoying, and hard.

Meantime, Mike tucked in the two boys, one in his little trundle with the side rails, the other incarcerated in his crib. Lucky them, their transitions were contained in one room. First, they called out to Mike loudly, their first move in the ritual release of consciousness. Then when they decided Mike wouldn't come back, each stuck a thumb in his mouth. Tova could hear tense sucking, memories of better moments consoling the present; the suckling child was all over the Psalms of David, the catchall metaphor for rootedness—physical, emotional. In minutes, as every night, she heard the boys' soft, irregular snoring.

Esther was able to sink roots like a weed. Sure, she'd have her first sharp, vocal responses, but then Esther never thought about the strange things another minute. It took her less than a week to fit in the nighttime rituals of the older kids, playing ball at the dead-end next door. They started the game when the day began to cool off and the men and the boys were on their way to *mincha* (afternoon) and *maariv* (evening) prayers. Between *mincha* and *maariv* the men would learn Talmud and the boys would wander out from shul. A few of the boys with lenient parents joined the girls and the game got a lot rougher: Esther knew the other kids well already: who hit the ball hard, who hit the ball low, who hit unfair. At some point, she would have to speak to Sandy and Nathan about their son Yossi. In one week, Yossi hit Esther with a ball twice—once in the face, once in the chest.

Tova walked over to the window and looked out at the dead end. In these ball games Debra's Shira had this grace, the grace of her mother, moving her body in waves and ripples so that no one could get her out. The delicate girls sat on the curb and cried. Neither Esther nor Shira was one of the delicate girls.

Tova walked to her front door and listened: no activity out in the hallway. Maybe no one else was going. No, that was a lie. Everyone else was going and no one else had the same kind of problem with Debra as she. Did they see something she didn't, or not see something she did?

Tova walked back into the kitchen and she heard Debra call

her girls from her kitchen window. "Change clothes, right now." Tova heard it, that lilt. That cadence. That something she couldn't figure out what it was. Tova put her hands over her ears, hummed out loud to herself.

Maybe the marrow of the situation was some kind of defiance. But Tova had nothing to defy and anyhow she would recognize defiance in a minute. She stared it in the face with those bedtime "no"s from Esther.

Resistance? Something more like resistance. But to what?

Number Four started pumping. Even the lift screeched with excitement.

Tova heard the girls scramble and slide into the foyer, running in to change clothes. Esther walked into the kitchen, red-faced, panting. She walked over to the kitchen sink and threw water onto her face. Then she grabbed a fresh mystery rag out of its cellophane.

Tova snatched the rag out of her hand. "For cleaning things, not faces." She handed Esther a paper napkin. Out in the hallway she heard women's voices. Doors slammed and echoed. Down on the blacktop, one car started. Another group billowed up to the bus stop. Yes, all the women and girls in the building were going to the concert. Esther hooked Tova's eyes with her own, sharp with instinct for hesitations and soft spots; in these six weeks Esther had become *extra* sharp—animal sharp.

"Aren't we going?"

To Esther's credit, it was a question, not a truth-or-dare statement. Esther was as yet a child and her world valanced by "yes" and "no," power, approval, parents, punishment, an active and passive at the same time.

Tova wasn't much different. "Get ready. We're out the door in five minutes."

For all the rumble of to-go-or-not-to-go, Tova missed a technical point. The concert didn't belong to Debra. The main act was the choir and accompaniment of the Gush Etzion women, who were supposed to be singing first, but the tunnel road to Jerusalem was shut because the cars were getting shot at, and though it should have taken twenty minutes it took an hour and a half to get into town. As Debra stepped onstage, the Gush women finally hoofed in, wearing identical denim skirts to the ankle, carrying cases of horn instruments, and shooshing back their excitement with a pageantry of forefingers to lips.

Debra started singing and she got everyone's attention by dunking the first note. But she was only preparing to launch. When she brought up the note, she brought it up like a window-wide call to dinner. Behind her, two pregnant women Tova didn't recognize were rigged out in identical black jumpers. They piped sax and keyboard, seven high notes synchronized, which hovered as Debra held hers—Tova counted, seven, yes, it sounded like "Respect." Then, she must have been mistaken because on the eighth note, when the scale rebounded, Tova recognized a *Shabbos* song: "Peace Be Unto You." Debra and her women bent into the mikes and their looping white head snoods tumbled around their shoulders like natural hair.

Then Debra's voice dipped and regulated and she spun out more *Shabbos* regulars: "Rest and Joy," "My Soul Thirsts."

Tova couldn't pin down the sound to one thing. Their music spliced and reglued, like a picture you made with a puzzle: a little Celt, fizzy as citrus fruit, a little bluegrass that was clear and melancholy, an edgy klezmer with a bite of wanderlust, forced wanderlust. Tova looked down and picked at a fleck of something white on her lap. When she looked back upstage, she looked up to a trompe l'oeil. As Debra hurled into "Blessed Is the Most High," Tova saw a huge dot matrix of black lice, dropping onto Debra's shoulders, draping, making a shawl. Tova gave up on herself in a minute. Go or not go; home or not home: they weren't the issues anymore. She had gone. Was there. And she was seeing something and missing it at the same time. She blinked. Of course the lice shawl disappeared. The real question was what was it she should be seeing instead?

In a reflex that she knew then and there was in fact a type of resistance, Tova tapped Esther on the arm and said they were leaving, immediately. They hopped outside and a city bus was practically waiting for them at the corner. Esther was unnaturally quiet and Tova braced herself for pointed questions she'd have to deflect with her dander up, but it turned out Esther was tired, real physical tired. She kept Esther moving long enough until they transferred buses at the Central Terminal, when Esther laid her head across Tova's stomach and hunched across the seat into a light sleep, her mouth open and wet on Tova's skirt.

The bus twisted up out of the corners of the city. In Jerusalem when Saturday night escorted out the *Shabbos* Queen, there was a little trail left, like afterflash when you closed your eyes. Even near midnight the navy sky sparked like a dawn or a twilight. Young people laughed on the sidewalks. Singles, groups, occasional couples, gathered at the pedestrian mall in town or strolled everywhere else. They had no fear of crime; night monsters were different in this country. Esther scrunched up tighter and Tova completed the curl with a mother hug around her rump. Until she felt a sharp prick at the top of her shoulder. "It'll hurt her neck. Sit her up so she doesn't get bent." It was a young, Hershey-skinned woman, with stone-encrusted rings on every finger of each hand, including her thumbs.

"No, it will pinch her spine," said the old man across the aisle. The collar of the white *Shabbos* shirt he still wore fanned wide open and lay across his shoulders like military epaulets.

"She should put on a sweater," said another dark woman, two seats forward.

Tova clutched Esther tighter around her rear, making a human shield with her forearms. But lumping Esther up woke her. She sat straight, wiped her mouth with her sweater, and then fished the sweater around her shoulders. She smiled back at the woman with the rings. The other passengers sat back, satisfied. But not Tova. Were they chiropractors? Orthopedists? What made these strangers think they could tell her how Esther should sit?

"We're all each other's kids," the bus driver said.

Was he talking to Tova? She looked to the front of the bus, expecting to meet the driver's eyes in his foot-long rearview mirror. But as his face furrowed roadward he continued counseling, "That's how people are friendly here."

Too friendly, Tova thought. But it hadn't escaped her that Esther took cues well and she never lost herself. In fact, she became more of herself. That seemed to be the job requirement.

By the time they got back to Number Four Tova's brain rattled more than it had in weeks, regressed to that just-arrived feeling. Her legs paddled as if her feet had been chopped off at the ankles. Mike and Dave were at the kitchen table eating leftover *cholent* and cold chicken. They'd baby-sat while they studied some esoterica on meditation. The book was pushed away but still open on the table. Mike steered Esther into her bed.

Tova looked for a book with which to read herself to sleep. She found an Agatha Christie. Though she had read them all, she couldn't recall a single plot. This book was called *Nemesis*. Miss Marple complained about the quality of newspapers and wondered if her gardener took too many days off. A stranger wandered into her garden with a question about flowers. Tova flipped to the last page. Since she was a girl she had the peculiar habit of reading endings first. Wasn't that a most human drive, to beg off the discovery and tension of a read? That need to know, understand, predict. Control.

An hour later, Mike came into the bedroom, trying to move quietly, although he was bursting with a kind of jumpy man-energy he got after group things—like ball games in the Old Country. He was surprised she was awake. "But relieved not to look for pajamas in the dark," he said, switching on the lamp.

By the time he turned off the lamp Tova lay in bed, getting it, finally, winnowing down to pertinent questions: all this time she'd thought the hard part was the separating, the move. What she needed was another arrival. Arrival, Act II. It wasn't as if she were resistant to the spiritual. She wouldn't be here if she were. But the theme of Act II was some kind of a change of perception. If this was really a play, could she use the name *Nemesis*? Or, better, the very definition: how to make a strange place your home. Tova spent the rest of the night feeling as if she were a speck of dust, lying in bed under a canopy sky, her legs cramping.

Next morning, Shira knocked on the door before school to ask for a cup of brown sugar—which Tova hadn't yet figured out how to buy. She didn't know what the package looked like. No, she said, she didn't have any. The girls wanted to do something for their mother. The concert had been so wonderful.

Shira took a big bite—top to bottom—of a peeled white fruit she had in her hand. The girls wanted to make their mother butterscotch brownies. Her favorite. They also needed baking soda.

Tova knew how to buy baking soda. It came in a little sack. Tova bent into the pantry and when she stood up again straight she realized that her legs and feet were planted. Steady. She wanted to tell Shira she was sorry, but to unlodge in any social way what she'd been thinking since before the concert till then was like coal mining, with the lights out. Tova would just be a good neighbor, the best she could be. She would pour some baking soda into a Baggie, maybe a paper cup. She laid the baking soda on the countertop. Shira grabbed the whole sack, hopping out into the doorway in two steps, like a quick bird.

"Did you enjoy last night?" Shira said. She was almost to the stairwell. Shira waited for an answer and settled her chin against her fruit. It was Debra's chin. This quick bird was Debra's girl.

Tova lifted her own chin in an answer, shooing her away. Outside the building there were small human sounds, a baby crying. A toddler laughing. Tova looked out the window. Jamal the delivery boy drove up in his boss's Mitsubishi van. He always carried the food crates high on his upper back and the kids said he urinated at the backs of the apartment buildings. Tova Zissie would be the good and *sweet* neighbor and she would make generous formulations with an eye to the good. Home was in the details. Details were like bricks; people were the mortar. Or maybe it was the other way around. She heard Jamal slam the door to the van and shuffle into the lift.

———

As soon as she saw the hydroponic cauliflower in the supermarket, Tova knew what to do. She heard it was coming and there it was that week, in the produce section three days before *Shabbos*, four days since the concert. Hadn't Debra, in her wisdom, told her the hydroponic vegetables were on their way? Hadn't it been Debra who had taught her about cleaning vegetables here, anyhow? Everyone knew there were countless prohibitions against eating bugs and crawling things and really only a couple of prohibitions against eating pork. And hadn't Debra—the first day—brought her down a vegetable brush and a plastic squirt bottle of aseptic pink rinse? The farmers here don't use bug spray, she had said. And they use human fertilizer on the potatoes. And when Tova had finally settled down to cook in her new kitchen, she dug and scraped the brown gook she would have sworn was mud. She made it a habit to breathe through her mouth. But with the hydroponic cauliflower there was no fertilizer and no dirt. No need to search for bugs. Just a light wash sufficed.

Tova could do a lot of things with cauliflower. First, she tried frying it, dipping small pieces in egg and then rolling it in flour with spices. Her grandmother had made it this way. But Tova couldn't figure out how to get the breading to stick. Then she tried boiling and mashing the cauliflower with a little tofu. Low-calorie, mock potato salad. Her mother's recipe. But the best recipe she'd gotten from Sandy—Yossi's mother—the cauliflower marinade with carrot and red pepper, wine vinegar and bay leaf. It was Tova's idea to add the cracked green olives. She took two bowls and divided the marinade in half, then, thinking about it again, put a little more than half in one of the bowls. She covered this one with plastic wrap. She would take it to Debra for *Shabbos*.

She waited until the next morning, Friday morning. She hadn't visited Debra in a week and she'd noticed how it hadn't been good for her, how proportionately her anxiety had grown.

Tova stepped out on her balcony. There on the crest of the farthest mountain, overlooking the two-lane from town, was the summer palace King Hussein had started to build before the Six-Day War when he thought Judea would be his backyard. He'd built the pillars, the facade, everything from the outside-in, and then after Judea was liberated in '67 the palace stood hollow and now he was dead.

Then Tova heard a voice, Debra's voice, laughing and then trilling privately. Tova tiptoed to the corner of the balcony where no one could look up and see her, but she could look down. She looked over the edge. Debra was hanging out her laundry.

It took a lot of effort, a lot of talking to herself to move her leaden feet. Tova forced herself out to the hallway, pressing the button for the lift, but decided to walk down instead. Some marinade sloshed up through the plastic wrap onto her shirt.

Dave met her at the door. "Debra is outside," he said. The laundry hung on the balcony like another world. Tova entered between two tablecloths.

"Here, this is for you. I made it for *Shabbos,*" said Tova, holding out the bowl. The box of odds and ends from the Burgers lay on its side in the corner; the Nancy Drew books in a stack on the porch floor. Could Debra have any idea why she was bearing a gift?

"Great," said Debra. "Thanks." She unclipped a wooden clothespin from one of the tablecloths, and repinned it to hold the corner of a blouse. "Distributing the wealth," she said, and Tova thought she was talking about the cauliflower salad because the hydroponic stuff was, after all, triple the price of the regular, but Debra was referring to the next clothespin that as she spoke flipped off her finger and dropped straight down onto Sandy's balcony. Tova looked over the railing. There it lay on the marble-chip tile, between Yossi's soccer ball and Yossi's skateboard.

"Always seem to lose a couple," said Debra. "I'll never see that one again. But hey, this salad looks pretty good."

So did Debra, Tova thought. A heavenly singing hillbilly lice-bearing earth mother. And Tova would never say it again to herself or anyone.


That night, after her *Shabbos* meal, Tova went out to her balcony alone. As she flattened a porch chair, Tova had an idea. She had read that if you sit still and look you can see one shooting star an hour. Mike said that besides that, Rabbi Shapiro had mentioned that this lunar month, *Av*, was auspicious for shooting stars.

Esther crept out with a blanket, in one of her random and unexplained attempts to be in Tova's good graces, do what her mother did. Esther lay on her blanket and said she saw one thing, perhaps a shooting star but it was so quick that she didn't know if she had really seen it.

Tova heard Dave and Debra and the girls eat a later meal. Dave prayed at a visiting Breslover minyan, with the Hasidim of Rebbe Nachman, the Dead Rebbe, where there was song and transcendence very late. Tova heard the *ping!* of the silver wine cups as Shira helped clear. Then the chink sound of stainless steel on china, then laughter. Sounded like Shira spilled soup on her foot. Then, while Tova was watching for stars, she heard their *Shabbos* songs, beautiful and harmonized. Dave and Debra and the all-girl choir, she smiled to herself. She had heard it before.

Tova continued to scan the stars but saw none in an hour. Sitting outside she felt filled up with goodwill toward her neighbors. If she could only withhold judgment and interpret their personalities like a family member, she could release something in herself.

Yossi slammed a door downstairs and his parents, Sandy and Nathan, yelled at him. If Tova were his parent, she would yell at him too. He went out anyhow, with the pitched arch voice of a pre-teen—a few words and then a question mark. She heard Debra and Dave finish their meal and sing the after-blessing. *"Ba'marom yilamdu, alay'hem v'alenu"*—"in the heavenly heights may they seek our good." They sang like that two floors below and instead of the stars Tova saw their music.

Esther had fallen asleep on her blanket. Tova began to get ready for bed, finally calm, folding and stacking the porch chairs to keep them dry against the morning dew. Then something caught her eye: the night birds, she thought at first, flying to their nests in the city. But then they lifted up, chaotically, like leaves driven loose, caught in a breeze off the mountains. When they flew past her railing she saw they were hooked, and silver-black, and they twisted straight up in a funnel, moving. The notes. Tova ran to the edge of the balcony and looked down over the railing to Debra's balcony to see if that was where they were coming from. But she knew that she knew it was so.

# A REAL HUMAN AMERICAN

THE WEEK BEFORE ROSH HASHANAH DEBRA SAID TO TOVA IN AN intimate way that didn't pretend to be a question, "You brought it all with you."

Tova answered, "Of course." They'd packed a forty-foot shipping container at the curb of their old brick house in Baltimore, waved it good-bye after two days' loading, greeted it again from the back side of a fenced security lot near Haifa's dock. They'd needed a lawyer to translate the bill of lading and to negotiate the customs. That was before they took delivery—which they were waiting for still.

But Debra wasn't talking about the *things*. She'd meant the personalities. "And the personalities are like seeds."

True: Tova's family was turning—preternaturally—each into some kind of animal: Tova had become a ladybug, skitting here and there, unable to land, and Esther, a lusty cat, with a high-minded caterwaul. The boys—was it their age or the atmosphere?—like puppies they tumbled and nipped to pass the tension. Mike, energy cresting the way people do when they imagine they control their fate, rode the next risk, tying up all their money in tech stock options, then struggling midnight faxes to their broker. Mike: a stressed and worrying crow cawed to the simplest questions. If that's what they turned into, what were they before?

That *Shabbos*, the setee of the women concentrated on this problem. This particular night the radar tower was dark, as were the lights on the new two-lane, and not a single helicopter swooped or circled. It probably meant something, but the religious newspapers, thick Friday editions, examined instead the Torah portion of the week and the rising heat from the American government about Judaizing Jerusalem—expanding the neighborhoods. All other news was blacked out.

"What do you think," Sandy said, finally, perforating the silence and the darkness, her voice like a sting. Being Yossi's mother entitled her to an affect like barbed wire. Sandy asked and answered a question at the same time. "Do you change or become more of yourself in a place where, when you get there, the neighbors say, 'Welcome home,' instead of 'Nice to meet you'?"

1985

The one time Sandy was inspired to metaphor they'd been discussing aliyah—moving to Israel—and she attacked Nathan's apprehension as some fundamental weakness. She said, "You remind me of one of those little silver balls in a pinball machine—something's shooting you off, you don't know for the life of you whether you're going to hit the numbers, or fall in the hole. You think we have any guarantees here in Hartford?" Even if it did come out as anger, her toughness secured him, was a strength for him, like strong roof beams or a three-foot poured-concrete foundation.

Nathan couldn't remember what he answered and he couldn't imagine for the life of him why he recalled that outburst now as he turned into the revolving door except that at best Sandy was indifferent to and at worst misunderstanding of his vision, and his sense of purpose.

She wouldn't be remotely interested, for example, that he could navigate to her hospital room with his eyes closed: floor one, septic, chemical, the smell of patients moving in and out of surgery; floor two, sudsy like Comet soft-scrub cleanser, and floor three (the women's ward) on the right of the landing, sweet, powdery, fecund. On the left it smelled like chlorine.

He turned to the left.

On her door hung the same sign as yesterday:

NO VISITORS

Underneath, new since yesterday, and handwritten in thin black marker:

NO ONE!!!
!!

—the exclamation marks falling off the edge of the page. He looked up the hallway for Nurse Cleaver, who would pluck him out by the neck for transgressing orders, even if they weren't her own. Then he ripped off the sign and entered.

Now if someone had told him beforehand that after this surgery, which had nothing to do with her mouth, Sandy would refuse to talk for an entire week, Nathan would have smiled behind his hand. But her silence was really depression and the silence greeted him, anyhow, as loud and regular as sharp words, and set off, in relief, her round face and eyes opaque as glass brick. She lifted her arm, paper white, and pointed to a pot of red geraniums sitting on top of the radiator cover.

"My rival?" he asked, kicking himself as he spoke. Irony would not snap her out of this. He saw what she meant, though.

The flowers sagged their dry heads. Another hour on top of the radiator they'd be tiptoed out on the trash dolly with leftovers from breakfast. Nathan moved the whole pot to the top of the Formica built-in, onto a white cloth doily next to Sandy's toothbrush, floss, toothpicks, baking soda, hydrogen peroxide, a little manicure kit in a red leather case; always removing, scraping off. In the case of this surgery, scraping out.

Sandy's roommate, Mrs. Stefanides, and her entire bed were not in this morning. Waiting on the bed table was Mrs. Stefanides's breakfast, a large plate under a large metal dome. "Looks just like the capitol building," he would tease Mrs. Stefanides. "You're eating legislation for breakfast."

Sandy's meals, of course, were double foil-wrapped (when hot) or (when cold) kosher odds-and-ends from the hospital pantry. Today she had Rice Krispies, again, in a peel-back disposable bowl. Sandy'd eaten so many Rice Krispies that she'd personalized her side of the bulletin board with the week's worth of peel-back lids. She'd also tacked up a doctored, aerial photo of Jerusalem where the Mosque of Omar had been rubbed out and the third Jewish Temple spliced in.

Since yesterday Mrs. Stefanides added a new Snoopy card to her side of the bulletin board to go with the picture of her grandson, her day-a-page calendar, and the two clippings from last week's *Hartford Courant*: "Michael Dukakis in Connecticut . . ." Mrs. Stefanides had a nephew-in-law who'd worked on the presidential campaign. Mrs. Stefanides was convinced that Michael Dukakis was coming to visit her.

As long as Nathan left the visitor's chair alone and stood up, Mrs. Stefanides liked his chatter better than Sandy did. Mrs. Stefanides, at least, would have a real conversation. Yesterday Mrs. Stefanides said she was "emptied, dished out. Shop closed. Shutters drawn. It is over."

"And Sandy is open for business," Nathan projected in Sandy's direction, loud as a cheerleader. "Ready to go. Come see us in Israel in six years. Three boys. Three girls."

Mrs. Stefanides opened her eyes very wide.

Now she wasn't there, and Nurse Cleaver was gone too, perhaps tied up or hanged or fired. Nathan pulled Michael Dukakis's chair away from Mrs. Stefanides's side of the room and sat down at the foot of Sandy's bed.

Dr. Warsi entered, knocking on the door as he pushed it back. Nathan recognized the medical students and the interns who made obeisance behind him, like embarrassed shadows. As Dr. Warsi dictated to them, he lifted Sandy's sheet and her hospital gown and traced the scar on her abdomen with his fingers. In a flat voice he asked Sandy to roll on her side, and since she refused to speak to him too, she sat up and rotated her legs with pursed lips. Outside, a single puff of snow whirled past the window, got caught in the sunlight, and shattered like glass.

"Just watch those—extra pounds," Dr. Warsi said, snapping the clip on his clipboard instead of inflecting his voice. He guaranteed nothing and threw in caveats, daily, as if to ground her. "No alcohol. Smoking. Too much eating."

Sandy laughed silently, humping the sound up in her shoulders, and Nathan knew why. She of all people had no temptations and she wasn't heavy, as you thought from first glance—just stuffed up looking like an emotional dam.

When Dr. Warsi left, Sandy held her Rice Krispies box up to the sunlight. She found what she was looking for, and squaring the plastic bowl on her bed table, broke the lapel of the peel-back lid with the handle of her plastic spoon. She poured in the milk.

The cereal crackled and Nathan thought: he had thirty minutes before he left for the office. If he was determined she would speak, he had to work quickly.

Warming up, he confessed his anxieties. His anxieties always got her going: they were leaving in two months and the house wasn't sold yet. "It wouldn't be real if I didn't have some anxieties," he said. "After all, I'm only human. A real human American." He laughed because maybe the real and American part weren't true. Another snowflake wandered against the window, piggybacked with a second, and fell down out of view.

"In Jerusalem," he continued, "do you remember? There are only two seasons? Winter, summer. How will I live without a New England fall?"

Sandy chewed her Rice Krispies with a circular movement of her jaw.

"The copper beech," Nathan declared. "This morning it hit our bedroom window, its leaves unrolled, plum purple."

Sandy bent her head to the bed table and looked into her cereal box as if there were something there that shouldn't be.

"I got the books I ordered," Nathan said, bringing his chair closer so that his knees rested on the bed frame. " 'How to be a scribe in ten easy lessons.' " It wasn't such a stretch. He'd taught Hebrew language, trained as a Judaica librarian. She looked over at him, still chewing. Her eyebrows lifted. Was he kidding? Nathan filled it right in. "Do you think Nathan ben Eliezer is a better name for a scribe than Nathan Hacker?"

Sandy opened her mouth, about to answer, then peeled the cellophane lid off her orange juice.

Nathan looked at his watch and continued, full blast. "Did you ever notice in Jerusalem the seasons are inverted? In the summer the trees are parched from the sun, all brown. In the winter the rain turns the forest to colors, like *tchotchkelas* on a mantel." He smiled and leaned into the foot of her bed. How did she like that?

Apparently, not much. Sandy wiggled her feet. Under her blanket her body rippled, knees-chest-head, and the entire motion ended when she crushed her juice cup into the Rice Krispies box. She turned to look at the wall over Mrs. Stefanides's bed, and when Nathan turned too, they watched shadows from outside buildings dance like a projectionist's hands. A bird, a plane, a torsoless duck. Nathan was tired, drained, but he had one more idea to try.

"I want to tell you what I read," he said.

Sandy grunted. Nathan knew it meant "go on, if you want."

"You know how you just feel that thing in Jerusalem? That buzz? I read this comparison to gravity, like it's something that's there. You just don't think about it a lot until you test it. Like the way you see gravity when you bounce a ball."

She turned her head 180 degrees, slow as an owl. "What are you talking about?" she said, grinding the words out of her mouth.

Nathan's heart leapt.

He pulled Michael Dukakis's chair around to the side of the bed and stroked her leg under the blanket. "That spiritual thing. Just say you're a ball . . ."

"Just say you're a ball," Sandy said. "And go bounce somewhere else."

Nathan pushed away from the bed, smiling. When she sank he knew how to revive her.

He lifted Michael Dukakis's chair back across the room so he wouldn't scrape the floor and bother her with any more noise. Sandy never did like his metaphors, his flowery talk. But Sandy would like them better—everything would be better when they moved. The rabbis said that the air in Jerusalem makes you wise.

PRESENT DAY

Nathan thought of his studio as a refuge. He loved the way the windows faced the pink light and the way the light rose over the mosque at Nabi Samwil predawn with the muezzin calling to prayer; the spirals at the distance, and the busyness in the dark morning reminded him of the little Connecticut towns he knew and lived in as a kid.

Behind his bulwark—his scribe's table—he'd arranged decanters of black gallnut ink, important as a blood supply, and on the narrow patches of wall between the windows he'd tacked odds and ends: an *aleph-bais* chain and a geometric border from an old wedding contract, so complex with minutiae he could travel galaxies just by sitting down on his stool. The studio would have been the third bedroom, but they'd never needed it—and now, after Sandy's operation last June, her second and her last, they never would. Licking their wounds, bitterly adjusting to divine will, they hadn't yet changed the emotional facts and the difference between Sandy and him remained: Sandy thought Yossi so good that she would clone him if she could, and Nathan thought Yossi took the work of an army and as widely as you could love that boy, his imagination collapsed before he could figure out what they would have done with another one of him.

One morning, about ten days before Rosh Hashanah, in an atmosphere naturally fraught with account-making (in the spiritual sense), Nathan ran directly home from morning prayer, ran into the studio, and tugged the metal chain on the fluorescent tube. Usually a happy moment, the light choked on with his feeling of potential: talent, exactitude. Design. A list of orders for mezuzahs from tourists who had gotten his name from clients in the States. When the light steadied, registering a buzz somewhere up against the ceiling, a business card emerged—his card—propped up in the middle of his table with one of the turkey quill pens he'd cut the day before. On it were two messages in Sandy's back-slanted script. One: "Our neighbor Tova called. Yossi! Ball!" Nathan squinted. The note did say *ball*. And two: "Rabbi Altman called." Yossi's principal. "He wants to see you."

The fluorescent tube swayed slightly again, hiccuping light. He would call their neighbor Tova—sometime, for whatever reason, about her ball. But Rabbi Altman . . . Rabbi Altman and Nathan had zigzagged, followed each other from neighborhood to neighborhood until they'd both ended up settling in Heavenly Heights. Even at simple times—like yesterday at the swimming pool—Rabbi Altman's eye had become inescapable. Rabbi Altman stood there in the shallow end, a pier; his three sons in a circle around him like mooring boats. Binny, Yossi's age, was doing handstands and Rabbi Altman counted the seconds. The second son practiced rhythmic breathing by the concrete steps. The youngest one bounced off his toes and restrained all his nervous energy against a nod from his father. And there was Nathan, tossing his father-instructions to Yossi: money for cola and a cone, meet at the bathhouse, four P.M. But Yossi had bolted even as

Nathan spoke. Nathan turned to see Rabbi Altman watch him finish up. "Have fun, don't run, don't swim right after your ice cream," admonishing, instead of the boy, blue pebbled concrete at the edge of the pool.

Nathan pushed Sandy's messages away and sat on his stool, bringing the stool up against the table, fixing his feet on the low bar. Orders for mezuzahs always set him back in balance. He opened the file drawer next to his table and chose a small square parchment. If he had no interruptions he could write one mezuzah in thirty minutes. Taking the quill Sandy had used for a weight, he dipped and drew the first stroke, clean. The black line struck out on the paper and the edge was perfect.

True, he'd promised Rabbi Altman the first day of school he would speak to Yossi, but true, when he spoke to his family it wasn't so clear that they listened. How many times had he told Sandy not to waste his business cards? He'd designed them himself, illuminated them with little curlicues and silver leaf.

Outside the window, little brown birds tumbled in a pair; then he heard them chirping from some hole in the grouting they'd found under the balcony wall. When the trees were dry and almost bare at the end of summer they found no leaves to nest in. The thought snagged him in the chest, like inspiration, and he dipped his quill again, bending to concentrate. "*Shema.*" The *shin*—the first letter—had three bars that made him think of the three in his family. Then, his favorite: three top strokes on the last bar made a little crown. Like kings, fathers should wear a crown.

Half the "4" was missing from the address sign. Disrepair, or maybe some kids playing too much ball against the overhang. The address was already hard enough to see at a glance and none of those new tourist-clients would ever be able to figure out which building Nathan was in.

It was Nathan's habit to work, concentrated and short, and to take frequent breaks, five minutes at a time. This was his mail break. He slid out a phone bill and a bank statement and, pressing gently on the back panel to his mailbox, coaxed the mailbox lock to click in as it did on a good day. The number "4" actually looked like a "1," or a backward "F." He made a point of explaining to clients that his apartment building was Number Four but the third building in. The contractors had built up the street backward, from inside out, high numbers to low, and they'd lost the first corner lot when the engineers finally noticed that the city buses would never make the first curve if it wasn't cut away.

The studio was a buffer to all these things, these aggravations, Nathan considered, walking inside and down the stairs. Back at his stool he knew that if he evaluated his year—he would even swear if he could—that none of these aggravations were his fault. Life had its own evolution, even in the emotional sense.

Two pictures came to mind. Often on *Erev Shabbos* (Friday afternoon), when the cooking and cleaning were finished early and the time hung empty between the parenthesis of preparation and sundown, he and Sandy and Yossi used to drive out the main road past the swimming pool, into the forest, past the cracked wooden arrows nailed to the pine trees, and past a boarded-up juice kiosk in order to visit the local wonder, the dinosaur footprints. Sandy would stand and worry the dates on the tourist plaque, calculating whether the time line for extinction was correct. But Nathan and Yossi would hopscotch the wide concrete toes—together—and roar.

But during this last *ben ha'zmanim*, the summer school break, they went and Sandy sat in the car by herself to hear the BBC news at one o'clock. There'd been a point-blank shooting between Gush Etzion and the tunnel road, a family car, both parents dead of head wounds and four newly hatched orphans, ages one to six; no new details, but Sandy listened to the whole broadcast again, wiping her eyes. The idea of orphans always ripped her apart. Yossi walked off, spent the entire time alone, hunting coins in the paper trash under the kiosk.

They'd come one time too many: Yossi was maturing, almost bar mitzvah, with a shadow on his face that didn't move away with the light.

Then, just yesterday, Nathan had one of those pictures, the kind of picture people like him were prone to, where a little scene had a big meaning. It happened when Sandy came to pick them up from swimming. Nathan and Yossi were just walking out of the bathhouse as Sandy tore the car into the parking lot, parked right next to the gated entry and security hut, making pebbles spray high in the air, over the small radio tower. She ran right off looking for them—ran right past them and looked so foolish, like a mother hen clucking after her wandering chick. Yossi stood under a pine tree, snickering, the little noises breaking out between his lips.

When Sandy saw Nathan and Yossi were behind her, she spun on her toes and called out to Yossi first (never Nathan). Her chest jutted forward, and her little splayed feet gave her a clownish look. The security guards made a joke to offer her their pistols but Sandy didn't hear. Yossi laughed, deeply.

Nathan agreed—her face looked funny. With all that earnestness Nathan could have been looking in a mirror, so when Nathan laughed with Yossi he felt as if he had betrayed all three of them.

"That Yossi should make it to school, every day and on time. That Yossi should speak to his teachers properly. That a father could better manage his son's behavior with rules to live by and boundaries that feed self-respect." The next morning Nathan woke up from a sleep that had wrestled a voice the entire night. A resonant voice that sounded like a book but it was Rabbi Altman's. Nathan got out of bed and through the open, screenless window smelled *Shabbos* cooking: chicken soup, chicken in soy sauce and honey, and from Debra's apartment upstairs, cilantro as sharp and familiar as fresh-cut grass. He looked out the window and saw nothing, not even the edge of the balcony. The morning cloud cover had mixed with the cooking fog. Certainly before the smell and the cloud moved off the balconies, and then off the mountain, it was impossible to tell what kind of day it would be.

He walked into Yossi's room and shook Yossi.

Both half asleep, they walked to morning services. Afterward, they walked back to Old Hana's *macolet*—the corner store. The trucks from the different city bakeries had already delivered their *Shabbos* challahs. There was no room in the *macolet* and the challahs lay about, haphazardly, in plastic bins lining the entire sidewalk at the storefront. Nathan picked out three seeded loaves from the tops of three different bins, guessing he'd picked the salty ones that Sandy liked best.

Side by side they joined the checkout line that curled through the tapered aisles and then out the door again. Yossi leaned back against a shelf crammed with olive oil and corn oil and started beating his forefingers on top of a waist-high display of canned corn, his right leg accompanying backbeat, the rhythm, like an intimacy, logged somewhere in his head. As Nathan came up to the register to pay, Nathan realized Yossi was tapping out a real song, a song that Nathan had heard Debra practicing late the night before for one of her concerts, but Nathan had never heard it sound like that. Nathan could barely restrain himself from grabbing Yossi's manic leg.

Outside, Tova's Mike stood, tearing off a plastic challah bag from the roll laying on an upturned milk crate. Rabbi Altman had also arrived, doing his Friday morning magic on the challah: divining sweet, salty, honey, with the power of touch. Rabbi Altman probed to the bottom of the pile if he had to, and when he rolled the loaf up on its tip he squeezed it, nodding yes or no.

Nathan stepped up, now second in line at the register. Just as Nathan lay his challahs on the counter, Yossi bolted, ran back to the refrigerator, grabbed a bag of Choco-milk, and bit the plastic corner of the bag with his sharp front teeth. He spat the plastic tip into his hand and pocketed it, then squeezed the milk into his mouth.

Both Nathan and Old Hana shook their heads at Yossi. Like a reflex, Nathan turned around to see if Rabbi Altman had noticed Yossi or Old Hana's face as she rang the register. Nathan was grateful when he saw that Rabbi Altman was busy, bending to his littlest son, counting out change spread across his palm.

Outside the *macolet* Nathan checked his watch for the first time in an hour. If they didn't hurry, Yossi would miss the *hasa'a*, the school bus. They ran one block, up to the little tinted-glass shelter that doubled as the Egged public stop. A cluster of boys stood in front of the shelter, already lined up at the curb.

Nathan stopped to catch his breath and walk the last few meters. His legs pumped at the calves, his chest heaved. Behind the line of boys, the sun had broken up the morning cloud cover and beamed, lemony strong; as Nathan moved under the tinted glass of the bus shelter, he always had the feeling he was putting on sunglasses, and concealed thoughts floated up to the surface. He looked at Binny Altman standing there (in his plaid shirt identical to Yossi's shirt) but Binny was so calm, so turned in on himself. Yossi always looked as if his skin were going to burst. What would it be like to have Binny as a son?

The bus arrived and the bus driver wound open the passenger door as the bus was still moving. Yossi jumped on. When it did stop the other boys filed in. Nathan saw that Yossi, all settled in the backseat, said something that made Binny Altman laugh even as Binny sat with the other boys in a group behind the driver.

Nathan pictured himself shot like a cannonball. Nathan pictured himself snatched by an eagle, flown straight over the school, and dropped out of the eagle's beak. As usual in Rabbi Altman's office, Nathan sat in the metal folding chair across from Rabbi Altman's desk, disciplining himself to sit upright.

On the wall behind the desk was a cabinet with two rifles for *shmira,* school security. Why two? Rabbi Altman wore a black suit, and under the orange light of a bare bulb his red beard turned in flames—as he spoke—like an autumn shrub.

Nathan felt his shirt stick to the back of the chair, entirely wet. And they hadn't even started yet.

Rabbi Altman answered one phone call buzzed in from his secretary and turned his body in toward the phone, speaking in low Hebrew, smiling.

Waiting, trying not to listen in to Rabbi Altman's business, Nathan noticed that there was a drawing on Rabbi Altman's desk: two hands clasped in prayer. It was one of those drawings made of Scriptures—popular with the tourists—with words in a shape that illustrated the content of the picture. "The prayer for rain," Nathan read the title, upside down. Why had Rabbi Altman bought this picture? And from whom? Leaning forward Nathan read the signature on the bottom. "Yecheskiel Alt . . ." Rabbi Altman had made this!

Rabbi Altman hung up the phone. He saw Nathan looking at the picture. "Eight hours," he said. "Took me eight hours. But I sell them for three hundred, sometimes four hundred shekels." This was more small talk than he ever made and he didn't smile.

"We found Yossi in the forest this morning, during Talmud class. He'd made himself a fort of pinecones and rocks. And some concrete blocks from the building sites."

Resourceful, thought Nathan. Resourceful and creative. He looked back at Rabbi Altman and saw Rabbi Altman had narrowed his eyes, was leaning forward. It was then Nathan realized he'd reacted with a smile though he hadn't meant to. Nathan wiped his palms on his pants and leaned forward, also, in order to unstick the back of his shirt from the chair.

"I can't really say who told me he was there," Rabbi Altman continued. "The most important thing is it's someone who is as interested in Yossi as we are. Someone who cares about him."

Binny. Of course, Binny, Nathan thought bitterly. One minute laughing at Yossi's jokes, the next minute Binny is his father's little boy. "I put him on the bus," Nathan said.

Rabbi Altman was silent. Nathan felt the heat of Rabbi Altman's beard, branding him. Perhaps Nathan's Hebrew was unclear. "I watched that he went on the bus today . . ." Nathan said, again, and realized he hadn't intended to bring the problem back to himself, to what he did or didn't do and to loop right into Rabbi Altman's logic. Then all of a sudden Nathan's Hebrew escaped him. He couldn't add another word. Why did Rabbi Altman force him to have these conversations in Hebrew anyhow? Rabbi Altman should know English well—his wife was American.

"Too much heart," Rabbi Altman said, finally locking on to Nathan's eyes and holding his gaze. "This is a problem I see over and over. Look, it is easier to avoid the tension of telling a child what to do. Some parents think that their only job is to enjoy their children. So much pleasure." Rabbi Altman shook his head, as if the thought amused him.

"It's not pleasure at all," said Nathan, bringing his Hebrew back and then realizing he hadn't quite said what he meant to. Or if he meant it he hadn't meant to *say* it. He laughed to himself and concentrated on the view out the window just past Rabbi Altman's head. Little boys, half Yossi's age, played soccer with their rebbe on a small blacktop court, surrounded by stacks of pink-stone building facade that hadn't been cleared away for over a year now. The boys kicked the ball again and again into the barbed wire, between the legs of the radar tower. But once it was under the radar tower, even the littlest boy knew the ball was out of bounds.

Rabbi Altman swiveled back and glanced toward the window. There was nothing out there worth pulling Nathan's attention away from him, so when he turned to face Nathan again his advice was notched up to exhortation, his voice granulating. "The Sages say you're supposed to balance," Rabbi Altman said. "Let the left hand push away while the right hand draws near."

Instead of wincing, Nathan leaned forward to cough, as if to shake an answer out of his throat.

Rabbi Altman interpreted it as blank space. He continued: "Chastise with the left hand—that's discipline. Pull close with the right hand—that's the expression of love. The two hands must work together."

Nathan hadn't realized he'd sat back until he found himself leaning forward again, the back of his shirt patchworking sweat off the chair.

"Children are a divine trust. *Abba shel* Yossi—Yossi's father—in my office that's who you are. It's that time of year. To reflect on what we're accountable for. Parenthood is a safety net of authority. And control . . . Give that to him. The right hand and left hand *should be* working together. You should be able to discipline him as much as you love him."

Rabbi Altman said the last words in English—or so Nathan thought—because what Nathan reacted so strongly to was so primary: a clarity, for just a second, that if the amount of discipline was equal to the amount of love, even Nathan could make math out of his failures. And where they came from.

When Nathan jumped up he was sure Rabbi Altman interpreted his reaction as the kind of shame you had when you were just set straight about something you could improve. His face was red, the backs of his ears aflame, from his mouth rose a puffy "Oh," which to Hebrew ears could sound plaintive as an "*Oy*," especially as the sound stretched out on his way through the office door.


Nathan found himself up on the sidewalk outside of the school building wondering how Rabbi Altman found the time to make those Scripture pictures. "Go figure who's a real artist," Nathan said out loud, then he laughed to see the only response he got. Above his head was a little rain cloud, shaking its finger at him, waiting to roll in the rain-in-season. In three weeks the rain would be on top of them but while the weather held, he could walk back home to Number Four.

As he approached the entrance he saw that another piece of the address number lay on the tile, inside the curb. The wind! Or one of the sonic booms of the F-13s on practice flights. Or what the newspapers *called* practice flights. He stepped back to look at the overhang. All that was left was a ', which looked like a dot to an i. He could ink a new number on cardboard (with permission from the *Va'ad Habayit*). The ink would run with the first rain but it was better than nothing.

He bent for the piece of the "4" and slipped it into his pocket even though he wasn't sure why anyone would want to keep it, just garbage really. Mike's Tova walked by. He concentrated on the piece of the "4" in his pocket, dodging the merest possibility of a conversation with Tova about her phone call. But Tova continued on, as if he looked so different from the back that she couldn't recognize him, and from behind herself, she gave the impression the old-timers did, ground down a little at the heels, a bend in the neck as if she were walking into a crosswind. He straightened up as Tova entered the lift, but like lightning, at the same moment, Debra's daughter Shira skidded out onto the walk, nearly knocking him over. Had Nathan, had he by chance seen a couple come, carrying a box? Her aunt in America, her father's sister, the one with one kid—a girl—was sending new holiday dresses with her dentist coming here for the holiday. Shira was late for school, she said, and she jumped away like a quick bird, all her movements looking as if they had a purpose, inspiring like her mother was.


Spiritual accounting and raising children should only be as easy as the *spongia,* Nathan thought, the way you sloshed the floor with water and scraped the dirt down a drain hole in the corner of the floor. Nathan poured more ammonia into the bucket, and rocked the edges of the bucket to mix the two. Then he stepped back and stood next to the open kitchen window, breathing fresh air. On Fridays, when Sandy worked late at The Book Mart, Nathan took care of the *Shabbos* cleaning. He usually liked housework, except today he felt a peculiar weight on his shoulders, dragging on his *spongia* stick; he kept thinking about Rabbi Altman. He knew he'd run out of the office quickly, but it wasn't all Nathan's fault. Not every parent can be told how to improve . . . Sandy would have given Rabbi Altman the what-for.

At one P.M., Yossi walked in from school. Yossi carried a cream-colored kitten in the crook of his left arm, tenderly, as if he were swaddling a baby. With his free hand he threw his knapsack on the tiny butcher-block island.

The kitten didn't belong inside. Nathan fumed and flamed. The cats were wild like squirrels here and Nathan had told Yossi a million times not to touch them. How could he discipline Yossi if Yossi never listened?

"I found her under the Dumpster, *Abba*," said Yossi, putting her down on the wet floor. He stroked the kitten and her feet spread as she flattened her stomach to the wet stone tile. The kitten took two small steps and touched its nose to the bucket of dirty water. "See. She's starving."

"Take it back to the street," Nathan said. He forced himself to look away from the kitten and tugged the *spongia* stick upright, full flag. He could discipline. He would be forceful—and the rest would fall into place. And if he'd gotten anything from Sandy it was how to be forceful. "Did you know Rabbi Altman really laid into me today? On your behalf?"

Yossi didn't answer at first. The question clearly stymied him;

the tone was his mother's, though not the way she spoke to him, the voice was clearly his father's. He bent to his knees, pulling the kitten back by its hips. After he leveled the kitten against his chest he stood up, almost as tall as Nathan, and answered, not the tone, not the voice, but the words. "I know, *Abba*," he said. "I heard how you ran out of there. I had to hear about it for the rest of the day."

"What do you mean?" Nathan asked, his offense wobbling. The *spongia* stick was dry and splintery as he held it straight up; his fingers stiffened around the tip.

"It's not like anything happens around here and it's a secret. Every time you come to school all the kids know it." Yossi squeezed the kitten hard. It opened a miniature, predatory mouth, but didn't make a sound.

"What were you doing in the woods?" Nathan asked, another offense, making his words safe. Sometimes a father's job was just to protect a son.

"I was planning to go into school."

Yossi sounded like a little boy and Nathan softened toward him, saying in a low voice, "How do you think I feel when Rabbi Altman calls me in?"

"How do you think I feel when I hear Rabbi Altman has scared my *abba* out of school?" Yossi's voice was entirely sincere.

Nathan watched a puddle that lay between them quiver on the floor.

"Go. Just go. Take that cat out of here and go," Nathan said, keeping his voice low. Maybe he was one of those little silver balls shooting off.

Yossi ran out.

Nathan dumped the entire bucket into the drain so violently that the water came right back up, gurgling over the floor tile. The worst of it was that little sob in Yossi's throat.

Four hours later, Nathan stood in the dining room, taking the good crystal out of the china cabinet. Yossi had run away. He'd gotten rid of Yossi. The rim of a glass hit the wooden frame of the cabinet door and Nathan touched his forefinger to the crystal in order to calm the pitch. Truth was, he had moved about quietly for hours, waiting to hear Yossi outside or out in the hallway. He hadn't heard any sound of him yet.

Sandy walked in the front door crowing out questions instead of a greeting as she headed straight to the shower. Did you call Tova? Did you call Rabbi Altman? Nathan heard the bathroom door slam and the shower turn on. The candle-lighting siren rang out from the civil defense station. Other times the siren was a signal to move into the shelters, but Fridays, at dusk, the siren announced a final get-ready for *Shabbos*. Today the siren ended so loud the crystal on the table rang along with it. Forty minutes until sundown.

Nathan walked to the bedroom to check that the lights were set on the *Shabbos* timer, to see if Sandy had noticed that Yossi wasn't around. What would she say if Yossi did not come home, eat *Shabbos* dinner with them?

Sandy was still in the shower, raising her voice, arguing with the candle-lighting siren. She always insisted that the civil defense station was mistaken by three minutes and she always lit *Shabbos* candles at her own time, though insisting as vociferously that she never once abrogated the boundaries, even the boundaries around the boundaries of the law.

Nathan stood, straight-toed against the threshold on the bedroom side of the bathroom door. Should he speak to her? Would she blame him for any Yossi business anyhow? He knocked very lightly on the bathroom door and turned the knob.

"I know, I know what time it is. I'm getting out in a minute," Sandy yelled. He heard her turn off the shower.

Nathan walked back to the kitchen. He set the final heat on the cooktop and laid down the *platta*, the aluminum cover that would keep their food warm until *Shabbos* lunch the next day. Earlier in the afternoon he'd added Sandy's cracker *kishke* to the *cholent* and it was time to strip off the tin foil. Was what he said to Yossi so terrible? Could life without Yossi be so bad? He slit the tin foil with a pointed knife and lifted the lid to the *cholent* pot, inhaling the smell of beef and beans, fatty and bitter.

Nathan knew Yossi could get dressed in two minutes. Standing in the Number Four lobby, ready to walk to services even before Sandy got dressed, Nathan watched Yossi run in from the forest as if something were chasing him from behind.

Shira skidded out through the door and waited on the sidewalk next to Nathan. Her box had come and she'd dipped in before Rosh Hashanah and she wore a new hand-me-down dress with a wine-colored stain on the bib. The bib made the dress too young for Shira and the sash was an add-on, a wine-red satin ribbon, Nathan couldn't help noticing. The sun, which had knocked back that little rain cloud, was wine-red too and hung like a child's ball, ready to drop on them.

Shira's father, Dave, came out the door and Shira jumped to his side; the only girl walking out to services. She worked hard to keep up with his long steps, practically two for his every one. Behind him Nathan heard the scrape of porch chairs. The Number Four women had begun their soiree, gathering on Debra's balcony.

Down the block Rabbi Altman floated out of his building

onto the sidewalk. Nathan began to walk quickly. He wouldn't mind if Rabbi Altman saw him now, not just father of Yossi, made some small talk. Rabbi Altman's boys scuffled, like ballplayers, fighting over who got to walk next to their father. Rabbi Altman finally took a firm position with the two older ones on either side. The youngest—the swimmer—fell in rank and even though Binny was the same age as Yossi, Binny held his father's hand as they walked.

Nathan slowed down, stopped a moment, and fingered the collar of his white *Shabbos* shirt. Yossi ran—in his *Shabbos* clothes—right past Nathan, straight out of Number Four and into the road. First Yossi caught up with Dave and Shira. Then Yossi yelled a yell: he wanted Binny Altman to wait up for him. Yossi ended up walking to shul with the Altmans. Nathan's thoughts broke off again, and he went so far to mouth a question, moving his lips as in the silent prayer: would Yossi be the same way if he were Rabbi Altman's son?

Nathan reached the shul the exact moment the sun dropped below the mountain line. Without light, either direct or reflected, there were seconds all the color disappeared from the sky. He watched Yossi part with the Altmans at the front door, holding up one finger. Either Yossi was letting them know that he was going somewhere or that he would be along in one minute. Nathan restrained himself from calling out. His eyes felt wet in back as if he'd made a sudden physical effort.

Inside shul Nathan and the other men slipped into a precise, quick set of motions, the *maariv* prayer service. Afterward, waiting to welcome the *Shabbos* Queen, Nathan moved over on the bench and opened up another space. Yossi would come of his own volition. Whenever. It didn't matter what Nathan felt. Or said. Or did. The thought of Sandy drifted in, as if he should react with some kind of fear. She always had an answer for his moods like that.

The men stood again and began to move their lips. Nathan picked up his prayer book off the windowsill. His eye followed the line of the window arch, two stories high. He loved this little synagogue, just finished six months ago, still breathing construction dust. Through the highest curve of the window arch the mountaintops etched a black line against deep purple, the color the sky had chosen for the night.

As the men began to sing Yossi slipped in on the bench. He smelled like dirt, fresh dirt. Under the fingernails on both hands were crusts of brown. Yossi sat, took off his shoe, shook out sand and pebbles from the instep.

The *Shabbos* Queen was splendid, like a bride. The men honored her with a bow. In front of Nathan, two rows closer to the Ark of Prayer, Rabbi Altman stood with his boys. Rabbi Altman showed his littlest son—the swimmer—something in the prayer book. Rabbi Altman and this boy swayed together, making the movement sweet, like a dance.

Forget it, Nathan thought. Yossi wouldn't be any different if he were Rabbi Altman's or anyone else's son. With that, something already cliff-hanging broke off inside Nathan completely and Nathan shuffled all the way over until he stood directly behind the littlest Altman boy. Then, from that place, that good place, Nathan joined the men in *Shabbos* prayer, moving forward and back.

# COOKIES, CANDIES, IN THE DISH

SINCE THERE WAS A CERTAIN PROVIDENCE IN THEIR RELATIONSHIP, THE English-speaking women of Number Four made a point of socializing and planned this get-together for one of the weekdays of *Succos,* the Festival of Booths. Tova had suggested going into town for dinner but what with all the car ambushes lately, and with *Shabbos* coming, and all the kids on *Succos* vacation anyhow, all the housework took double—no, triple—time and no one could spare more than an hour.

So they sat in Debra's *succah* on her balcony; three canvas sheets and one hippie bedspread hanging for *succah* walls. The bedspread was oriental, garnet red with a blue and gold medallion in the center. The fabric had gotten so thin in spots that when the sun came in from the west side, the bedspread cast down colored shields on the table as if it were stained glass.

"See that," Debra said, running her hand under the spot of blue light, tapping into the center of the shield with one finger, "that is the exact shade of ratbane blue. Where I'm from in Kentucky it's the color of the flowers and the color of the sky."

"What is ratbane?" Tova said.

"Never heard of it," said Sandy and Ahuva. Tova knew that

there was no verifying. Debra could say anything because no one had been to where she came from, or could even point it out on a map.

Anyhow, in Tova's opinion, there was no blue like this Judean sky, posing picture-clear half a year for the journalists and politicians and hanging over these settlers like this, a stained ceiling or—it occurred to Tova that morning—an eye restraining itself from tears. But the discussion was moot. In a couple of days the rains would start and until then they lived in these *succah* huts. So, baby blue, ratbane blue, powder blue, they didn't see much sky anyhow.


Among these four mothers sitting in the *succah* Tova could count eleven daughters jumping rope on beats two stories below, in a blacktop circle protected from through traffic:

    "Nine he comes,
      Ten he tarries,
      Eleven he courts,
      Twelve he marries . . ."


Tova, jumping every step with her Esther, wearied of the rhythm. She took in her breath with the fragrant back breeze off the Judean hills, and noticed, with alarm, that her Esther's voice had become louder than anyone's. Tova wondered what she'd done to uncage Esther since they'd arrived. It had only been four months.

There was a loud whir outside the *succah*. Tova stood up and poked her head through the bedspread door, where the end flap was tied back with a cord. The helicopters patrolled every hour or so and number 513 was hanging a hundred meters away from the railing. Tova reached out to touch it, then seeing how she mistook the distance, waved like a child. Number 513 bowed its head and bent southeast to patrol deeper in the territories.

Tova came back to the table and looked at her neighbors. She couldn't resist the urge to make them a group. First of all, they were good mothers: they might be sitting and talking, but like paparazzi with their extra sense, they could pan to children's events at the moment they happened. Or they could tune themselves out to the large noises and concentrate on each other. But it occurred to Tova that she was projecting desire because she might want to be a good mother, and so might the rest but what they really had in common—at least on the surface—was the desire to rebuild and reclaim what was theirs. But, noble outpost in Judea or penthouse in town, they had to survive the transitions.

"Where I'm from," Debra said, "the hostess is in charge of the food as well as the stories."

She pushed a yellow and green Crayola tin across the table. Inside was her *kesuba*—her marriage contract—and a couple of $25 U.S. Savings Bonds. "My safe-deposit box," Debra joked. Debra pulled out a black-and-white Kodak from under the bonds: looking at the hair, laid under a flower wreath, looking at the hang of her lips about to sing off, the Kodak was unmistakable. Debra as a little girl. She sat on a log next to a tree-stump table, giant acorn caps and pinecones for a tea set.

"In this place," Debra said, "it's like nothing you've ever seen. The mountain streams glow—red like tomatoes—all mining waste. My granny had to raise me and she made us a steady life, everything the same. Till I found out I didn't belong in the first place."

They knew that Debra's father had been Jewish and that's what she was referring to. Tova leaned forward to take the picture. Then she sent the picture down the table to Sandy who quickly passed it along to Ahuva. Debra pulled it back before Ahuva had a good look and Ahuva didn't even notice. She was busy curling a paper napkin between her fingers, making the ends into mush.

"This isn't the most important one," Debra said, and she slipped it back into the Crayola tin. She pulled out another picture, color this time, and displayed it at angles as if she were making a confession. In this picture Debra wore striped bell-bottoms and a midriff top with tied ends. Half her stomach showed and her hair was a one-shade blond and ironed. She stood on a stage in the picture, her arms spread, pointing downward, mouth a knot. "Like a human pine tree," she said. Funny, the exact words came to Tova at the same time.

"What is this?" Ahuva asked, coming to life.

"*Hair*," Debra said. "I was singing in a production of *Hair*."

"What is *Hair*?" Ahuva asked, her voice gaining pitch, like the ring of an alarm. In the literal sense, for the married women in their community, hair had taken the quality of any other body part that was regularly covered. No wonder she was shocked: Ahuva was the only one of them who'd never been out there. Sheltered. More like their own daughters here, and she was too young to know about *Hair*, anyhow.

"*Hair* was a musical play. I left the backwoods as soon as I could to look for my father's folks so I went to Cincinnati. I typed at a law office, four days a week. One night I tried out for a community theater show and there I was."

Ahuva leaned forward to look at the picture, stirred in her chair, and began to push it back.

"Something special must've happened when I sang," Debra said, "because when I did I drew men to me with looks on their faces like they were in pain."

Tova found herself slightly embarrassed, unsure whether Debra should continue. No telling what Ahuva could say, sheltered as she was. To protect Debra as much as to preserve the sitting together, Tova pointed suddenly to the *succah* door and called out, "Look at the artwork." Debra's girls—all seven of them—had created a welcome sign, BLESSED ARE THOSE WHO COME, and the letters were formed by hand-drawn, miniature citrons—*esrogim*—the fruit that is part of the *Succos* holiday. Some of the older girls had made an accurate job of the *esrog*, a bumpy lemon with exaggerated tips.

Debra laid the second picture back into the Crayola tin, walked out of the *succah*.

With the door flap opened, Tova could hear Sandy's Yossi down on the blacktop taking one end of the jump rope. All the children—even Esther—sang the jump rope rhymes in a funny English, contracted as if they weren't sure whether the vowels were long or short.

Tova sat back, satisfied, figuring she'd distracted Debra enough, that next perhaps Debra would talk about her daughters, or something like that. Debra walked back in carrying red plastic bowls and sat again, pushing the bowls to her guests. "Did you ever wonder," Debra asked, "how I got from there to here?" She spun her finger in one clear arc, west to east.

Tova saw Sandy's eyebrows wing up. Tova considered nodding no but Sandy said yes, after all, she did wonder. Ahuva didn't say or do a thing. Debra continued, determined. "When they said things like 'blood flows thick,' I used to picture how the rain swelled Lower Back Creek and the water rushed through. The water left sediment, took sediment as it went, leaving and taking, working both ways until the water and sediment altered each other. Nowadays I imagine a roving Jewish soul, sailing about in the Upper World, looking for a place to come back in, reassert itself. It was all logical because of my blood. I had this Jewish soul placed in a backwoods girl."

"What do you mean?" Sandy asked.

Tova sat on the edge of the chair. She knew exactly what Debra was talking about: the force—when it happens—that gulps up your place and who you are until it turns into something you have to do. Her heart filled like a sponge.

Down on the blacktop they started a new round:

"Teddy bear, teddy bear,
Turn around
Teddy bear, teddy bear,
Touch the ground . . ."

Tova heard Yossi roar, "Teddy bear! Stoopid." Then a little girl started crying, *huh huh huh,* and the cry walked closer, just under the balcony. The mothers practically sprang antennas: Debra pushed back her chair and rose in stages, head then neck then shoulders then body, and what amazed Tova was the lag between her intent and her energy. Debra looked through a seam where the canvas was sewn together. She pawed her head scarf against the light wind that had picked up with a thrumming sound, and her dun-colored bangs lifted to show blonder roots.

Tova jumped—it could have been Esther crying—and then what? The response with pitted fear was a new one, but on the other hand, since they'd come, Esther didn't need any comfort from her.

Ahuva stayed seated. Three of the girls outside were hers, but her attitude, pouty, was that if it belonged to her it would come to her. With relief Tova discovered it wasn't one of Ahuva's girls. Sometimes Ahuva used kids' fights to not talk to a neighbor or not lend salt or sugar or her flour sifter (the one that trapped the flour mites). Ahuva was pretty and Tova didn't know if it was true since she'd just known her a couple of months, but Ahuva kept saying her sixth child had made her heavy, and she spread in the chair. Sandy had no daughters and she stood up instead, appearing to inspect the tier of the balconies that were built and staggered for this very festival so that each *succah*, each booth, took its own lease from the sky.

Certainly from Sandy's view, with all the greens and bamboo thrown on to make the *succah* roofs, each family's *succah* was like a person, with an outside look and an inside. Debra, for example, could be just a typical religious housewife in a head scarf, high collar, sleeves below the elbow, hemline past the knees.

The *huh-huh-huh* crying off the blacktop receded, finally, and Debra continued a shy pass-around of pickled kohlrabi and carrot with lemon juice and cilantro. Then, crossing the table was a slightly bitter smell that opened the nostrils. Debra had stewed peaches in horehound. She had a pot for "boiling up." "Granny used to boil herbs too," Debra added. "She could make up a tea that repaired you from bosom to bowel."

Before anyone could eat or reject the peaches, Debra said, "I'm not finished hostessing." She went out the door flap once more and came back with paper cups and peach wine, Hebron white wine, and brandy in a little cello-shaped bottle. Ahuva said she never needed any alcohol. Tova wondered that *needed* was a word she would never have chosen and had a feeling the liquor was for Debra and her, the ones for whom discovery was like a navigation.

Neither Ahuva nor Sandy touched the peaches either as the bowl went around. Tova served herself a couple of tablespoons full. As she ate it her throat widened and flamed, almost minty, and she nodded as she swallowed, mute.

Debra took the silence and filled it in. She continued: "One night after a performance, I'm dreaming in my sleep and I see a rabbi with a black beard sitting on my bed. He was just sitting."

Sandy smacked her thigh with her hand. "You're making this up," Ahuva said. "How did you know it was a rabbi?"

"Why couldn't she know?" Sandy asked. Her impatience was pointed, clearly not a defense of Debra but a loss of restraint against Ahuva's one-world, one-type point of view.

Tova pictured the rabbi sitting, ethereal, barely making an impression on the bed.

"As if he had no weight," Debra said quickly, turning to Tova. "The rabbi was holding a little silver box but in the dream I didn't get to see what was in it.

"The next day I was off to a short rehearsal of *Hair*. We performed at the JCC, a beautiful old stone building with a deep auditorium, wide stage, maroon and red curtains of velvet, heavier than two people could lift. So I'm walking over to the rehearsal and I see the rabbi from my dream walking by with that little silver box in his hand.

"Now it still surprises me that a whole lifetime can revolve on a single moment."

Tova felt her neck tingle. Then she realized she'd been staring so hard at Debra's face that her eyes hurt underneath, as if she hadn't blinked.

Sandy drummed her fingers on the back of Tova's chair. Ahuva's face was impossible to read.

"I asked the rabbi what was in the box. When he opened it the smell hit my face with the force of a wind. 'A citron,' I said. I knew right away. He was as curious now too. I told him how my father was Jewish. I told him that my father brought this little citron tree that grew in my granny's kitchen. Did I ever tell you about that?"

Ahuva, Sandy, and Tova nodded no.

"This rabbi and I eyed each other and continued a conversation where one line didn't tag off of the other. He said my father planted me a symbol. I told him how I knew the citrons' lemon candy smell and how the inside was mostly seeds, more potential than anything.

" 'Did I realize,' " he asked, " 'that's like the human heart? And that a citron is just the size of a human heart?' "

They had been sitting less than an hour, but the children's voices sounded thin, even Esther's.

"One I love,
Two I love,
Three I love I say . . ."

Tova felt tired, but more relaxed, as if the tired had descended upon her instead of coming from the inside. Suddenly they heard: "This is the last game!"

Could that really have been Esther commanding?

"Cookies, candy, in the dish
How many pieces do you wish,
One, two, three, four . . ."

Sandy picked up a glass and chipped at a small crust at the mouth edge.

Ahuva rolled her eyes. "Did I tell you my parents are coming from America next week?" Tova thought she'd just seen them visiting last month. Turned out they had been but it wasn't as if money were a problem so why not come as often as they could? Ahuva asked, and she began to describe various ruses to pass small appliances through airport customs.

Debra picked up her story with a rush, as if she had to cram it all in. "This man I met was Rabbi Sandler."

"Rabbi Isaac Sandler? Of Cincinnati?" Ahuva asked. "I know him. My cousin is married to his daughter."

"So then you know what he's like. And Rebbetzin Sandler too. Lots of guests, the seeking types. I started going to their house on *Shabbos*. I was drawn to their house on *Shabbos*. First I was the *Shabbos goy*. I turned a light off and on, ran errands up to the drugstore or the doctor. Did you know Elvis was a *Shabbos goy* in Memphis?"

"You're kidding," Sandy said, slapping her leg. She hadn't looked as if she had been listening. Tova couldn't tell if Debra was joking.

"I'd hear Rabbi Sandler say things like '*Shabbos* is like the World to Come.' Or Rebbetzin Sandler would say the minute she lit *Shabbos* candles she felt like she'd been deflated, then repumped with something else. Not air like the rest of the week. Every time I went to their house on *Shabbos* I felt like I'd been traveling and I'd finally got to where I was going. I'd been traveling to their house, to *Shabbos,* my whole lifetime.

"I wanted to convert. They tried to dissuade me, you know, three times, like it says in the books. When Rebbetzin Sandler said I would have to give up singing in public, to men, I told her I wasn't worried, that I have all that song stuffed up inside me, bound up like a kernel ready to explode. I knew I'd find a place for it."

"Oh," Ahuva said, retreating to the same passive face she'd sat down to the table with. "Well, I guess you did find a place for it—your song, I'm talking about." Ahuva, apparently, thought the story was over. After a moment's silence she moved out of her chair. "I've got to do some baby wash." As she left, the bedspread door snagged on the corner of a chair and pinned itself open.

A helicopter (was it 513?) buzzed back again, out over the highway down past the balcony. It dropped a little, seemed to chase a few cars, then bent away and off.

"Every once in a while," Debra said, "I remember how young our soldiers are." She opened the peach wine that had a twist cap and scraped her finger on a rough wiggle of tin.

Debra poured wine for Tova and herself into two of the cleanest glasses and offered to pour for Sandy.

"I have to start dinner. Yossi gets so hungry after these outside games," Sandy said, looking nervous.

In five minutes Tova and Debra were alone and Debra poured more peach wine. They drank. Debra started to talk again but stopped herself.

Tova knew Debra was waiting to be asked to go on. "What was the conversion like?" Tova said.

"Well, the Sandlers sent me to New York twice. The first time I met a big rabbi in his office in a part of Staten Island. The second time I went to Brooklyn and sat with three rabbis before I went to the *mikveh*. They asked me questions for hours. A lot about the Jewish calendar and holidays. How to keep food warm on *Shabbos*. The only question I did not know was how to make liver kosher. Rabbi Sandler watched his cholesterol and the Sandlers never ate liver.

"On the way to the *mikveh* the three rabbis sat in front of the car and I sat in the backseat alone, shivering. I wore a robe into the *mikveh* water and they stood back against the wall. I took the robe off under the water, then they shouted questions at me, mostly things like 'Is this your own free will?' I wanted to say really I never planned this, but this was the way it had to be."

"Then how did you meet Dave?" Tova asked.

"I went back to Cincinnati, converted, koshered, pedigreed, and marked. All I was missing was the kosher clip the Empire chickens get on their wings."

"And Dave?"

"The Sandlers had him in mind for a while. He'd been staying in yeshiva in Jerusalem and he was just dying to get back here. It was more him than me, though I knew it was the right thing. You know how that goes."

Yes, Tova knew how that goes.

Out on the blacktop Yossi was kicking a ball and shouting at someone. Sandy called him from her kitchen window. Ahuva was upstairs, clipping baby wash on her clothesline. A sleeper with footies, a bib.

Sitting inside a *succah* created a type of mystique and Tova's mind spun off questions and tailgated answers: who she was, who she would be, how was it that what you are or what you must do just announces itself to you sometimes.

"You know what Granny used to say?" Debra said, after her glass was empty. "It's an old Kentucky thing but it goes for Jerusalem too. When a woman is hanging out her wash, then all is right with the world."

# CLEAR AND LIGHT

ON THE LAST DAY OF *SUCCOS* THE *KHAMSIN* CAME RIDING IN LIKE THE headless horseman. Sand was the symptom, a fine grit like fairy dust. The men, duty-bound by mitzvahs of time, carried on inside the *succahs*. The women and young children stuck it out inside the apartments.

"The normal response to all this stuffiness," Tova complained, "is to open the windows." It wasn't only the stuffy breathing; her whole body was a complaint.

"Don't open those windows," Debra said. She crept up from the sofa and screwed the blinds shut so tightly the winding rod creaked. She was making a point. "It'll kill you. Like chemical weapons."

Tova looked over at Debra. Debra was never prone to hyperbole and Tova had never taken the position of adjusting *her* down a notch. "Don't even say anything like that. No one would use a chemical weapon," Tova said.

Debra rolled her eyes. The *khamsin* roiled up innocence, doomsaying, real advice. Debra returned to her sofa that lay perpendicular to Tova's love seat. The kids were reading books Tova's mother had sent. Esther curled on Debra's sofa edge with the latest Harry Potter. Three of Debra's youngest girls squatted on the floor with a pop-up edition of *Goodnight Moon*.

"This is worse than a chemical weapon," Tova said. She didn't care what she sounded like; the lowered blinds didn't make breathing—or thinking about breathing—any easier, and she had a point of reality to prove.

"That's what you think." Debra closed her eyes, signaling *not* a concession, but more like a refusal to engage.


The morning after the *khamsin,* Tova woke up in a fine grit, her body outlined in her bed like the chalked outline of a crime victim. Mike had been to shul and back, bought a *Jerusalem Post*. The *khamsin* had knocked out a Ferris wheel in Beirut, Lebanon, the same Ferris wheel that had survived a Hezbollah ambush and civil war.

Standing in the shower, she remembered some of yesterday's whole body kvetch. Then, the thought occurred to her, how often did she get a chance to, literally, wipe off a yesterday? She stood under the running water. She measured out her Pert Plus carefully. They weren't running out of their American toiletries yet—but the idea had crept up on her. A neighborly bandwagon, the communal test of faith—sometimes the sacrifices were large, sometimes small. What she'd understood since she'd been here was that Debra and Dave had run out of money, period. Sandy and Nathan had run out of savings and possibilities of more little Yossies, though they still had their income. Ahuva, she'd heard, had run out of Hellmann's mayonnaise and Celestial Seasonings tea, but her parents visited from the States every month or so and replenished her and she could always afford to buy it at the rip-off prices in town, anyhow.

Tova finished rinsing her hair. For some quirk of his own, in one of the small negotiations Tova and Mike had lost, their contractor had insisted on building a little window into the back of the shower wall, small as a ship's porthole but square. She soaped the tracks as she'd learned to do and slid open the glass. The contractor had known something. From her porthole she entered the rear world of Number Four and heard the scrape of families dismantling their *succahs* and putting them back into their storage rooms. Mike had decided he would roll theirs onto an awning he rigged above the porch door. His work-at-home plan had decelerated, his formal Talmud learning on vacation since Yom Kippur, and his puttering time blown up in direct proportion. Tova, on the other hand, had made some decisions. After another nasty bout with Esther's school notes, she'd decided to take a Hebrew class in town. If she didn't watch it, she would drive the teacher crazy with neediness.

Dressed, Tova wrapped her head scarf around with a braid on the top, the way Debra had taught her to do. What if she became a Lyudmilla or a Yvegenia, Tova thought, walking out to their balcony. There, the *succah* lay in pieces at Mike's feet, dismembered like a mosaic of memory: where he sat, where she'd sat, where they'd dragged out a mattress to properly dwell there.

"I'm starting the NordicTrack today," Mike said, standing in a patch of sunlight with the *succah* pieces. It wasn't like him to railroad his projects, but Tova knew he was driven to keep busy. On top of that, she noticed for the second time in a month how badly he needed a haircut, or how badly he looked like he needed one. "I'm fixing it for you," he said. He meant the NordicTrack. Several weeks earlier, after they'd cleared the legalities at customs, they'd waited daily, weekly, for the delivery of their shipping container. Back in Baltimore, back in the early summer of that other lifetime, that other universe, they'd paid and insured-in-full for door-to-door delivery. The bill of lading still sat in her carry-on valise. When the container finally arrived, the moving men took out the gears of the machine and asked her for a box. In Hebrew. Tova didn't process the request fast enough. So the taller moving man cupped his hands and motioned for Tova to do the same. He dipped into a carton and then emptied his hands into hers, like some child's game where you closed your eyes and guessed. But Tova felt a dozen bolts, screws, gears, all the parts of the NordicTrack fall through her fingers. Next, the man produced the torso stem and the handle bars (intact). Impatient, he lay them in the Number Four foyer. Tova hadn't found a box for them fast enough. What had customs been looking for? Drugs? Bombs?

At least they'd been able to recycle the plywood from the china crates for the fourth *succah* wall. Now Mike showed her how he looped a rope and the frame and roof pieces of the *succah* went up, over the porch door. Mike grinned; he'd reinvented the wheel. But the plywood of course didn't roll. He lay the wood against the porch door.


*Isru Hag* used to be a symbolic word on the Jewish calendar, the name of the day after a holiday. In *Eretz Yisrael, Isru Hag* had meaning, the whole place shaking off the season like a hangover. "The hair of the dog that bit you," Debra predicted. She'd insisted they would be a little down, that the antidote was more inspiration. She'd ordered tickets, for an afternoon tour of the Old City. Mike demurred; he needed to wait at home for the afternoon hour here when the business day started in the States, in order to conference call to his old boss and possibly a new client. Debra's Dave had set off first thing that morning for his reserve duty near Dimona, in the Negev. Tomorrow school began once more. When Tova turned back into her kitchen it looked as if all the children of Number Four had landed there. They'd spread out a Monopoly game on Tova's glass kitchen table. Esther wasn't as much the draw as—Tova suspected—the ice maker, and the endless supply of ice cubes to suck. As Shira handed out the metal play pieces, she announced that later all the kids would bus over to the Super Cheap Market to race the automatic doors.

Yossi raked in a heap of Monopoly money. At last, it actually looked like toy money to Tova when the entire first month all the shekels in her purse made her think precisely of Monopoly. She watched as Yossi stretched his whole body across the glass tabletop, on the way past "Go." "Get down from there," Tova said, sharper than she intended to. But regarding Yossi she was rather pent-up already. Yossi wasn't bad. There was something about Mike in him or vice versa: when his eye attached itself to a thing the rest of his body folded right after it like an accordion. Debra called it impulse. Sandy, Yossi's mother, called it life.

Yossi slid back onto his chair, counting hundred-dollar bills. As long as Yossi was under control she could walk out of the kitchen.

Then, from the living room, Tova heard a thousand separate tinkly noises. Symphonized. She heard Esther yell and every human noise that could be made was ejected at the same time.

The glass tabletop had broken.

———

"*Mazel tov*. Like at a Jewish wedding," Debra said, appearing at the door with a handy vac. How did she know what happened the same moment Tova did?

Tova was boiling mad. "Should I call Sandy?" Tova asked, following Debra into the kitchen. Shards and slivers bedazzled the floor. The children had already climbed out of the room.

"How do you know it was Yossi who did it? Call Gary the Glass Man," Debra said. From the counter she grabbed Tova's Heavenly Heights' *madrich*, and flipped to the index of the ads in the English to Hebrew side. "Who knows when he can come, though. I was standing behind his wife at the *macolet* and I heard her say to Old Hana that she hadn't seen her husband in weeks because of all the business."

Indeed, Gary the Glass Man was unreachable. "Be patient," his answering machine said in English. With all the requests for protective windshield sealant, please be patient. And now he'd expanded the business to metal work, armoring cars, school buses. He repeated the whole message in Long Island Hebrew. He would return all calls within a week or so. Tova slammed down the phone.

The floor glittered like mica, even after two vacuumings and two *spongias*. The frame of the table stood empty, hollow, and lonely—Tova thought—if she could use lonely to describe a thing. Mike innovated. He carried the plywood from the china crate, fresh from its second incarnation as a *succah* wall, and gave it new life. A tabletop. He was clearly pleased with himself, satisfied altogether by his problem solving. Tova, on the other hand, bloated with frustration—and anger. She found a vinyl tablecloth and whipped it out over the splintery wood. She didn't begin to exhale until she and Debra rode the number two directly to the Old City, and even then she felt as if she were spewing more exhaust than that old bus.

"You were right," Tova said to Debra. With her tongue she shaped her ice cream cone into a mound, remounded it, actually. The Old City tour was fine inspiration and the ice cream—of all things—was the final toast to the hair of the dog.

They sat, knees touching, at a small table, outside a small kiosk, two stories and a turn up from the Wall. During the tour they'd joined a dozen real tourists, and the tour, sponsored by the *Ateret Cohanim* group, was an orchestrated and moving introduction to what was called the Moslem quarter, but was in fact the oldest of Jewish neighborhoods before the outward fan into the "new" city. Moshe the tour guide wore his *tzitzis* outside his belt and they swung like cattails as the tour strolled behind him. He was built like a linebacker, or two. So were the *shomrim*, the guards who flanked them through the unnamed streets, streets no wider than alleys and curled so curiously you would need a special language to decode them. Though the adults eyed them uncomfortably, the little Arab children approached them. Did Tova want to buy film? Did Debra want a Water of Eden bottle? The point of the tour was to make a point. The *Ateret Cohanim* were buying back the homes and settling back there, in between the Moslem families who had homesteaded when the Jews were expelled in '48. Then, doorway after doorway, Moshe pointed out the cleft of a ripped-out mezuzah; until '48 Jewish families had lived here for hundreds, or a thousand, or two thousand years. "There"—Tova had raised her hand like a schoolgirl, pointing to an Arab home with laundry stretched in a line

87

between two TV antennas—"is probably where my grandmother lived." Next door a Jewish family was taking down its own *succah*, which stretched across the entrance to two or three apartments.

"There is," Moshe reminded them, "an American entrepreneur—no names please—who has recently sponsored four of these purchases."

Their last stop was a small square, where this entrepreneur had built a playground, mostly metal climbing structures and the same exact red and blue horses-on-a-spring they had in the playground in Heavenly Heights. A dozen or more screaming children spent their *Isru Hag* hanging upside down and inside out, riding, riding.

Their kiosk was the only one Debra knew of, besides the Carvels in town, that served soft ice cream. Tova's whole body had given way again, as if she were a set of bellows and had two modes only, the in and the out. She was relaxed. Around them, more real tourists swarmed, wrapping up their *Succos* vacations.

"Down and back to the *Kosel*. Time to say good-bye, no doubt," Tova said. She couldn't remember when she had stopped referring to it as the Wall and had begun the familiar, the *Kosel*.

"You have to start saying *Kotel*," Debra said. She licked her ice cream quickly, all around, and it turned into a mini-cone, sinking fast.

"*Kosel. Kotel*," Tova said. Debra made a proper observation, though. Debra was referring to the European pronunciation, a thousand years in Diaspora making, where the "t" had evolved to an "s." The modern, Israeli pronunciation, *Kotel*, was a sign of acculturation—in two directions at once: back to far tradition and onward to the modern language of the nonreligious. Some people spoke one Hebrew in the street, prayed in the other; some never spoke the language in the street. In Heavenly Heights, half the population persevered with the traditional "s," saying *Shabbos,* not *Shabbat.*

"It's a political question too," Debra began. What was left of the ice cream in her cone listed to one side, dripped on her fingers. She rose to grab a napkin when the ice cream man turned up the volume of his countertop radio. Who else but a bunch of Jews, Tova thought, would conjure such a language conundrum?

The call signals began for the news broadcast. The nontourists in the small plaza quieted naturally; the news was a national pastime. Everyone listened, all the time here. Tova flattened the top of her cone with her tongue. The news began with local stories: Tova could audio-skim, catch the nouns: Gaza, soldiers, day laborers. New road, Beitar Illit. Then world news: American medical high tech. *Nafal.* Fell? They named two companies that were *p'shoot-regel.* One was Digital Imaging. That was based in Massachusetts, actually the parent company of Mike's. Then the other name, she thought, but maybe she didn't hear right, was his, Bio Optics, based in Washington, D.C. The announcer said, "Vashinton, Deecy."

"What did he say?" Tova asked Debra.

Debra's Hebrew wasn't much better than Tova's but she did know a term or two. "I think *p'shoot-regel* means bankrupt." With that she ate the bottom "V" and the last of her cone. "And he said Vashinton. For Washington."

Tova's body filled up again, on the inhale this time and she felt as if she were going to burst. Mike had sunk seventy percent, maybe eighty percent of their money back into the company. Into their stock options. Tova had to get home, speak to Mike. What would happen to them without their money? What was this little twist? Something to make them like their neighbors?

*"Meod haval,"* the announcer clucked, "too bad." Then he moved on to the weather. Today and tomorrow, *bahir*.

*Bahir*. Tova knew that word, a Hebrew combo word for clear and light, as if the two were inseparable, she thought, pushing back her chair, as if they were always the same thing.

# IN THOSE DAYS, IN THIS TIME

SUNDAY MORNING WHEN, IN BALTIMORE, THE NEWSPAPER WOULD JUST be landing on the front porch, Jerusalem stirred from its *Shabbos* slumber collectively, like the waking scene in *Sleeping Beauty*. The soldiers lumped up at the bus stop, saying good-bye to parents after *Shabbos* leave; the Angel bakery, already at full crank since the night before, pumped a manna of sugar in the air, and Tova bused in to her Hebrew class.

She'd tested into *gimmel* level, the middle of five. After *Succos*, that first week in class had been a debacle. Tova and her desk mate translated a chocolate-chip cookie recipe and included a half cup of *nozelet*. When they read it out loud, the class roared. They'd made a mistake and the mistake was more than a consonant sound. They'd meant to say *nozele*. Liquid. Instead they'd used the word for mucus. Snot.

Tova rode the bus to town, to save the gas money and to save the wear and tear on their van that they were going to have to drive (now) for the rest of their lifetime. At the Central Bus Station she boarded a number three to Sharei Chesed. Unlike Heavenly Heights, Sharei Chesed was a mature neighborhood. Once there'd been a street plan, an even grid, and now it was buried to a hieroglyphic of overgrown foliage, trees, and bushes wild as an uncut head of hair. The thought filled Tova with optimism: Heavenly Heights wouldn't always be so bald, so exposed.

In the classroom, Ilanna ruled. She slapped palms for each English word used instead of Hebrew and demanded a shekel. She was saving for a trip at the end of the semester, to where else? America. When Ilanna moved her head her blond hair veiled the side of her face and this morning Tova watched Ilanna's hair inch across her cheek, her mouth, her chin. Ilanna opened the class by checking short comprehension questions on a story by S. Agnon. Then, together on the blackboard they constructed the last exercise. Find ten phrases that were Agnon's language and put it into modern Hebrew.

What was Agnon's language anyhow? Tova wondered. Archaic? Literary? But she made a concerted effort, refused to be a Yvegenia, wagging her hand all day.

Ilanna was a better teacher than Tova. She didn't suffer forlorn faces and she switched gears every twenty minutes. Her students acted like adults.

They opened their homework: verb conjugations came easier to Tova than stories. Most verbs began with a three-letter root that you hauled through paradigm constructions. If she knew a word at its root she could guess a new word and its meaning in all the permutations. For homework Tova chose thematically, she told herself, but not bitterly: *shekah*—in its simplest form meaning "to sink." In the passive construction, "to be sunk," in the causative, "to invest," in the reflexive, "to be sunk, to settle permanently."

Finally, five minutes before the end of every class they closed their grammar and story books while Ilanna schmoozed. The first week Tova puzzled it out, but with no result. Was Ilanna's daily sign-off calibrated, part of a master plan, or just a Rorschach of her own daily life? Today, Ilanna began by talking about newspapers. In Israel the newspapers were too expensive to buy every day—and family budgets so tight—that advertising was instead localized. Hadn't they noticed the sell-swap-buy-lessons-taught signs hanging in the building lobbies? And on public bulletin boards? Tova had seen the busiest bulletin board outside of Old Hana's *macolet*. How did she come to walk out of class thinking about Old Hana's *macolet*? Tova found the stream-of-consciousness relaxing, even if she didn't have energy left to connect the dots.

After class, the number three bus wound back to the Central Bus Station where Tova waited for her transfer. The groups of soldiers had thinned out, just enough to walk and patrol and scout *hefetz hashood*, suspicious objects. *Hefetz hashood* was the first object lesson a toddler—or a new immigrant—learned, similar to, in the States, dialing 911. *Hefetz hashood* was Ilanna's last week's schmooze: Report all suspicious objects and never kick a soda can in the road or overturn a rock. As Tova watched, the soldiers stopped and discussed a large shopping bag, rolled loosely and set on top of a trash barrel. Tova noticed, too, the small ads plastered on the bus-stop walls: concerts, death and funeral notices. Ilanna's Kulturkampf put Tova in focus, like adjusting the lens on a camera. She climbed her transfer bus and as the bus pulled out of the stop she saw a trio of city policemen approach the trash can, then step back a couple of feet, as a soldier barked orders into a walkie-talkie, his face whiter than white. The latest fashion bombs were jam-packed with nails and bolts and screws that could turn a victim into a hardware store.

Back at Number Four Tova gravitated to Debra's apartment instead of her own. With Mike in the States time had a taffy feeling, stretchy, her schedule and obligations free-floated, her relief from his little projects admissible. Though, hearing what he had to say from Baltimore, it sounded like he floated too: the optics project that wasn't, the buildings so tall, the drugstores' aisles so wide. Costco. Target. Debra sat at her kitchen table like a magistrate, sorting newspapers. Thanks to Ilanna, Tova understood the weight of the task—which newspapers to keep, which were old enough to set under the potato peels.

Debra startled her; she jumped up as soon as Tova came in. "I've been waiting to see you. Look," Debra said. When Debra sat back down she knocked the table and her coffee cup began to tumble: it balanced on an edge, threatened to dump on the newspaper, a *New York Times*, but, with a glance from Debra, it righted itself, like a dreidel. Tova leaned over to see an AP photo of a wide-faced, white-haired man.

She knew him. They all knew him. Their neighbor downstairs, sixtyish, a survivor, widowed three years. "What's Mr. Stanetsky doing here? And where did the *Times* come from?"

"Ahuva's parents. They'd thrown it out."

Was Mr. S in some kind of trouble? All she knew of Mr. S was that he liked to work around the building; he was the volunteer manager. Tova read the headline out loud: "CONDO KING FROM QUEENS TO CITY OF KINGS."

"What's a Condo King?" Tova asked.

"Read." Debra pointed.

Tova skimmed. Mr. S had developed condos and co-ops. He'd started in Queens, moved to Westchester County, northern Jersey, a little southern Connecticut. A real estate tycoon. A major Jewish philanthropist.

"Mr. S?" Tova asked. "So he has money. What's the problem?"

"It's what he does with it. He's been buying up land . . . and houses. Read," Debra commanded.

Tova read the first paragraph out loud. " 'Are purchases in Jerusalem legal and binding?' " She moved a stack of papers off the second chair and sat down, scanning to the bottom of the column. "It says that Mr. S refuses to speak to the press about it but his business manager quotes him. 'Since the dispersion in 586 BCE Jerusalem has been occupied thirty-five times and destroyed nineteen times. All these years the Jews have been quietly and legally buying back their rightful home, *Eretz Yisrael.'* " The newspaper, of course, put *Eretz Yisrael* in italics. To the rest of the world, the vision, the greater Israel, was the real problem.

Debra grabbed the paper from Tova. She'd already read, already summarized, already hyper-summarized. "He's got a case with the Supreme Court in Israel. You know that land off Hebron Road, outside of the Old City? The land on the far side of Mount Zion that's been some big controversy? He was the one who bought it and who's trying to turn it back to a Jewish neighborhood."

Tova grabbed the paper back and skimmed the facts in a sidebar next to Mr. S's picture: In 1910 a Hungarian businessman bought a twelve-*dunam* plot to build on—one day. He never got around to the building and the title just sat while local squatter types were there planting and selling vegetables to passing pilgrims. After '48 the land got lumped into Jordan, but the Hungarian family saved the original deed and all these years later Mr. S bought the land from the Hungarian family, the real owners, and he wanted to build a neighborhood.

"Like a Heavenly Heights. So what's the problem? Everything he did was legal." Tova looked up.

"That's why they're in court, to prove it *is* legal."

Tova wasn't sure why anyone needed proof. Wasn't possession simple as child's play, that at the end of the day, I'll take my toys and you take your toys and then we all go home?

"Did Dave see this?" Tova asked, finally. "Does everyone know this? Is he the mortgage Godfather?"

"I'm not sure it matters," Debra said. She took the paper from Tova's hand and crushed it. Then she stuffed it deep into the trash can, stomping in with one foot, then the other.

## 1964

Mr. Stanetsky's life is made of parts, not all equal: his search for memory, the money, his buildings in Queens, the kids, Malka.

He and Malka have come so far. When they crawled out of Europe he never knew the next step until she showed him or how much he could dig out of himself until she dug with him. Now he has a chance to give it back to her: Last week he emptied the coin wash on Park Street and brought home two hundred dollars of quarters in a canvas sack, and when he swung the sack onto the kitchen table Malka announced—in one of her leaps of logic—that because they were getting rich they would move again, to Jerusalem, and live near her sister. If it's Jerusalem and her sister she wants, she will get them.

Wherever she is, Malka creates a present tense and launches the family. She bagged up some quarters, ran out to the A & P, and bought peaches, plums, thick-skinned oranges with a dent like a *poopik*, a belly button, all that fruit out of season. She made fruit bread, fruit soup, fruit kugel.

Malka says she's too busy to look back. So, they don't share everything: Mr. Stanetsky strains to retrieve pictures, and he thinks he'll go mad because he can't call up a single one. When he sits and tries, Malka tells him maybe he should eat some more.

Just past the ticket gate at the World's Fair, Mr. Stanetsky rubs back his white hair. He is twenty-nine years old and he has been white for ten years. He seizes Danny's hand and orders Linda's elbows inside the stroller. Malka thinks he brought the kids to the World's Fair to give her a break before *Shabbos*. If he told her what he has in mind, if he told her that going to the Bell pavilion where all kinds of communication are possible, that it is like a pilgrimage—like Jerusalem too—she would say take a nap.

The very idea of a world coming together in peacetime piques his interest. From the roof of the building on Park Street, he's watched the World's Fair crop up in Flushing Meadows like a glass-and-steel garden; watched them coil sidewalks into the miles of tiny interior paths, important as capillaries. He's followed the openings and the ceremonies and the first week news: how the New Orleans chorus show was closed for indecency, how a nine-year-old boy from Port Washington was lost to his family three days until police found him asleep in a Pepsi-Cola boat.

Linda leans out of the stroller, limbering her elbows up and back as if she is going to dive. He reaches into a crochet bag on the back of the stroller and pulls out a peach. She shakes her head; she's eaten her fill of peaches. He fishes out Malka's *mandel* bread cookies he planned to save at the end for the drive home. He gives them each two but Linda's pieces are, plain to see, larger. Danny says thanks, then bends into the stroller and gets even. He fingernails Linda on her upper arm. She cries and points to two shallow pricks under her sleeve. Their fights are petty, spring from having too much (not too little), and Mr. Stanetsky doesn't have the heart to chastise them.

The colored arrows and little street signs shimmer like neon in the noon sun. He couldn't see these signs from the perch on the Park Street roof, or the new trees in pots, or the pools of silver water beneath them. The unisphere looked like a landed spider from above. At ground level it resembles a giant, ugly, high-legged beast, and the Bell pavilion, when he arrives there, reminds him of a shul.

Mr. Stanetsky pauses—hopeful, submissive. The crowd funnels in from two directions, right and left, and they obscure the entrance. Like in front of shul he does a little account-making that starts with questions. Malka would say brush the *mandel* bread crumbs off the shirts of both kids—which he does. He grinds down on the stroller wheels and rolls straight ahead into an exhibition hall.

A small crowd concentrates its attention on a young woman dressed in a hot pink skirt that puffs out and ends just above her kneecaps. The skirt makes her look like Linda when she's dressed as a ballerina, and he wonders if he'll be able to take her seriously. She stands in front of a display of screens and phones and points to a small man sitting at the table next to them. She says: "He is speaking to a scientist in Anaheim, California." Her Brooklyn accent breaks the word "California" into foreign syllables even Mr. Stanetsky can't recognize as belonging somewhere.

But this is just the kind of thing Mr. Stanetsky came to see. He pushes forward with the stroller; if breathing was voluntary he would have to force his breath to go on. The man at the table has a camera aimed at his face like a gun and he is moving his lips. The woman in the pink skirt is reading everything she says from index cards. The man at the table is talking to a man on the TV screen. They are having a conversation about weather and types of clouds. The man in California says they don't allow clouds there in California.

The two men laugh with each other. When their lips move the sounds they make match their lips; for all that distance there is no significant time lag. If this is a trick, it's a good one, like that talking horse the kids watch on TV.

Silence lays on the crowd, unnatural, thick as smoke. Linda's hand, filled with *mandel* bread, is frozen against her mouth. Mr. Stanetsky feels as if he has seen this kind of thing before. Then the woman in the pink skirt suggests the audience try out the phone for themselves. The crowd breaks into action. A family of children, all matched with short blond heads so you can't tell if they're boy, girl, Jew, Gentile, tries one machine. They mime and monkey into a little movie camera and their faces appear piled on top of each other on the telephone screen.

Back on the TV, the scientist in California is in the middle of shaking hands with Jiminy Cricket when his image spurts like a Bronx cheer. He evaporates, instantly, in a quick fuzz. The crowd sighs loud *aahs*. The blond-heads think it's hysterical. Something breaks away in Mr. Stanetsky and when he tries to name it, it feels as if he has a child's block lodged in his windpipe.

The woman in the pink skirt is flustered because she has never seen people evaporate. It's not in her cards, either, so she proceeds to the end of her little canned speech. "The instrument will not be available for public use in the near future." Her knees joggle when she says the word "future." The man in front of Mr. Stanetsky bends to tie his shoe. "It is beyond future," he says to his wife.

"Futuristic," she answers. Mr. Stanetsky has never heard this word "futuristic," and the woman, dressed in slacks with stovepipe legs, grabs her husband's hand. From the back, walking

99

away, they look like two men. Has she made up this word "futuristic"?

Malka would say "future, schmuture"; that his problem is, was, will be, that though he is anchored in one place his mind searches all over, flies like a homing pigeon that has lost its landing place. When he gets like that Malka says to stop: he has everything, right here, right now. A voice guides him back. To come.

"Come." It is Danny.

"Daddy, with these phones what if you're talking to someone and you want to turn the person off? Like the TV?" Danny walks behind the display to examine the wires. He lifts a cable. Danny's fat fists look more like boxing gloves than on any child he ever remembers. "Or can you just pull the plug?"

Mr. Stanetsky can't believe his son is asking these questions. "Why would you ever turn the thing off if you had the choice?"

Danny rolls his eyes and makes an "O" with his mouth. He's perfected a whine that has no sound and he reaches into the *mandel* bread without asking. Mr. Stanetsky wants to say he knows, how well he knows that children hate when you answer a question with a question.

But adults, like him, they can go crazy from it too.

PRESENT DAY

Singing wakes Mr. Stanetsky up from his nap. *"Ba'yamim ha'hame, ba'zman ha'zeh,"* in those days, in this time. It's almost Chanukah and Debra is on her balcony one floor up hanging out her laundry—or taking it in—and singing about miracles.

Mr. Stanetsky sits up and looks out the bare window at the side of his bed. The moment is like a window too—one dry winter hour in Jerusalem. A cankered blue cloud waits to strike off the farthest mountain.

Mr. Stanetsky leans forward and pulls up his knees. He remembers that he has napped because he has a hard job this afternoon. Because he's the most experienced, he is the *Va'ad Habayit,* building manager. Someone has to be anyhow—and a couple of days a month it makes him very busy. Today will be a day of chastising; he will hang a new set of *Va'ad Habayit* rules. He will also collect the *Va'ad Habayit* fee.

Thinking of the *Va'ad Habayit* makes it even harder to get out of bed. His feet are cold. They never stay inside the sheet. He bends to the right and can see through the window that the puddled rain from yesterday laps at the pine needles that have blown in from the forest. Together they make a tea at the edge of the porch drain.

*"Ba'yamim ha'hame, ba'zman ha'zeh."*

Debra moves into her apartment and is doing something different with her voice now. This version strikes him as more authentic than the one that he woke to. He hears the twang of her native Kentucky. She is a strange bird who has changed colors. She has flown here.

In his own way, he sees now, he has flown here too.

Like a homing pigeon, Malka used to say. Until three weeks ago he imagined he had just begun when he was sixteen. But then he got this: he pulls the picture out of his left shirt pocket. He has slept with it; this picture of his parents and his sister—of Blessed Memory—and himself as a little boy. It was taken in front of their house a good five years before anyone ever heard of a transport.

He'll show it to anyone but he always hands it over in the envelope, which is stained with red flecks where his cuticles cut against the edge of the flap. Now he rubs the envelope between his fingers. It has lost the grainy feel of paper and it is soft like tissue. He doesn't even have to look at the picture half the time, just rubbing the envelope is enough.

But now, suddenly, the paper rips on the long side, then down one of the gummed folds. He feels a pang from his head to his chest, as if he were ripping too. He is glad that the woman's music has stopped. O silence! The envelope is shapeless like a cotton ball and it takes both hands to wrap it around the picture and slip it back into his pocket. Mr. Stanetsky feels like crying.

Mr. Stanetsky walks to the kitchen thinking of the envelope. He doesn't have another in the apartment.

He plugs in the electric pot, and it clicks off right back at him as if it has been waiting. The steam pushes out of the kettle spout and he stirs the Nescafé into his cup. The coffee is especially black but not a thousand cups of coffee will get rid of this weariness now. The envelope . . . It has taken him sixty years to get tired. All the years, all the moving around and finally moving here, like a retirement, it never got to him. But now this: he drinks his coffee and pats his shirt pocket, where, before, he kept pens and a Swiss army knife.


Mr. Stanetsky will say there is nothing exceptional about Number Four. Number Four looks just like it's supposed to, for a Judean outpost. It is a stone-face, concrete high-rise with bars on the windows up to the penthouse.

It's a low-rise, rather. Four floors and eight units, one still unoccupied. It's easier for him to calculate what the couples owe for their common fees when he figures on eight apartments, but there are really seven because Mike and Tova own a double.

He is standing in the lobby jiggling the key ring that hangs off his belt loop. Mr. Stanetsky knows from experience how hard work is healing. His children always complain the menial labor should be beneath a man of his means, but he likes, as he says, "to putter." He walks past the bomb shelter to the broom closet. The *Rav-Bariach* lock takes two hands to pull down but if he doesn't keep it locked the children will play in there too. The broom closet is mostly his and it isn't neat. He knows he will need the old boxes for something and he would never throw out the dowels. The room is about the size of a small bathroom, and it has a utility sink that is the width of the long wall. Where is the *spongia* stick? Part broom, part rake, it is the best thing to pull in the *schmootz* those kids leave all over the floor. He bends to look for it under the sink and he knows to come back up with a curl in his neck so he doesn't hit his head on the drainpipe.

"*Baa—ya—mim—ha—hame.*"

Suddenly Debra's singing is everywhere again, even under the sink down in his closet. The singing bothers some of the men, but she's doing it in the privacy of her own apartment, and he gets the same kind of picture in his head like the one he woke up to: colors, and the music skidding over the mountains.

Then he has a black thought. Is he the only one who notices? Puts it together? How every holiday time it happens, or before one of Debra's shows. The music. Then the stuff that falls and stays on the floors. It's too crazy. After all, mud is seasonal too, and so is the way tree blossoms turn to mulch. And the construction dust, more like meteor showers. It has to land somewhere.

Nevertheless, as he straightens up, he thinks that he should empty one of these old boxes, that he might need it. What a *shmegegge* he is, walking to the lobby. In one hand he has the *spongia* stick and a box, in the other his condo ledger, and the new flyers he will tack on the bulletin board. The flyers took him the entire morning to make:

## VA'AD HABAYIT RULES: CONDO RULES

The residents are almost all English speakers, so writing it first in Hebrew is political. The ones who don't speak Hebrew yet should learn already. He has learned both Hebrew and English and before he writes he still has to think out his zayins כ, gimmels c, s's s, and fives 5.

## NO CHILDREN UNDER TWELVE
## UNACCOMPANIED ON THE LIFT

He would speak to Debra again.

## NO PLAYING IN THE BOMB SHELTER
## NO DUMPING TRASH IN THE BOMB SHELTER
## NO STRAY CATS LOCKED IN THE BOMB SHELTER

He told Yossi he would make him clean it up. He would speak to him again.

Overnight two new notices had appeared. Sale: American clothes, gently used. NordicTrack elliptical trainer. Plywood from shipping crates. And English lessons: Reading. Writing. Conversation. Both notices have telephone tags hanging off the bottom margin and the same phone number for each. Not that it should make a difference but he wonders if the advertiser is from Number Four. Mr. Stanetsky pangs for the insolvency of others; he's devoted his life to it. He pulls down one of the telephone number tags for himself. He can store some lift wood in his basement room. He lines up the notices with his own notices and centers his biggest one underneath them all:

## ALL TRASH IN RECEPTACLES

He's fussy about the cleaning. The lobby floor will be the end of him. Jamal comes to wash the floor twice a week but it is never enough.

Then he sees the black stuff all over the place. The stuff! His heart practically jumps out of his shirt and over his pocket. It is exactly what he is worried about.

He is *Va'ad Habayit*. He will get the stuff up and out of there before anyone sees. He works the *spongia* stick quickly and makes a pile by raking two sides. But the black stuff has a shine when it turns under the light. What in the world can it be? He bends down to push it into the box. The stuff is flat on one side and heavier than he thought. He uses his hands to scoop it into the box and prints his fingertips on the cardboard. A last little bit is left on the floor and this he pushes around with his feet.

Except for the shine it could look like the mud prints. The floor is dirty like this for months, until Passover when the rain stops.

Now, the rain *is* like something supernatural! Through the lobby glass he can see it move from beyond the mountains and close over the city like a theater curtain. The rain floods the curb and collects ankle deep at the dead end where the children play ball.

He discovers his reflection in the lobby glass. It is half-light outside and the fact that he sees his reflection means it is too dark inside. And it is only the afternoon. The thought has occurred to him to replace the light timers with photo cells. But anytime he spends anything extra the condo fees go up and the couples complain and that hurts him. He does everything he can to make it right.

He hasn't come to the lobby too soon: Debra's girls skid out into their hallway on the top floor. Their canvas shoes screech the stone tile and he can almost see the black pit marks they make. They are working on a harmony for their Chanukah show: ". . . *V'al ha'purkan, V'al ha'gvuros . . .*"

He bends in to listen and in one hand he has the *spongia* stick and in the other he is holding the ledger. He leans against the stair tread to write: 22 Kislev. December 11. He collects the condo fee the middle of the English month.

The rest of the harmony continues as the lift whirs down to the first floor. "*V'al ha't'shuos . . .*" He hears the mechanics of the pulley. Debra and her girls always put him in a funny position. They have to be the right age to use the lift; he really hopes that the oldest sister who is seventeen accompanies them.

He pats his shirt pocket. The picture is still there in the torn envelope. It is obvious to him why the whole thing, envelope too, is so important. He crunches his body over the top of the *spongia* stick. It has something to do with the shock of it. From nothing to something. It's the oddest thing. The craziest thing. Three weeks ago his cousin is visiting from Argentina and tells him she has this picture. She's just had it, she says, although they've visited half a dozen times before. It is decades since he saw his parents' faces—and his little sister. The worst part, the very worst part, was having remembered wrong. A smudge instead of a face, a smile where there wasn't one. And who was he angry at? He puts the picture back in the envelope and carries it in his shirt pocket. He keeps thinking he will make copies. Yes, he can get copies made in town and it will be back in his pocket in an hour. He will do it soon.

Outside, at the curb, a little white taxi with a green blinking top bulb pulls up. The taxi is framed by the lobby window and it looks like a picture itself. He hears that the lift is landing and Debra's girls have stopped singing. They try to open the inside door before the safety latch lets go. When the door jerks forward the girls practically tumble out on top of each other. The oldest is with them.

"*Erev tov*, Mr. Stanetsky." They are still wearing their school uniforms—blue skirts, white blouses—and as they straighten themselves up they shove their blouses in at the waist. Not one of them ever seems to have clothes that fit her.

"*Erev tov*, girls," he says. He lifts his hand with the *spongia* stick and waves.

They flip up the hoods of their winter jackets and discuss the direction of the rain and the power of the wind gusts. Should they open their umbrellas or not? In the end they decide no and sling the umbrella straps over their shoulders, wearing them like rifles. Usually when they see Mr. Stanetsky the younger ones ask if they can hang off his upper arm. He can even hold two and give them a ride. No one asks today. They are rushing.

The rain is like a tempest. He sees Ahuva getting out of the cab, trying to keep herself dry. She has nothing to say to Debra's girls as they pass. She has that kind of shine that the tourists have even though she's lived here all her married life. Her parents are visiting from America; she's wearing suede boots and a new leather coat. She pushes the cab door shut with her booted foot and then her umbrella blows out. She can't close the umbrella. She walks into the foyer shaking water, busy trying to pat the umbrella down, as if it has come alive. Mr. Stanetsky is glad, at least, to have gotten all the black stuff up off the foyer floor before she walks in.

"Mr. Stanetsky," says Ahuva. She holds open the inner door of the lift when she calls him. She has a kitten voice. "The mud is impossible out there. Right inside the curb. I almost lost my boot in it."

When he hears Ahuva say the word "mud" he is relieved. If it's really something more she won't restrain herself from commenting. Ahuva is a little spoiled, like his children. The children of survivors who made good. But her father's money comes from retail and Mr. Stanetsky has the real estate.

While things are under control in the lobby it's best to start collecting the condo fee with Sandy and Nathan. They live on the bottom floor and he opens the lift door.

The lift trembles when it stops at a floor, gets the women scared sometimes. All the more reason that children under twelve shouldn't ride unaccompanied. He touches the picture in his breast pocket. Underneath it, his heart is tumbling fast. He is healthy and strong but he sees in the little mirror that his face is white. Can it be a coincidence that the black stuff has started with the singing? Aah, in his world, in this world they never use the word "coincidence" and after all it could be nothing.

The Gernokovskys live on the bottom floor, but they are out of town for the week. Sandy and Nathan live across the hall from them where the stairway ends in a railed-in well. A Ping-Pong table with white highway lines lies up on its side and brushes the case of the hallway safety light. Mr. S wants to move the Ping-Pong table over six inches; he thinks to hide the *spongia* stick and the trash box behind the Ping-Pong table before he knocks on the door. No telling what can set Sandy off. He will get in there and out as fast as he can. He has lost any mood he has for this today.

Sandy opens the door. Nathan is not home. *Oy*, he is surprised at himself for forgetting such a thing. None of the men will be home. Rabbi Shapiro down the street has lost his mother and the men make a quorum for afternoon prayers at his apartment. Yossi doesn't count in the quorum yet. He is not bar mitzvah. He is on the stone floor—wearing a T-shirt in weather like this—rolling knee-hip-elbow, playing some twist game all by himself. Yossi is half man, half boy and he stands up when he sees Mr. Stanetsky. Mr. Stanetsky thinks to mention the cat but he can't say anything in front of Sandy anyhow. Mr. Stanetsky shakes his head and crosses his arms. He is not giving rides today. Yossi rolls back down to the floor.

Sandy looks all stuffed up in a tight sweater. But she looks all stuffed up anyhow, and uncomfortable. He's not the only one who notices she isn't herself since her latest operation. Last summer she went back to the doctor in Connecticut who operated on her years ago, and Mr. Stanetsky took the brunt of it already. She tried to rent out her apartment for the month and when she couldn't he had to convince her that she still had to pay the *Va'ad Habayit* fee.

"Mr. Stanetsky, you look positively gray today," says Sandy. He follows her into the kitchen. She looks at his face and in her own way backs off. "Not that I'm the expert on skin tone."

Sandy has her food processor lying open on the counter. She turns her back to him and cleans the blades with a spoon. She bangs the spoon into a stainless-steel bowl full of white potato grounds. "Latkes," she says. She is freezing them for Saturday night.

Mr. Stanetsky thinks of something he hasn't thought of for at least fifty years; how his mother used to fry the latkes with onion and how he used to eat the sweet burnt pieces out of the pan as soon as he could touch them.

She is also frying ground turkey patties. He hears the sizzle and smells them at the same time.

"How are you?" Mr. Stanetsky asks. He notices this time how he pats the picture in his shirt pocket. He doesn't want to call attention to it and in her home he is, anyhow, always feeling like he is waiting for something to explode.

"You showed me already," says Sandy. "Did you make a million copies yet?"

He is surprised, even from Sandy. He didn't want to talk to her about it but the edge in her voice . . . all the more reason to get in and out of here in a hurry.

She bangs the processor blade on the counter edge. "You'll have to wait a minute. I'm doing fifteen things at once." She runs back to the doorway. "Yossi, I'm making these turkey burgers for you." Yossi doesn't answer.

Sandy flops her purse up on the kitchen counter and pulls out a curly cardboard checkbook.

"Two twenty?" she asks as she starts to write.

Then they both turn to the outside. It is unmistakable that there is singing. He wishes it would wait another minute.

"Nothing's changed," he says. He is positive he sees something float by the kitchen window. But it is white, not black.

"Do you hear that?" says Sandy. "Debra's singing." She finishes and caps her pen. Has she seen it too? If she hands her check over any slower it will sink back into her checkbook.

"And the construction dirt," she says, finally. *And* means it's different from the singing. "The construction dirt is all over the lobby. Outside too. Take a look out on my porch."

He walks to the back wall. He knows where the light switch is on the side of the pantry. There is no natural light left outside and under the porch bulb he sees the wind has picked up and the rain blows in horizontal sheets. There is something there, but it is glossy in the rain and the lightbulb. The pile flattens as he watches.

In a reflex he pats his picture in his pocket. Sandy is so stuffed up and agitated but he's the *Va'ad Habayit*.

"I'll get someone to clean it up," he says. He knows and she knows that the cleaner is him. He looks at the door. He can't think of another thing to say.

When he leaves Sandy's apartment he sees Yossi behind the stairwell where his mother will have to walk out if she wants to find him. Mr. Stanetsky hopes Yossi hasn't discovered the trash box.

Yossi hasn't noticed a thing. He is using an American skateboard. It is against the rules. There is to be no skating, dancing, ball playing, etc. in the common areas.

Maybe Mr. Stanetsky will only try to get a couple of checks. There is nothing that says he has to do it all in a day. The electric bill, which is the biggest, is not due until next week. He clips Sandy's check to the top of the ledger and notices some black stuff and some white stuff on the floor. He grabs at it and tries to throw it in the box. But these little piles have no weight at all and it lands back on the floor. He toes it against the folded Ping-Pong table and presses the button for the lift and the door lights up right away. He waits the second for the door to disengage and takes the lift back to ground level.

Tova's door is decorated with a cardboard menorah and computer signs: WELCOME, ABBA and WE MISSED YOU, ABBA. Scribbled in pencil, in some tricky hand, is "What did you bring us, *Abba*?" Tova answers the door. Mr. Stanetsky points down to the pencil marks. Tova bends and shakes her head; her gold jewelry shaking down at her wrists. This graffiti is one of those things that really gets to her.

"Mike came home from Baltimore an hour ago," she says. "Business," she adds, because she's learned that no one goes back or admits he goes back for any pleasure. He follows her inside and gets the feeling that he is bothering her.

She and Mike are the only ones with the luxury of a foyer, which is now covered with suitcases—open and closed—and duty-free liquor store bags.

He follows Tova into the kitchen where Mike is slumped in a kitchen chair. He turns when Mr. Stanetsky enters and his eyes are wide open but red all around. If Mike was away on business the business isn't very good.

"You want I should come back later?" asks Mr. Stanetsky.

"No," Tova answers. "We're not so private—he's still wired from the flight."

Mike pulls out a chair and points. It is a wood chair with a flimsy cane back and seat. On Tova's kitchen counter Mr. Stanetsky sees layers of potato latkes draining on paper towels. As a matter of fact she has a new roll of American Scott Towels. Behind her, her children are excited and they slosh back and forth in pajamas with foot pieces. They start in the foyer and slide down the marble hallway back and forth past the kitchen door.

"I don't know if I can stand it," she says.

Mr. Stanetsky thinks she is talking about her children but he doesn't feel any sympathy. This bothers him. In truth they are more polite than all the rest of them put together. He presses the picture in his pocket against his chest.

"Did you make copies of your picture yet?" asks Tova. She is pressing latkes between paper towels and holding the oil-blotted sheets up in the air.

"What picture is that?" Mike's speech is sluggish. As if Mr.

Stanetsky is invisible, Mike drops his face into his hands and seems to sleep sitting up.

"Show him," says Tova. "It's unbelievable." She drops the oily towels into the trash. Mike follows her voice and lifts his head.

Mr. Stanetsky puts down the ledger and unswaddles the picture. The envelope is practically a lump. "It's the first one I've had—the only one . . ."

"That you? On the rocking horse?" Mike asks. Like the scientist he is supposed to be his eyes zero in and his focus is clear. He is very serious.

"The little blondie . . ." Mr. Stanetsky wants to say he looks like his mother but Mike hands it right back to him.

There is no real relating to this couple. The best thing is that Tova will pay two months' fee if he asks.

Her kids are screaming so loudly he can't begin to speak.

"Will you kids stop it!" She didn't yell when she first came.

Tova is organized. She has a desk in her kitchen with a Formica top that matches her cabinets. She keeps her records in a file cabinet built into a drawer. She sits at her desk and pulls out a large folding checkbook and starts to write. "You want another envelope for that? We've got plenty," she asks.

He knows it is Tova's nature to pay three months' fee if he asks her but he's heard some noise about Tova and Mike, about their savings or something, and an envelope, anything but what's obligated, is the last thing he'd take from them. He shakes his head no.

"By the way, have you noticed anything weird going on?" she asks when she hands him the check.

He turns up his head. Now that she stands she is a full head taller than he. On purpose he makes his face a blank page.

"I keep finding this stuff," she continues, "like mica chips all over my balcony. The kids bring them in on their shoes. I sweep them over the side but they seem to appear from out of nowhere."

"You know what you told me," Mike says. He must be very tired because his voice is very rude. "Tova says it's Debra, Mr. Stanetsky." Mike gets up from his chair. "She says that it comes from her singing. If that's true, then you have to do something. I didn't come back here to find all this craziness."

"Mike—you're tired . . ." says Tova. The word "tired" is loaded and Mr. S of all people knows tired that's not just physical.

She walks Mr. Stanetsky to the door and is clearly embarrassed. "Mike needs some rest. We can talk about this later," she says.

Mr. Stanetsky walks out the door and feels so twisted, like he can't even do his job right. He has a huff in his chest as if he's been climbing but he's just pushing the button for the lift. It's just seasonal *schmootz*. But he's *Va'ad Habayit*. He's the one who has to do something about it.

Before he can knock, Debra opens her door. Her undecorated door. As a matter of fact there is not a decorated thing in Debra's apartment. It is odd because she and Dave know from these things. They work a framing business out of their storage room. Debra points her head toward the kitchen and as she walks pushes back her dun-colored bangs. She rights the elastic waist of her skirt.

He follows her and notices right away that there is no oil smell here. Instead he can smell the rain from outside. They walk into the kitchen. On the floor are half a dozen red plastic bowls filled with water and peeled potatoes. There is a half-chewed potato on the kitchen table. He looks into the living room. The piano is pushed against the wall. Where a sofa might be are wooden drying racks with girls' laundry stretching across.

He sits at the kitchen table and pushes the potato away with the back of his hand. It rolls to the center and balances on its bitten edge. Debra knows, of course, he has come for the *Va'ad Habayit* check. He wants to say something more to her. He touches the picture in his pocket. He can admit it is something like a nervous habit. *Oy*, he has left the *spongia* stick and trash box somewhere. He looks around, on the floor, out the window. Does he need his trash box at all? Did he leave it at Tova's? Is it back in the lift? He is more upset now. He should get the check and get out of here.

Debra opens a deep drawer next to the sink. He half expects that she won't find her checkbook. She pulls out a corkscrew, cough drops, and twist-tied bags with dried leaves in them. She lays them up on the counter. "You know, Mr. Stanetsky, I have never bought a plastic bag since I've been in this country," she says.

Indeed, sometimes he comes up and he sees her wash bags and hangs them inside out to dry on her line. It is probably her nature to do things like that but her budget is so small she usually makes her month's payment in two checks. These thoughts make him feel small and dry like the leaves in the twist bags. He has come in an official capacity. He can get his check and leave. He shouldn't have to sit for a minute!

She must be preparing to ask him if she can make it in three checks.

"I have something special for you," she says instead when she turns around. The kitchen is small and she is standing one meter away from him.

He looks at her mouth when she talks. There is nothing so different or even strange about it. It's just that chirr in her voice that unnerves everyone. This strange, unadorned bird has been many places and she is happy.

"It's something special I've been saving," she says. But she isn't speaking it. Is she singing? She looks like she is talking but he hears the exact thing that woke him up from his nap. Maybe he's right. There is something weird.

But not like he thinks. He hears that the voice does not dust the mountains this time. It comes from a place that feels more familiar, like the pleat of the mountain. Her mouth is like a crevice and the weird stuff is coming out of it.

He shakes his head wildly. He doesn't see such things, ever.

She is holding a stiff plastic bag with a green line across the top. "It's a Ziploc. I've been saving it for something special. Give me your picture, Mr. Stanetsky. I will take care of it." She holds out her hand. "I'll copy it and frame it for you. I'll make you a Chanukah present."

He flattens his hand against his shirt pocket and looks at his shoes, which crosshatch black prints on the stone floor. He is afraid if he looks up at her face the stuff will come out again.

"I don't want to," he says.

"I'll give you my *Va'ad Habayit* check if you give me the picture," she says. Her voice is singing again.

"No," says Mr. Stanetsky.

"The whole month at a time," she says. She is singing.

With her voice like that he imagines two frames hanging. The picture of his family in one frame and—it looks funny—the envelope in another. Which wall is this?

She takes the picture from his hand. His fingertips tingle and burn and hers feel wet.

"I'll take that too," she says, putting the envelope in the bag with the picture.

He is sure she is singing this last line and he will not look at her mouth. That he hears is enough. She must know that her voice is a show.

Outside, beyond her head, and under the porch light, the ash and the glossy white marble up into a funnel. They blow out with the rain and head in the direction of the city.

# FREEMASONRY

IN HEAVENLY HEIGHTS THERE WERE TWO SHULS, THE MAIN AND THE Little, enough for variety and not enough (as the old joke went) to have one that everyone could refuse to go to.

In the Main, structure and pattern were pride and joy: steel beams anchored deep into the bedrock of the Judean ridge and soared three stories high until the whole interior was a Star of David. Where the peaks broke against the skylights, the *oys* and *aahs* of the worshipers rose like body heat and tangled with the conviviality.

The men who chose the Main for their daily prayers chose for the schmooze factor, before and after prayers of course: someone always knew the next *YESHA* council meeting, or that Old Hana's *macolet* hadn't, like yesterday, received the fresh milk delivery. Today, Mike knew the probabilities of another baseball season for Cal Ripken Jr. and what his salary might be—if anyone was interested. He'd returned at four A.M. from his second money mission to Baltimore in one month, the optics cable project for the break-off start-up company finally nudged to a grant-writing stage. "Now," he'd told Tova, "it's like a holding pattern when an airplane's waiting to land. But you're sure it's going to land." He knew how she depended on his optimism and then how he reckoned on her dependence to buoy them both. Mike unzipped his tefillin bag and reran the grant schedule—two months to write, one month to send. He shook the folds out of his tallis—three weeks for approval is what he'd told Tova but it could be as much as three months. Unfolding his own tallis, Rabbi Altman *klopped* him on the upper back and declared affection in his puckered English, "Haven't seen you. Around. Some time now." Mike nodded.

Mr. Stanetsky walked in. He bent to take his tallis bag out of the cubby in the back of the bench. In this shul the tallis was a symbol of marriage, and though Mr. S was a widower, the law never dismantled a former status. Mr. S unzipped his tallis bag. He'd missed seeing Mike every day too, though the way he downturned his tone every couple of syllables sounded mournful. "Yeah, *boychik*," he said. "You going . . . to be around . . . for a while . . . or what?"

If it were really a question it expected no more of an answer than a shrug. And it was enough for Mike that the men noticed and cared. As he sat to extract his tefillin from the bag a fat cloud moved over the center skylight and plugged it up, neat as a lid to a cooking pot. Instead of throwing their own shadows, the men stood inside them so that when Nathan Hacker walked in, dragging Yossi, and Yossi broke away, it was his shadow that sprang loose into the chandelier light. Nathan, though, caught the sad drag of Mr. S's question, then, like reading a headline and not finishing the article, Mike thought, Nathan misunderstood. Nathan pulled the collar of his shirt away from his neck, and visions of mortality dancing in his head, he asked, "What's wrong with Mike? I hope he's not sick. Or that sick."

The group of men froze, then calculated the error. It was logical—illness was one of the real reasons a person could leave town, or backtrack on an aliyah—or not come to begin with. Mike bent his head under his tallis. Mr. Gernokovsky, who had no chitchat English, stepped a light quadrille and spread his tallis like a wing. Debra's Dave, Mr. S, and Rabbi Altman followed, choreographed like fan dancers. Then Dave deduced the whole picture first. Nathan thought that Mike was mortally ill. Under his tallis his chest bumped up and back with stifled laughter.

Nathan realized in a flash they were laughing with him. At him. And he laughed along as he scuttled off to the side wall. Rabbi Altman banged on the podium with one heavy fist and motioned to Mr. S to climb the risers. Two more *klops* meant *enough schmoozing now.* A third, single *klop,* like an exclamation mark, meant prayers would begin.

On the bare tile floor of the shul, early comers like Rabbi Altman shuffled around the concrete dust so thoroughly the stragglers-in barely had dust to leave their footprints in. Rabbi Altman always began his day the moment the day began, even on *Asarah Be-Tevet,* a fast day when not a drop of morning coffee would pass his lips.

Rabbi Altman's solid hairless forearms and square neck made his neighbors think of a cut of stone when they saw him. His red beard was fire. For that image he got paid. He was the perfect boys' school principal. Parents begged him to turn their sons into men like him, little chips of stone. Rabbi Altman knew that what the Sages said was true: if he educated these boys, he was also their father. They were the myriads of children he and Shaindy had been on their way to, had hoped to have themselves, *boom-boom-boom* like a litter of puppies.

When Rabbi Altman opened his mouth to pray his own small *oy* escaped. Rabbi Altman never expected physical challenge so he knew right away it wasn't the missed cup of coffee; after convincing both Shaindy and the medical service that she was more than ready, Shaindy's wheelchair had arrived at the medical service. He had to pick up the wheelchair this morning, between nine and eleven.

After *Alenuu,* Rabbi Altman's neighbor, Mr. Stanetsky, brushed past. Mr. S had led the morning services. Turned out this fast day was also the third *yortzeit,* the very anniversary of the death of Mrs. Stanetsky. Rabbi Altman put out his hand to shake Mr. S's hand. "*Yasher koach,*" good work—a prayer job well done.

Rabbi Altman expected the common response: a wisdom for the day, a quote from the Sages, a quote from the Talmud, a thank you.

But Mr. Stanetsky was snagged back by memory and answered as if the *yasher koach* was about his wife, not about his prayer-in-honor-of-her-memory. "Yes she was good, I was good, and now?"

"I didn't mean her. Or that," Rabbi Altman said.

"*Boychik,* I'm not all here." To Mr. Stanetsky, Rabbi Altman was still a *boychik*.

In Jerusalem on a fast day you could cross from history to memory to the realm of the day all in one moment. Mr. Stanetsky had some errands, and lately since all his publicity he had become more assertive, like a person who had already arrived somewhere. "Are you perhaps going into town today? I'm looking for a ride."

"As a matter of fact." The medical service office was located right in the center of town.

"Fifteen minutes?"

"I need twenty. I'll meet you at my car."

In the foyer, the men who carried weapons picked them out of a cardboard box next to the stack of extra prayer books.

Outside of the main shul, Mr. S walked off in the opposite direction of his own apartment, whistling a tag from *Alenu*, hands in his pockets.

The ground was hard, not quite frozen, but yesterday's rain had trapped a brown crystal at the forest edge. A sailor's sun, ringed in bile, hung over Rabbi Altman's shoulder. Thinking about coffee on a fast day was natural, not a lapse into a wish for what the Almighty didn't give him. Rabbi Altman never did that. He remembered: last fall he'd had the best of times and the worst of times, drinking cappuccino with whipped cream, and the cream trickled down to the bottom of the cup and he'd tipped back his head for the last drop, knowing that was the way to get it all.

They had sat at a small table in the garden of the Ticho House—an oasis the Jerusalem way, where a little water and care brings up absolute potential. Rabbi Altman and Shaindy weren't used to any nightlife or leisure or recreation and the irregular noise through the palm trees annoyed him: two right turns away, the hawkers on the pedestrian mall had set up their kiosks of silver jewelry and army memorabilia, and teenagers—religious and nonreligious—poured in from all the city neighborhoods. They were only in town because Shaindy's brother and sister-in-law were visiting from America, a fraught pilgrimage to cram in the heavenly sites and like all tourists they could draw a personal map of the local restaurants. When the waitress came, Rabbi Altman and Shaindy ordered drinks, the brother and sister-in-law ordered Greek salad, Princess of the Nile fillet, pecan cake for dessert.

They sat under a hanging nut tree. Shaindy's brother and sister-in-law ate, steadily. Rabbi Altman watched two grandmothers play with a baby on the crafted lawn, green and uninterrupted as carpet. The baby was just learning to walk and they pushed her back and forth between them as if she were a ball. Shaindy laid her cane against the nut tree and made nuggets for the folks back in the States, describing each of their children, oldest to youngest, smiling every time she said Binny's name and using Binny as the standard for the younger boys. She popped saliva at her lips every time she smiled.

Then she spilled orange juice on her blouse. Rabbi Altman watched the stain spread across her chest, an ocher butterfly, trying to decide whether to jump up and blot it for her or to let it go. He felt everyone watching him, as many opinions about what he should do as there were eyes.

Then Shaindy's brother and sister-in-law looked at each other and started in gently. They knew a good neurologist. Shaindy should come back to a neurologist in the States.

"MS is MS. This is no exotic disease," Shaindy said, all the *s*'s in a row making a hiss. "And leaving the country is *yerida*, a stepping down." Desertion.

"Not every rabbi agrees with that. This"—Shaindy's brother was pointing to her chest but speaking of her passion—"is what got you here to begin with." He pushed back his chair. He was the youngest in Shaindy's family, had always been short-fused, making leaps of logic that had to be padded out—the very opposite of Shaindy. What he meant was that Shaindy's passion to come to *Eretz Yisrael* and her passion to stay were the same religion. "And let me guess, you're earning *Eretz Yisrael* by your trials and tribulations.

"True," Shaindy said. "Some people have the problems with money, some . . ."

"What does it hurt to have another medical opinion?" Shaindy's sister-in-law asked, finessing the discussion before a real philosophical argument began. *Eretz Yisrael*, at least like this, was not for everyone. Would Hashem have even made the Diaspora communities? With her fork she reached across the table and picked at her husband's cake. Rabbi Altman looked away; in their home sharing a plate of food was an intimacy, a private act.

"We've made our decision—together," Rabbi Altman said, for the record back in the States, making their position clear.

Shaindy looked at him, wrapped her hand around her cane, pushed back a little in her chair.

"That's right," Shaindy spit out.

He looked up. Shaindy wiped her own mouth. They were still a couple with their *Eretz Yisrael* in common.


The first years they were married Shaindy taught high school in the mornings. Afternoons, between babies, she tutored American college girls—religious neophytes—in Jewish outlook. Sometimes the college girls stayed to fold laundry or hold a baby or if it was Thursday night, clean vegetables for *Shabbos* or learn to bake *Shabbos* challah. And for the privilege of helping Shaindy the girls were grateful.

Six days a week Shaindy rose at dawn to her devotions. She called her morning prayers "a word to the Sponsor" and she'd had to explain the joke to him. Then, she took care of the babies, cooked their midday meal, took the babies to their *metapelot*. When Rabbi Altman would return from shul she'd be gone, but he would open the front door to the smell of red lentil soup, potato *bourekas,* brown mushroom gravy.

Now, as he opened the front door to their apartment, the smell of urine smacked him in the face.

On a fast day without coffee there was bound to be a moment of nausea. But like a nightmare, if he avoided closing his eyes it would not come back.

Rabbi Altman took a bottle of bleach from under the kitchen sink, and a rag. In the bathroom he plugged the sink, poured bleach and ran the water, wiped the toilet. He could clean the toilet in two strokes. If she'd made it to the bathroom it actually indicated one of the better mornings. After wringing out the rag, he gathered the top of the thin white trash bag (lemon scent). How many times had he prayed? Visited *mekubalim*? Changed the letters in their names, their marriage contract? First he thought it was just a matter of *mazel*—plain luck, the way the heavenly wheel turned—and there were ways to affect the *mazel,* to stop the wheel.

He unrolled another trash bag into the garbage can and swung the old one next to the front door with one finger. Far cry from prayer, work, his myriads of boys—little cuts of stone. These days he was the one who bought the children their holiday clothes, ironed his own *Shabbos* shirts. He'd learned how to cook one-egg omelettes and spread them thin across the pan, answer the phone, strap sandals. All at the same time, like a woman.

In their bedroom, Shaindy sat in a chair by the window, crying about what to wear for Binny's bar mitzvah. The bar mitzvah was ten months away, but her mind—like her body—had few places to go.

She wiped at her mouth and said, "There's a fly going around my face. Get it for me?" Even though she had range of hand movement she couldn't coordinate the hand with the eye. Rabbi Altman cupped his hand against her shoulder and trapped the fly. The fact that she didn't complain made them a perfect match and she watched him toss the fly in the trash can, step down on the trash with his foot.

"You okay?" Shaindy asked. "There's something on your face." She always made little efforts toward him.

"It's *Asarah Be-Tevet*. Without a cup of coffee my head feels like a helium balloon."

She nodded. Another time she might have laughed at him and his dependency on coffee. He picked up yesterday's newspaper she'd dropped on the floor and spun open the horizontal blinds. Sunlight dashed across her lap like arrowheads and she clutched the armrests against the illusion of sudden motion.

"Today is the day. Your wheelchair is in," he said.

"I'll make my debut." Shaindy laughed, no trace of her anger in her voice. Her fingers drummed the armrest as she relaxed them one by one. Her right eye drooped against her cheekbone. As he walked to the door she turned her whole body to look at him. "I'll be a *debutante*."

Rabbi Altman fluttered defensively. He didn't know this word "debutante" and she could still have that effect on him. Shaindy used to say they had a mixed marriage, American-Israeli. Only Shaindy knew that he kept the Alcalay dictionary, English to Hebrew, under his bed. *Debutante*. Judging from the irony in her voice he could guess what the word meant.

He turned back to say another good-bye. The blinds had settled, and the light around her head made a crown the color of sand. In that moment sat Shaindy Sternberg, twenty years old, sitting at the *Shabbos* table of Dan'il and Merielle, their mutual cousins, expounding the entire *machloket*—the dispute—between the RambaN and the RambaM, on whether moving to *Eretz Yisrael* or living in *Eretz Yisrael* was the mitzvah, then whether the mitzvah was a biblical command or a rabbinical command. He couldn't wait to hear how she would untangle it, lay up the arguments of each tradition—not that there was clear resolution. Her eyes were rich, gray like stainless steel; her hair, gold and red like polished brass, little gold freckles all over the backs of her hands. And when she'd stood up he'd thought he would faint at first, then he suddenly had felt hungry all over.

She waved good-bye to him with her right arm and stretched it slowly to flick on the radio next to the window. He could force the *mazel*, stop the wheel, drive the future. He'd learn English—for her, for them, better than ever.

Three electronic beeps erupted from the radio and stalled his vows, suspended the wheel in one of those moments he hated because not moving forward meant moving backward instead.

After the three beeps a pause, then the facile announcement all the same whether there was something raw on the other side of it or not. "The voice of Israel." Shaindy listened to the news, on the hour, every hour, checking to see if in the outside world it had gotten any worse.


Before he left the house Rabbi Altman checked the kitchen one more time. An empty carton of Depends lay against the trash. He grabbed the carton and began to crush it into small squares. *Adult Protection* (fold over), *Double Thick* (fold over), *Concealed*—

until the box was as small as a sheet of notebook paper. At first he'd added these adjectives to his long mental list of adjectives; then he began to hate them and all the euphemisms for disaster, English or not. He would never use one of those words if he were forced to. He slid the cardboard into the trash bag at the door. This illness had happened to both of them; they shared every bit of it. In the first years hadn't they marveled at the perfect formula of the *beshert,* one's intended? Rabbi Altman had said it many times himself. *Forty days before a baby is conceived a voice rings out in the World of Souls: The daughter of so and so will marry so and so.*

He ran into the bathroom to bring in another carton of Depends. He tore the perforation and lay the box on the floor.

The children had finally stopped asking what Depends means but the word had an expanded meaning for Rabbi Altman. The doctors were messengers of the Almighty; the wheelchair a tool. You mustn't depend on miracles but on this fact: the Almighty's rescue could come in the blink of an eye.


When Rabbi Altman walked outside his building lobby he saw Mr. Stanetsky and remembered he'd promised Mr. S a ride. Meanwhile Mr. S had made himself busy, chasing (alas) used foam coffee cups from the lobby trash can and advertising flyers that were swirling loose out of the mailboxes, blowing around in the entranceway. Mr. S handed the stack to Rabbi Altman, who shrugged and put them in the Dumpster with his scented white trash bag.

When they got in the car Rabbi Altman pulled the seat belt across Mr. S's chest and the numbers on Mr. S's arm rippled with his high, blue puffy veins. Mr. S wouldn't have used the seat belt if Rabbi Altman hadn't insisted. Rabbi Altman knew his type: Mr. S didn't dare fate. It was just that he'd seen so much of it he knew the outcome was not in his hands.

It took all of a minute to drive out of the main road. The forest, watered hours a day by winter rains, was fake-looking, crayon green. White almond blossoms had drifted to the edge of the blacktop making a soft ridge, like snow.

When he saw Rabbi Altman looking at the almond blossoms, Mr. S said, "Smells like coffee."

Mr. Stanetsky's imagination surprised him but didn't strike any recognition. Rabbi Altman drove.

Then Mr. S surprised him again, asking advice of him even though he wasn't the father of a school-age son, even though a half hour ago he had called Rabbi Altman a *boychik*. Mr. S wanted to know: What do you think? If your wife is your *beshert*, what about a second marriage?

In his job Rabbi Altman was used to having quick answers for everything, even if he wasn't always right. "They say the first wife you get what you need. If you have a second wife you get what you deserve," he said. They turned off the blacktop to a wide road and the almond smell stopped, abruptly. Army tanks propped up at the intersection sorted and slowed the traffic in the right lanes. Rabbi Altman looked straight ahead and drove through.

Mr. Stanetsky spoke, "She came to me twice, my Malka. On her *yortzeit*. The first time she was dressed in white. I said, 'Malka, what are you doing here?' She said, 'Danny'—that's our oldest—'get him married already and set him up.' So Danny got married and I bought him a store."

"Did she say anything else?"

"The second time—last year—she said, 'I will help you.' And then we had this conversation just like couples do when they're both of them alive—each word it's like the tip of an iceberg, you don't have to explain much. I was thinking and she answered before I got all the words out. I lay there wondering, it had been on my mind, if I should tell her I won't get married again and she said, 'Don't be ridiculous.' But how was I supposed to know? She's in the World of Souls. I'm in this world. Did she mean ridiculous to get married or ridiculous not to get married?"

"You didn't ask her?"

"I woke up."

"She didn't come last night?"

"No. I was having a hard time falling asleep but I waited, though," Mr. Stanetsky said, inflecting the last phrase as a question.

Silently, Rabbi Altman turned the car into the Street of the Prophets. The traffic slowed.

"I'll wait another night, I guess," Mr. Stanetsky said.

At the third stoplight, Mr. S asked Rabbi Altman to pull over and let him out. Rabbi Altman jerked the car to the right and, misjudging the curb, scraped his tire. Mr. S walked directly through a group of girl soldiers; the excited swaggering kind of girl soldiers, very feminine, not in spite of but because of their slacks and their khakis. Mr. S said something to the girl soldiers as he cut past and as he pulled ahead of them they put their heads together and appreciated something about him.

Two blocks farther, Rabbi Altman turned into the parking lot next to the medical service. Leaning against the kiosk at the edge of the lot were two pregnant Hasidic women, barely out of their teens, the same age as the girl soldiers. They drank cola from cans, and the little box-shaped hats perched on their marriage wigs tilted back with their heads, defying gravity.

———

Turning back out of the parking lot, the wheelchair slapped against the side windows in the backseat of the car. Rabbi Altman turned around, afraid the foot pieces that hadn't folded in neatly would plain fall off. He'd suspected immediately that the medical service had given him a used wheelchair.

Turning onto the Street of the Prophets, as he came up to the first stoplight, Rabbi Altman had a thought about *beshert*. Perhaps the two parts are from the same source-soul. What could explain their attraction? What else could explain the fact that they knew how to fight, for whatever they had to do, even if they'd been given one of the lousier jobs?

Just past the stoplight, Mr. S's face emerged, waiting at an outbound bus stop, heading home. In his right hand Mr. S held a striped paper bag. Rabbi Altman pulled the car over and a dozen hopeful faces turned to him. Rabbi Altman thought for a generous moment he should cram in as many passengers as he could but Mr. S got in, suddenly all bends and folds like a young man, and slammed the door. The little striped bag was folded over neatly at the top and small enough to rest in Mr. S's palm. Mr. S continued the conversation they'd begun earlier.

"You know when I was walking I remembered a story."

"Yes?" said Rabbi Altman. He concentrated on the rearview mirror, finding the wheelchair again, watching the way the wheelchair bounced across the seat.

"In my hometown, Krakow, when I was a boy they used to tell a story I never understood why they told it. It was an *Asarah Be-Tevet* story though and they told it once a year because it happened then. There was a plague, back five hundred years ago. The rabbi had lost his mother, his whole family. Then he lost his wife. The wife was young and the rabbi wanted another wife. So he went to his father-in-law and asked for the next sister. And do you know what happened?"

Rabbi Altman didn't know.

"The father-in-law said, 'No.' Why? Not because he wasn't a good son-in-law. Or a good man. That was a different relationship. The father-in-law said that at the first wife's funeral, the rabbi made a eulogy so wonderful and eloquent, it was as if the rabbi had had it planned."

"You do what you have to do." The words flew out of Rabbi Altman's mouth. He sat upright in the car seat and lost focus of the wheelchair in the rearview mirror.

On a fast day without coffee there was a moment of madness but if you hung on and rode it the madness would subside. To Rabbi Altman Mr. S's face looked fresh and open out of his collar, as if Mr. S had just woken up and it wasn't clear who was explaining to whom.


Pulling the wheelchair out of the car made a whole day's excitement for the preschool children, the mothers, the *metapelot*. From Building Number Four to Building Number Sixteen, apartment by apartment the blinds shook in the front windows of each living room overlooking the parking lot. The Arab day laborers stopped jack-hammering in the corner where they were building another new shul.

"*Oy,*" said Mr. S, once they righted the wheelchair on the blacktop and opened it up. Mr. S stuffed the striped bag into his pants pocket and bent down. "I can fix the footrests," he said. "It was used already, you know, probably not so good." With that, he sighed.

Rabbi Altman sighed too. He didn't see a wheelchair, but

another vision of *beshert*. The souls were fat like cherubim and they tried to come together. They bounced, broke away, couldn't quite meet up face-to-face. But they knew each other well and would recognize each other anywhere in any world. Mr. Stanetsky looked over to the spot where the cherubim were. Mr. S lingered there for a minute, then roped Rabbi Altman back with his eyes. "This world, *boychik,* this world."

# LITTLE *SHEFFELAS*

RAIN FELL LIKE SOMETHING ELSE AFTER *TU BI-SHEVAT*, THE NEW YEAR of the trees: three winter storms knocked back to back in an evening, a morning, and an afternoon. Just one week earlier, the schoolchildren had marched out, spades and sand toys in hand, planting baby date palms and infant yews on the bald ridge between the building backs and the road. Now the water ran off, a meter deep in the level spots, flushing out the new two-lanes to town, and the baby trees clung for their lives with the last strength of their spongy tubers.

By Friday afternoon the water receded halfway, and the roadside swelled, fat as a cracked baked cake: loose tar and rubble turned up crumbs; the almond blossoms and what was left of the baby trees iced across the travel lanes. Unless they had business in Tel Aviv or some hankering to visit Amman, Jordan, they were trapped, literally trapped in Heavenly Heights.

*Shabbos* night, on Debra's balcony underneath high stars and the kind of cellophane sky that stretched clear sapphire as far as the eye could see, Debra, Sandy, Ahuva, and Tova sat in a circle near the railing, keeping an eye on the blacktop where the children rolled their own way out of cabin fever, turning strollers into chariots and racing curb to curb through the standing puddles.

Debra pointed to the sky where the stars peppered through steadily; the sapphire changed into diamond pave. "Dry weather. Soon," Debra announced. Predicted.

"Then what?" Sandy challenged, turning her chair directly across from Debra's.

"I'll tell you then what," Debra began. "When we get out of here I want a trip to Uri's pizza. They have that hot sauce in bowls on the counter that you spread on top."

Sandy and Ahuva smiled, nodded.

Tova asked, "Uri's?" How come she'd never heard of it?

Sandy snorted. "You think you know everything already. You just got here."

Tova dropped her jaw. But she should know by now to armor herself against Sandy's little scimitars.

Debra and Ahuva turned their chairs for a complete face-off. The children weren't the only ones with cabin fever games.

Sandy understood, at least, the cue to take a turn. "When I get back to town," she began with a whisper, then amplified into a rhapsody, "I want to buy Yossi a fancy tefillin bag for his bar mitzvah, the silk ones the women make in the caravan communities and they bring them in for pennies. You know, and they sell them to the tourists at two hundred percent profit."

Neither Ahuva nor Debra responded, a kind of getting even because the strength of reaction was the score.

Debra took pains to set her mouth into a straight line. For a moment it even looked as if she were roosting, and since Sandy was sidelined the conversation would end. Then, as Debra leaned forward to broaden the lay of her skirt across her knees, she said,

"Ahuva?" If a woman could drop the prickliness, restore equilibrium, maybe pick up the mother theme, it was Ahuva, who'd had five children in six years.

Ahuva didn't blink an eye. She straightened the beaded front of her velour-and-sequin *Shabbos* robe. On her feet were heeled, leather slippers that she suspended off her toes and slapped back onto her arch. "Maybe it's safer anyhow that we stay off the roads and don't go anywhere, but if I could I would go to Marshall's," Ahuva said.

Debra hooted. Sandy raised her eyebrows so high, they lifted her ears against her little pointy hat and her hat slipped back, a small chain reaction. Even the stars stirred up a commotion, lowering, moving, purring like something alive.

"Or Loehmann's," Ahuva added, pleased with herself. "When you go get bargains it's like you're winning, getting some release."

Who could top this, Tova thought. But the women turned to her; it was Tova's turn, ready or not.

"I want a Sunday," Tova said. Sunday! The word just popped out, to her surprise as well as the others'. Sunday was a concept, a leftover from Diaspora land. Tova should be happy with the six-day-then-*Shabbos* week. But *Shabbos* was so intense and so was after *Shabbos* with all the effort to rope Esther in from her ball games, to get to bed early, to get ready for school the next morning. "One Sunday a month?" she said, softening the complaint into a question, into the womanly need for consensus. Below on the main road, the *Shabbos shomrim* drove by in their Jeep and perforated her moment. In a sudden heat Tova unbuttoned the top button of her blouse, then the second and third and fanned her exposed neck—there were no men around. When she looked up Sandy and Debra were nodding. Ahuva made a point of averting her eyes.

That Sunday, road declared dry and passable, slick almond blossoms and sticks that had been trees plowed to the side like crests of snow, summer stole from winter, making a dry day—warm— in the eighties. Mike and Tova stole the day too. They headed north to go rafting on the Jordan River. Mike folded over the corner of a page in his tourist book. *Kids Love Israel, Israel Loves Kids*. Climbing into the van Tova sorted three supermarket bags at her feet: towels, *petel* water and paper cups, sandwiches, packaged salty crackers (expensive), and American peanut butter, a treat.

The south to north roads were even numbered, the east to west odd, and here and there the highways stretched their shoulders, emergency landing pads for military aircraft. Tova slipped a tape in the cassette player: *Uncle Moishy and His Mitzvah Men*. Uncle Moishy ended every set yearning for Jerusalem. Poor Uncle Moishy; Jerusalem was receding in the rearview mirror.

For over an hour they drove along on Route 2. Then they turned east and followed the signs—no more numbers, just arrows—pointing this way and that to Kibbutz Sde Menachem. Halfway into the kibbutz the tarred road turned into a dirt road; gravel whipped up into the exhaust and pattered, inhaled into the engine.

They parked a few meters from a young man, sitting on a folding lawn chair, smoking a cigarette. Boaz (name written across his T-shirt) was tanned, blond, blue-eyed, and he looked surprised when they said they'd come to go rafting. But Boaz wore warm-weather clothes: cutoff jean shorts and navy Bass sneakers without socks. Why was he so surprised? That on this window into summer they had come for summer sport? He rose and walked into an open, adjacent booth where he leaned on the wooden counter to greet them officially. Behind him, life vests clustered off hooks, like fat biblical grapes. He pointed to a chalkboard, prices listed in two straight lines, then without a word held his hand back out to Mike for shekels. Forty per person. Tova cringed. It cleaned out Mike's pockets and they would travel back to Heavenly Heights with only the coins in the bottom of her purse.

After Mike paid, Boaz pointed to a stack of rafts on the floor behind him. Mike leaned over the counter and chose a red and orange raft, starboard painted toothy, a smiling shark. Boaz dragged the raft out of the booth, pointed the whole family up a dry weedy path, and asked them to wait, exactly in a patch of sunlight. To the left, through a meter-deep bramble, the river trickled along. To the right was a field, full of small, woody, twisted plants alit with white puffs. Cotton? Tova wondered. Dreamy cotton like the old south. "Cotton *balls*," Esther cried out loud with certainty, clipping Tova's reverie. At that moment Boaz, a pointed blue tembo hat set on his head, drove up in a tractor with two hitched-on sections. Bringing up the rear was a flatbed with the raft and the life vests; directly behind him was a cart with benches. They climbed on and he drove them, rickety and bending about fifteen minutes to a flat entry point on the Jordan, fifteen or twenty miles beneath the Banias, where the water combined with winter runoff and the natural spins and waterfalls flowed down from Mt. Hermon, the highest point in the country. Where they stopped, the cotton fields turned a corner and met a cornfield—lush, green, ready for winter harvest. Boaz laid the raft on the small shore. They climbed in one by one, according to weight. Mike and Tova at either end, Avi and Yoni rigged up like Ghostbusters in their puffy vests balanced the inside, and Esther anchored the middle. Boaz pushed them off and Tova leaned back, first things first running her forefingers in the Jordan—icy cold, arctic cold.

The first twenty minutes conjured all the Sunday adjectives Tova came for—calm, smooth, relaxing. The raft rolled and dipped—the bends and rocks calibrated by the Creator better than any roller coaster, any man-made ride.

"This is too slow." Esther spewed a complaint, or an accurate observation, depending on how you looked at it, bound to be the first of many. She bent up on her knees and made a T with her arms. Because the ride was slow and Esther was bored she was going to fly instead. Yoni rolled upright in his vest, beginning to imitate her. "Esther," Mike said. She turned to face Mike, but before she sat back down, if she was going to sit back down, a rocky hump spun them sideways into the side bramble and Esther fell back against the baby. Yoni laughed. When she righted herself she looked back at Mike. It was all his fault. They barely settled back in when a small waterfall spun them again, this time 360 degrees, three—maybe four—times until they steadied against low trees and stopped.

"There's a scratch on my eye," Esther whined. Tova kneed forward and picked leaves out of Esther's hair, and a beetle—which she didn't dare mention—then she froze Esther's whipping face between her hands. How could she examine her eye if she didn't calm down? The wildness was new, natural in this country, and also the fact that she expressed it. All the time. They didn't grow Jews like that in America.

Mike took an oar and pushed off of the trees. Now that they'd seen real action, Yoni and Avi sat up straight, eyes wide and laughing.

"It hurts," Esther announced again. The tree scratched her head too. The raft wasn't fast enough, the raft wasn't level enough: Esther, the straight shooter. Her complaints were like Muzak—would that it were ignorable as Muzak, Tova thought.

When the water calmed again, the baby lay back, sunning himself. He looked like a belly-up bug. They'd been riding for thirty or forty minutes. Boaz said the entire trip was no more than an hour and Tova was glad she'd come, and that no one else was around. Part of the release was the privacy, part of it the still beauty; they'd floated into a photograph in Mike's tourist book.

From the first high spot against the first bald waterside they caught sight of the northernmost peak of Mt. Hermon and beneath it the cluster of red roofs, the solar panels, and the forest of *doodai shemesh*—the water heaters—of Kiryat Shemona. The water trickled and rushed. In the rest of the world the sound was turned off. Tova looked at all three of her children and saw herself with three more, and three more than that. Tova relaxed her body against the inner bulge of the raft rim. Esther opened her mouth; Tova flinched. Esther was about to whine again, or proclaim some truth about dead fish in the water or that they'd brushed past a hornet's nest. Above them, an airplane distracted. It circled, lazed, puttered with the exact, natural noise that the boys made with their mouths when they ran their toy cars against the bedroom wall.

Then, from the direction of Kiryat Shemona, they heard crashing. Crashing and booms. *Ka booms* in two syllables.

At first Tova thought, How did that little, lazy plane get so loud?

Then, another *ka boom*, and time slowed so that each thought had a thought of its own hitched onto it. It wasn't that litttle plane. For, streaks of light shot over Kiryat Shemona. Meteors? She turned to Mike.

"*Katyusha* rockets," Mike said, ducking and grabbing Yoni.

"They're bombing Kiryat Shemona." A couple of miles away.

Tova dove toward Avi. "*Sheffela,*" she said. Little lamb—she'd brought him to a slaughter.

And Esther sat in the center of the raft, alone, bereft of either parent, and in what was not her last ballyhoo of the day, crowned their success and underscored their failure. "I want to go home to Heavenly Heights. How could you take us to such a dangerous place?" she wailed.

Later, the imprint remained on Tova's inner eye: the way they dove for the boys, the way Esther's barbed-wire disposition had trained their reflexes. They sat in the kitchen. When Tova uncrossed her leg her thigh hurt where a branch gouged her—probably on one of their spins though she hadn't felt it at the time. "Don't lean on the table," she said to Mike. The new glass had finally come in—1,200 shekels.

"It's actually funny," Tova said.

"What's funny?"

"What Esther said." That Esther was secure enough in general to feel angry when she didn't know what she was talking about. Or maybe she was more right than they.

"I guess we're just the paradigm of success," Mike said. This sarcasm was brand-new. He got up and opened the refrigerator, moved some jars around. Maybe he was just hungry. They'd never really eaten lunch and they were a meal behind.

"There's fruit."

"That's not what I wanted," he said. He gave up on the refrigerator and sat down with nothing to eat. Tova got up and foraged the pantry. She found the crackers they'd brought in the car, lay the open pack on the table, and pushed the pack toward Mike whose sour face reminded her precisely of Esther's, a little template of reality. Only when you're feeling safe, she told herself, do you also feel safe to act out and complain.

It was Purim day, fourteenth of Adar, year 5759 from creation, Jerusalem, Israel, Earth, World, Milky Way, Universe. Yossi felt like a speck.

He watched the 7:20 bus chugging uphill, blowing exhaust, running regular schedule. He stood outside Old Hana's *macolet*. He wanted to just go in already, it was so hard to wait for Binny Altman.

Yossi adjusted the lump of fur at the back of his neck. This was the gorilla suit he'd wanted for a couple of years now. He'd wear something like this every day, but Purim was costume time. Why Purim, anyhow? It was something deep about appearance and reality, but those kinds of words in the same sentence made him stop paying attention.

He adjusted the lump back in the other direction. Maybe the gorilla costume was more trouble than it was worth; it was one-man-size-fits-all and he'd had to pull the tie strings tightly till the shoulder pads crossed at the back. And on his way out the door Mother said he should have gotten the boy's suit. But the man's gorilla had the full mask with that chunky fur head and besides, he'd spent the whole year between sizes, between ages even—it was eight months till his bar mitzvah.

Look at that, Yossi thought, the next bus driver, the 7:25, he knew how to do it. He'd gotten a gorilla costume too. There were a couple of early riders scattered around the bus seats. Were they in costume? Or maybe they looked like that anyhow. Sometimes when he was excited, even if he could control himself he couldn't control his legs or his eyes. Where the heck was Binny?

When he was little, nine or ten, he'd spent a Purim picking from the food baskets the families sent to each other as gifts, and the mothers, especially the mothers, worried "Was it enough?" and "Did they remember to give to so-and-so?" and "Who gave to them last year?" He straightened the fur at his knees where the leggings had twisted around. Who cared who the baskets came from? The way they piled up on the dining-room table, the packing cello looked like colored straw—until it was almost a chore to sort the suckies from the licorice, the hazelnut from the almond chocolate, the carob sticks and the oranges and the pomegranates. Then the little bottles of wine and brandy and the miniature whiskeys and Le Roux liqueurs from America. Had they always gotten them or just last year? He tried to hold his leg down with his furry arm. It was so hard to wait. This year was going to be different.

But maybe Binny couldn't come. Maybe Binny wouldn't come. Part of getting older meant it wasn't just the chocolate, but doing some of the things you wouldn't normally do—maybe just acting like someone else. He didn't think he had to convince Binny. Binny liked him. He liked everybody, that was true, but he liked Yossi more. And there wasn't anyone in the world Yossi would like to hang out with more on a day like today; to drink a little, get a pack of cigarettes like the older boys did.

The clouds were breaking up in hunks over the mountains. This neighborhood, almost a town itself, was built so high on the hills he was even standing in a cloud. They'd had no choice, Mother and *Abba* said, with the families booming. They had to stretch these neighborhoods into the mountains winding out of the city. But you could still get to the center of town in fifteen minutes, Mother said. He almost never left the place anyhow; all ten blocks of it. Everything he wanted to do was always here.

The wet from the clouds gave his fur a real animal smell. Maybe Binny didn't want to come. Maybe his father knew who he was meeting and didn't let him come. A million times when he thought of good, he thought of how much Binny liked him. He'd wait for Binny, he'd wait for him here and not start without him.

"What are you, a camel or a gorilla?" Binny asked, smacking the fur lump on his back when he finally showed up. He'd slid in through the cloud mist. Good trick. Yossi filled up with feeling for Binny. Loved him for coming, loved him in the pirate costume. Binny had blackened in his gingy eyebrows and dotted some stubble on his face. He wore a red shiny sash and a plastic eye patch.

Okay. It wasn't so original. There'd be at least a dozen pirates in shul. But that wasn't why he liked Binny anyhow. Binny just had this way he could make other people happy for him.

"I told you to be here at seven-fifteen," said Yossi.

"I couldn't help it. I couldn't just slip out. There's no reason for me to be going anywhere and I can't lie. I had to tell them I was taking a walk and they couldn't figure out why I was going . . ."

He didn't have to say any more. What terrible luck his best friend had a father who was principal of the school. Rabbi Altman made it clear that he watched what was going on. Sometimes he let Binny be with Yossi, sometimes not. Like it was some kind of gift. It just depended on how Yossi had been, what kind of "period" he'd been going through, like his parents said. But Binny told him no matter what Yossi always made him have fun. Yossi jerked his head toward the *macolet* door. "Let's get started."

"I thought you weren't allowed in there," said Binny.

"Old Hana wouldn't have the heart to shoo me away today,"

said Yossi. He was really hoping that Old Hana would never recognize who was in the gorilla suit.

The last mist wheezed off the mountaintops. The sky had bumped in, all blue. He rubbed some water off the *macolet* door with his rubber fingers. Old Hana was at the register, a little book of Psalms in her hand. Yes, she was open. She smiled. Either at his gorilla or probably because she recognized Binny.

A clown man rushed by him and pushed into the door. His legs and arms were all bony and he'd hung a pillow belly on his front. He wore an umbrella skirt over his trousers. Was his costume done or not? He had a red bulb nose on his face. The man turned back and his nose rolled up toward his eyes as he said hi to Binny. A second man rushed in ahead of them. Moses—Yossi was pretty sure because of the staff in his hand and a thin weave gown with blue fringes. These were some of the family men on morning errands, looking for *leben* and bags of milk. And since it was an obligation to drink to obliteration today, each of them bought a bottle of liqueur. Old Hana tossed out double plastic bags for the bottles. Usually she was so cheap. But the clown man wasn't happy. He would have to come back because the fresh bread wasn't in yet. He almost growled at Old Hana when he walked out the door.

Yossi and Binny walked in.

"A packet of Kents." Yossi pointed up to the cigarette shelf rigged up on the ceiling. Old Hana couldn't figure out who he was. Old Hana didn't even have to dress up, he thought, as she climbed down the step stool and cranked her bent old witch body back down to the register. She lay the Kents on the counter and put out her hand for the shekels.

Then the thing popped into Yossi's head: "Grab some matches," he said to Binny.

Binny dug his hand into the plastic canister on the counter.

Yossi nodded to the door so Binny would see what he meant.

Binny knew exactly what he meant. "You can't do that, she knows me," he said. "She'll think I'm . . ."

"You already took the matches, didn't you?" asked Yossi. Old Hana scrunched up her face like dried fruit; she wanted her shekels. Yossi grabbed the Kents off the counter. "Run!" he said to Binny.

He ran out the door and Binny had to follow. Old Hana made it after them as far as the sidewalk. Yossi ran uphill and jumped the stone wall next to the trash Dumpster. Binny was right behind and crouched down with him. They breathed in the trash smell: citrus peels, mashed cucumbers rotting on old newspapers.

The bakery men arrived, Yossi could hear them around the corner and Old Hana cackling in her cackle Hebrew asking them to bring it in the store. They tossed their plastic crates out of their open trucks. Yossi could smell the fresh seed rolls and the sweet cheese buns. He wanted one of them too.

"Why'd you do that, you idiot?" asked Binny. "Why *did* you do that?"

"I don't know. I couldn't help it," said Yossi. The cucumber smell made his face tickle and blurred his eyes. He tried to lift his mask to wipe his nose but it was tight at the neck and he left it on. If he squinted he could see okay anyhow, and when he squinted his vision did a trick and bent around a corner: there, by the bulletin board at Old Hana's, Rabbi Altman, all in one motion, stopped, read a poster, tore a phone number, pocketed it, and bounded off to shul.

"Well, I didn't come here for this," Binny said. He straightened his sash that had twisted off center when he ran away from Old Hana's.

Sometimes Yossi couldn't tell if Binny was really mad. Binny shifted his sword to the other side. It wasn't staying in because the sash had ripped. "I've got to go meet my father, to go to shul."

Yossi watched him walk away on stiff pirate legs, as if his foot were a peg. The stones on the wall felt like plates of ice. Binny never stayed angry at him for long.

Yossi had to meet *Abba* at shul too. But he wanted to figure out one thing first. If it was going to be too hard to take the mask off and on, he had to figure out how to smoke with his mask on. He pursed his lips through the little tongue hole and pushed away the fur on either side of his mouth, making two fingers into a V. He liked that part, reminded him of the way the men pushed at their beards before they said important things.

Yossi was so late he skidded into shul. The first thing he noticed was all the human color. The boys were all dressed up. Some of the young men were too. And of course, his *Abba*, who could never decide how serious to be—even when he was supposed to be having fun. *Abba* wore a half costume. A cowboy hat whose wide brim made shadows on his face and made the bones stick out on his cheeks. He wore a little string tie that clipped shut with a metal horse. He should have dressed up all the way or nothing at all.

"How-dee, Yossi," he said in his drawl, "is it really you?"

Yossi didn't answer. There was Binny, with his little brothers dressed like a pair of dice, and his father, Rabbi Altman, sitting one row ahead and a couple of places over. They sat directly across from the shul rabbi who came over and shook Binny's hand and pinched the cheeks of the faces poking out of the dice. The old men on the left side of Rabbi Altman fingered Binny's sash. *Ooh* and *aah*. Oh, *brother,* Yossi thought.

The half-dozen men on *Abba*'s bench looked up at Yossi. The bench was not well balanced and everyone had to get up—it was like a seesaw—so that Yossi could slip in. They had to sit back down all together. The jerks. *Abba* looked like he was going to use that drawl again. Yossi grabbed a prayer book and turned his face into a page. He moved his lips: Leave-me-a-lone. *Abba* would think he was praying.

Binny switched his eye patch to the other eye, so he could turn, just a little, and look at him. Binny's father jerked Binny around as the beadle opened the ark. They bounced up to say the prayers before the special reading of the Purim story.

All the boys were nervous and excited. The Purim story was really about good guys and bad guys. Haman wanted to wipe out the Jews but the Jews were saved. So when the story was read out loud, they wiped out Haman's name instead. It was the only time you could go crazy in shul.

The little boys had squeegee hammers and wooden cloppers. The first time Haman's name came it was about a third of the way into the reading. Binny had an electronic toy that made crash sounds, bells, ambulance sirens, glass breaking. Yossi had his roar. When the bad guy's name was read he roared until the rubber piece shook at his mouth. It was hard to remember that he had to stop once he got started. *Abba* had to shake him.

After the reading, Rabbi Altman motioned to Binny to lift a brown paper bag onto the bench. He pulled out a bottle of American scotch whiskey and handed the bag back to Binny to refold and lay by his coat. He set up little plastic thimble cups on the bench and nodded toward all the men, including *Abba*. *Abba* the cowboy. *Abba* started to wave his hand in front of his face. He never drank. The men from the bench took full cups. The dice boys watched their father and knocked their heads together. They fell over and laughed. The men laughed too. The men thought all the boys were funny when they were seven or eight and did things like that.

Rabbi Altman poured a quarter of a thimble cup for Binny. Go on, boy, he nodded.

"You too, Yossi," he said. So Rabbi Altman could tell who he was. Yossi grabbed the cup and pushed the fur off his mouth with his fingers. The whiskey was wet on his lips but felt like dry fire on his tongue.

*Abba* steered him out of shul with hands on his shoulders. With the hair on top of his gorilla head, they were almost the same height. The sun out the window was a dot now, it was almost midmorning. Across the way Binny looked back with his right eye, the one without the eye patch. He shrugged. He had the same feeling Yossi did: helpless and he had to go home.

Just a couple of hours later, at the party at school, it was exactly how he'd wanted to be: the gorilla beat his chest and linked arms with the pirate, dancing. Yossi started to sing, "*La-Yehudim, La-Yehudim, ha-a-saw ora, sasson v'yikar.*" The Jews were full of light and gladness, joy and honor. The Purim song.

The teachers had made the party outside. The school was built so low down the mountain that they were almost below ground level and the balloons that hung on the edge of the basketball court looked like a forest of lollipop trees.

The teachers came forward in a lumpy group. They began taking the balloons off the fence and handing them out. The fat round balloons looked like bunches of flowers. They gave Binny three and Yossi three that he took and pinched. *POP, POP, POP.* "Want mine too?" said Binny, handing his to Yossi. *POP, POP, POP.* One of the younger boys started crying.

"I'm ready to get out of here," said Yossi. "I've got a present for us anyhow."

"Cigarettes," said Binny. "Whatever happened to the cigarettes?"

Yossi barely remembered the cigarettes himself. Instead he pulled a cello-shaped bottle of brandy out of his gorilla pocket and flashed it up quickly so the teachers wouldn't see. "100 Proof." He pulled Binny by the sash and they ran outside and up the school steps, until they were at street level. "I've been saving this all day."

He snapped open the aluminum cap and took the first sip. It sizzled the back of his throat. "Your turn." Out on the street they could see Old Hana's was closed, the door held back by an iron grille.

"That's not for me," said Binny.

"You'll like it," said Yossi. "And if you don't like it you don't have to have any more."

Binny drank and made a squeezy face. "It's the way it feels afterward," he said.

They looped the whole neighborhood passing the bottle. Binny seemed, but maybe not, to take a double sip for Yossi's every one. They walked up the highest street and leaned against an unsecured guardrail. They were building new apartments here. Around their feet lay the rubble of stone cuts, concrete balls, and old chicken wire. Beyond the settlement, toward the desert, the radar towers looked like UFOs with their landing gear extended.

Yossi pulled a cigarette out of the pack, lit it, and passed it to Binny. The hair on his gorilla chin smelled crispy.

"Give me one of my own," said Binny. "I like the way it feels when you do the first light." He lit a cigarette and puffed for a minute, then stomped it out. "Another." He held his hand out to Yossi. The cigarettes didn't seem to bother Binny the way they bothered Yossi. He could hold the smoke but they made him kind of sick. Binny took another. Then another. He went through the whole pack. Lit, puffed, and dropped. Yossi looked down. At his feet lay the whole pack like shredded sticks in the concrete dust.

It was nighttime and they came back to roost, to their little park tucked into a man-made hump with a couple of baby olive trees, new with the new year of the trees, stuck in the dirt. They were baby trees from last year or the year before but their trunks were already knotted and they had faces like old men. They were a block from each of their apartment buildings.

The grown-ups thought they were still at the school party. Yossi bent forward a little to adjust the fur at the back of his neck. He was inside the sandbox. He twisted the bottle of brandy out of his gorilla pocket. That should get Binny going again. Binny was just lying there, hanging his head, using the bottom step of the sliding board ladder as his pillow, his eyes closed and his lids jumping as if he were seeing things in the dark. He and Binny . . . it figured they would end their day here.

Like on a million other nights Yossi watched the Jerusalem sky crash down on the mountains, like a falling blue curtain. Did Binny know that it looked like a curtain? And now it was black. Binny didn't seem to notice anything.

The sand brimmed over the edge of the sandbox, down his back, into his undershirt.

They'd grown up in a little park, just like this. Come with their teacher when they were three years old and lined up like little *sheffelas*—"little lambs"—he used to mimic—for their twisted seed rolls and bags of chocolate milk. It used to drive the teacher crazy when he pushed but he was the first to figure out that to be first in line meant a roll from the top of the bag, not a doughy one pressed at the bottom. Him showing the other boys, even as they stayed away from him—it was like a calling. They must have been three or four when he figured out how to bite off the tip of the milk sack and spit it at the teacher's feet so she'd be hopping back in the sand.

"Hey, Binny," he said, scraping some sand off the cap of his brandy bottle with the tip of his rubber fingers. "Want to see me spit?"

"To the slide?" asked Binny, trying to sit up a little, using the ladder to steady himself. His eye patch hung by its elastic on his neck and lay like an open collar.

Yossi gargled the brandy. Then he spit in a high stream. A geyser. A volcano. Beyond the playground wall and into the parking lot behind it. "A real fountain, huh?" he asked. "What did you think of that?"

"I think you've got to get me home," said Binny.

"Me? Home?" asked Yossi, blotting his furry chin with his hand. The brandy made him smell like fire. "Binny, you need some more of this."

Yossi balanced the open bottle on a flat palm, high in the air. He could do tricks too. He took another drink, a long drink, then crawled across the sand. The least he could do was take care of old Binny.

"You smell like real gorilla." Binny sat upright, pushing Yossi back, his chest starting to pump. He wasn't going to cry or anything. "How can you keep going?"

"Me? It's like it's the beginning of the day," Yossi said, and it seized him. He didn't feel any different than he had first thing in the morning. Just less excited.

Binny sat up again, pushing his hands around in the sand. "You've got to get me home. I wasn't counting on this." He went down on his elbows, then laid his head across the ladder again.

They were supposed to be doing this together. "Hey, wake up. Binny, watch this." Yossi squeezed off the gorilla head. The head was as tight as the costume was loose. All that pressure around his neck, all the junk he'd taken from the food baskets—the red Twizzler licorice, hazelnut chocolate bar, honey sesame chunks— they bunched up at the top of his stomach and flowered at the back of his mouth. He swallowed it back. He would never throw up. Binny looked like he was sleeping. But he couldn't go to sleep now.

"Hey, Binny, watch this," Yossi said. He sat his gorilla head on the baby swing, snapped it safe with the chain belt. Binny straightened up and opened his eyes. Yossi gave the gorilla head a pinch on the cheek and laughed. "Little *sheffcla*." Then he gave it a push.

Binny sat up from the waist and laughed. He could always make Binny laugh.

It was worth all the trouble. The way the eye slits and the flat nostrils caught the apartments' light from behind. Looked like the gorilla head was really alive. "What do you think, Binny?"

Binny made a frittery, tinny noise. His chest was pumping up and down. "Binny, are you crying?" Yossi couldn't believe it. What would make Binny cry?

"I want—to—go—home," said Binny. He was really crying.

Yossi grabbed the gorilla head off the swing and crawled across the sand, pushing shallow tracks with his furry legs. He bent over Binny and pulled his head up onto his furry arms. Binny looked like a little doll. He could tip back Binny's head and his eyes closed; when he tipped it down his eyelids flapped open. Binny never looked so heavy.

"You're a good friend," said Binny.

He wasn't but he wanted to be.

He was able to swing him to his feet and it wasn't so far to Binny's building, shorter if he got him across the parking lot and into the side door. The side door was good but there was no elevator there. He stopped for a minute. It would be better to push him into the front foyer and push him on the elevator. He could shove him in and hit the floor button. No. Someone would see them. Maybe Rabbi Altman, who would say . . . who wouldn't dare say it was Binny's fault as well as his.

There was less light at the side door. It was safer to get there and for sure someone would find him there by morning. Binny's right leg was walking faster than his left. "You're really a friend, a good friend," Binny said. He balanced himself by rubbing his head into Yossi's chest.

"What are you doing? You're gross," said Yossi, pulling him across the parking lot to save a couple of meters or so. Binny's eyes were closed and he didn't answer.

The lights were on in each apartment. The way they were stacked, they looked like cubes all glowing. It was best to scuttle at the building edge, under the shadow of the porches, and he decided to aim for the side door. There it was. It had a little round bulb with a wire net cover. What if he couldn't open it from this side? On the ground there was a little broken glass, some crumpled blue paper napkins, and Twizzler wrappers. Yossi and Binny used this door sometimes when they didn't want anyone to see them. He opened the door with his left hand, and thrust Binny forward with his right shoulder. Just inside the door they slid, together, to the cold concrete floor. Binny pulled the gorilla head out from under Yossi's arm and snuggled it under his head. He curled his body to a C, rubbed his face in the fur, and smiled.

No way. He wasn't leaving the gorilla head there; that was a fact. Yossi pulled the head out from under Binny's face. "Is cold. Too cold," said Binny, rolling on his back. His voice was kind of bubbly and a little spit leaked out of the corner of his mouth. Yossi noticed his own leg was shaking. It occurred to him not to leave Binny on his back. But he had trouble thinking it out that far. Couldn't someone vomit or swallow it or something? He stretched the eye patch off of Binny's neck and placed it under Binny's cheek, rolling him over. "No, no good," Binny said, rolling onto his back.

Yossi's leg was jiggling so fast he thought it was making noise. He couldn't think that far. He could never think any farther than what he saw. He saw Binny lying on his side and he looked okay.

The door crushed closed behind him; a heavy door, with thick rubber sealers that made a sucking sound like a refrigerator. Almost caught the gorilla head in the jamb. Yossi shook it out a little. It wasn't worth it to put it back on. He felt around and steadied his legs and felt the brandy bottle in his pocket. He didn't even remember putting it back there. The night clouds barreled in over the mountains and between them the sky was liquid black, the way it curled around with no edges. Made the windows of the apartment houses look like shiny eyes. He wondered what they saw when they ogled like that and why they were crying.

# HEAT

THE MARRIAGE BOOKS HAD SEVERAL NAMES FOR *MIKVEH* NIGHT: night of immersion, night of ritual purity, night to resume marital relations, but the hands-down favorite was "another wedding night" because after two weeks *off*, *mikveh* began the two weeks *on*, and all that waiting and buildup reminded them of their younger days.

The couples in Number Four were courting.

Debra's Dave made a point of bringing home a basil plant before *Shabbos*, a plant that meant more to Debra dried up but she didn't delve into symbolism, and meanwhile the wide heavy leaves shed a trail, like Hansel and Gretel crumbs, all the way from the lift to Debra's apartment door. Saturday night and Sunday, Debra put her feet up while Dave handled the framing business himself, humming and hammering down in the storage-room shop.

Ahuva's husband returned from Brussels early that morning and slept all day while she forced her children to play, then eat outside. Late afternoon they sat on the bench at the park in the dead end next door, eating store-bought falafel. Another ten minutes they would start to argue about the relative value of the wooden hand toys their father had brought from the airport.

Toward dusk Dave took out the trash, took in the stroller for the night, and locked up the bicycles—with the whites of his eyes showing. Mike napped for an hour, read through half the instruction book to build the Lego pirate castle from Grandma-in-Florida. He read Esther and the boys two stories and one comic book, including the one where he turned Mighty Mouse into Mighty Michael. He stood as he read, pacing and bouncing and stretching off his arches the way he did, as if all his energy were located in his legs. Then he tucked the kids into bed a half hour early.

Near sundown the husbands rubbed their hands.

The *mikveh* of Heavenly Heights was tucked away in a small, tile-roofed, concrete building on the mountainside of the high road, the privacy of the women protected on three sides by the forest, the privacy protected by an etiquette of invisibility. Even when they *knew,* the best of friends and neighbors didn't tell each other that they were going to the *mikveh* even though it was common for neighbors, cycles in sync, to go the same night. Tova had seen everyone from the neighborhood at least once, except, maybe, Rabbi Altman's wife. Anyhow, a woman never returned home and remarked on who she saw there. Some women didn't chatter idly when they got there, either.

This night Tova saw Ahuva's blue Volvo in the lot but not Ahuva. Debra sat in the anteroom, a couple of numbered turns ahead, wearing a black dress Tova never saw before. Tova seated herself on a plastic chair opposite Debra and picked through the bridal books on *mikveh*: the-waters-of-Eden. Hebrew, English. French. Farsi?

Down a narrow corridor on the left, a single bell chimed behind a door, signaling the *mikveh* attendants that a woman was ready for immersion. Down the opposite side was a dressing room donated by the French women, two walls of mirrors, dryers, combs, swivel chairs, lipstick samples. There, blow dryers clicked off and on, roared. Ahuva emerged, with full makeup, her eyes like dripping honey. She looked Tova and Debra right in the face and turned out the door without a word. Debra didn't flicker an eyelid. Finally Tova broke etiquette and leaned toward Debra. "Will you need a ride home?"

Debra said, simply, "I walk."

Tonight they were wives, not women.

The morning after—without any lightning, without any rain—thunder began beyond the mountains.

A large gray cloud peeled back over the horizon, exposing a sky the color of ash. A morning of blocked light.

Tova lay in her bed, rolled over. She'd slept deeply between body impressions enough for two. Mike was in the shower. Out on the balcony a family of zebra-striped birds hopped and pecked a late breakfast where the baby had fed his sandwich into the porch drain.

Tova heard knocking at the apartment door, short solid taps. She washed quickly, pulled on her heavy terry robe, snapped the buttons. "Who's there?" She looked through the peephole.

Debra stood, all neck and face, distorted through the fish-eye lens. Tova unlocked the door and opened it. Debra wore a yellow summer robe with green and white daisies. She was barefoot.

"Are you sending the children to school?" Debra asked, walking inside.

"What's the question?" Tova asked.

Then Tova heard the helicopters that hadn't come to her lying in bed, lolling in her own world. A bedlam of motors and propellers bounced in the stone doorway. They couldn't speak again until the whole group passed.

"What's going on?" Tova flipped the kitchen switch. The room yellowed slightly without brightening. The thunder was siphoning off the natural light.

Debra high-stepped behind her. The stone floor stung her feet. Tova's feet were bare too, but her night heat still warmed her under her robe.

Another group of helicopters—or planes—passed overhead. Debra and Tova stood a moment, unable to speak. Tova pointed to the Nescafé jar as Debra shook her head no.

When the thundering died, it turned out the phone was ringing. Tova had been standing right next to it but hadn't heard a thing. Had it been ringing all that time?

"Hello," she yelled into the receiver.

Her parents from America. Both of them shouted at once, on extensions in the kitchen and bedroom, though they knew two extensions diluted the connection. They just wanted to hear her voice, they said, then must have forgotten that was all when they both screamed. "Are you okay? We heard the news, then we read the *Jerusalem Post* on-line and it said there'd been a kidnapping of reserve soldiers. Then they were hatcheted . . ."

Tova's mother spoke above her father's voice. "Killed."

That sounded better. Thanks, Mom, Tova thought.

"And their bodies dragged—"

"Taken," Tova's mother corrected.

"In the back of a Jeep," her father continued. "Through the town. And it's right up the road from you."

So they'd watched the TV news half the night and read news on-line while she and Mike played wedding.

"We're fine, normal." Tova wasn't lying—at least not yet. Weren't the lines clearly drawn? *They* were there, up the road, and Heavenly Heights was down here. Her parents' pitch calmed and they turned the call into a regular one. Her father hung up. Her mother wanted to know if the baby was walking yet because last week he stood up and pushed his own stroller.

Debra waved and ducked out. Tova's body felt all bubbled up, like she was still waiting for something; Mike must be out of the shower by now. She stretched the phone cord to a near snap, filled the kettle, coffee for two. The gas flame refused to rise higher than an inch, a simmer. She promised to call her parents back later but they said not to bother and she spooned Nescafé into a cup. The phone rang again. Debra. "School is open. I'm sending." By the time the kettle sang her night heat was spiring up, thin as vapor. Tova realized she'd comforted her parents' anxiety by containing it, inhaling it. But now what did *she* do with it?

What did anyone do with it? How does the country respond? Mike went on-line and saw the pictures they'd seen in America: the reserve soldiers, or what was left of them, dragged, not taken, behind a Jeep, and after morning prayers Mike sat at the kitchen table, pushed aside the Telma Flakes, the plastic bowls, the breakfast cheese, and got into an argument on the telephone. He wanted to find his package from Shigur express; his grant was finally on its way from his old boss at Bio Optics.

Mike's mood, since before today, was agitated anyhow. His Hebrew was fast and sharp. Listening to him argue, watching him get up and pace, was like listening to one side of a tennis match. She knew he could do it. But it got Mike nowhere. The package was waiting but Shigur wasn't sending. No trucks out today or who knows when?

He would come himself, he said, slamming down the phone.

Tova looked at him.

"The action's in the other direction," Mike said. He looked at her and sat. Then he rose to clear the breakfast dishes into the sink.

Tova took the dairy sponge and slowly began to wipe cheese and cereal off the plastic tablecloth.

"It's not a problem," Mike said.

"At least try to convince me. You're *telling* me."

Tova filled the sponge, wiped the excess into her hand. "No one belongs out there," she said. "The radio said they've put roadblocks all the way into town, and they have them there for a reason." She threw the sponge into the sink.

Mike jumped back. "Don't listen to the radio anymore today. Okay?" He looked into her face and grabbed her shoulders. "Dave will go with me. Dave has *clay-nesheck*." A gun.

Outside, the thunder rumbled low, like body noises, anonymous and polite.

"The action's far away," Mike said. "At least a mile."

"Not even a mile," Tova said. "And we've got to be nuts if a mile or part of a mile is far away."

"I'm going in the other direction. They—this—should stop me from doing business in my own country?" Mike said. He could put everything on the line in one minute—their purpose, their children, their politics, their lives. Would he walk out on her while he was doing it? "You're fine here," he said.

And she couldn't argue with him because she had to believe what he said was right because it was what she'd been believing all along.

Tova began to scrub the plastic tablecloth. It was dirtier than she'd ever noticed. Specks and grit. Most were little nicks with dirt ground inside and they were the hardest to scrub out and they made the cloth look filthy. What if people had to come back to the house to visit her at shiva, a new widow and the house was dirty? She shuddered and stood up. She had to remember the difference between negativities and real prophecies. No one made real prophecies anymore.

Except, perhaps, the ones who wished them harm.

From the living-room window, Tova watched Dave and Mike climb into their van. Dave's pistol was tucked in his belt at the back of his pants. The heroes. Could be Tova would do the same thing but Mike had just drawn his conclusions too quickly, turned himself into a creature of action, knowing exactly what to do as if he had been through this kind of thing before.

Then, most predictable, like a teenager, with that energy coursing down his legs Mike revved up the van to a frenzy. Not that the van needed Mike because it had a national purpose of its own, had received a draft notice that, in case of emergency, it would be "taken" for military transport. The van spat out two fat bullets of exhaust, turned around in the dead end, and swung heroically out to the main road.


The wild, wild West Bank.

When your stomach is riddled with pits do you make a normal day or not? The children decided it for her, in a way. Like any Monday Esther got out of school at one. The boys needed lunch at twelve. Tova counted the must-do tasks on one hand: dry cleaners, stamps to buy. The van was not only drafted, but they'd received a tax bill for the radio cassette and she could pay that at the post office too. She'd dispose of what she'd wanted to do most: in Hebrew class they were reading *My Michael,* by Amos Oz, and she'd come to the part where the main character shopped at Mayan Shtub, a department store in town, and Tova, still making Jerusalem her own, had in mind to find it, still extant.

Returning from the post office, she met Mr. Stanetsky puttering next to the mailbox on the curbside of the lobby. A gray Sears toolbox lay open on the floor. He'd unhinged the front drop-down panel of the mailbox and explained he was taking it up to his apartment to flatten, bend it back into the right shape so that it closed enough to keep the mail in. "A good day to do this," he said, cheerily. "With everything going on there won't be any mail delivery."

When she came back through the lobby to get the boys from *gan,* Mr. Stanetsky was puttering again, loading cleaning supplies out of the service closet. Trash bags. Bleach. *Spongia* sticks. Cotton rags.

"A good day to air out the shelter. Not that we need it for anything," he made a point of adding.

"Good," she said. "Good. A good day." She looked at him. Was he for real? Maybe he had turned his radio off too. Maybe he never turned it on. Before stepping into the lift she couldn't help noticing that there had been some action on her notice for English lessons, beyond the one call she'd gotten from the man who mangled the verb phrases and said he'd get her back when he probably meant he'd get back to her, which he never did. But no more calls—perhaps the ones who needed the lessons couldn't make the calls. Perhaps the Russians who'd moved in downstairs needed Tova. But it wasn't Tova's culture the Gernokovskys needed. They were all on the same side of need. Especially on a day like today.

When the older children began to come home from school Yossi helped Mr. S mop out the shelter. Yossi walked through the lobby, like the sorcerer's apprentice, balancing two buckets of steamy water except he looked like he'd grown three feet since Tova last really looked at him. Mr. S carried big, lemon-scented trash bags and two *spongia* sticks.

All afternoon the older children played close to the building. At first they made a game to count the troop movement out on the road away from town, putting aside a pebble for each tank. Two for a helicopter. Five for a plane. Apparently, they lost interest and started the ball games. Where was Mike?

He never said what time he would be back. Or that he would call. Calling didn't matter because cell phone service, especially out to here, was all jammed. But the funny thing was that as angry and upset as she felt, even as he soared out on the road she was proud of his choice to not be held back.

The children didn't count a single pebble for civilian cars on the road. There weren't any. Tova put up water to boil noodles but it would take twice as long. Turned out the low flame meant that the gas supply was cut back—for some kind of security reasons.

As if they lived next to a landing field, the thunder was the background noise. Then, as she ripped open the noodle bags, thinking how her nerves were so bad she couldn't even think and open a bag of noodles at the same time, she heard screams, bloody screams from the dead end below.

Esther? The screams struck her chest like a sudden punch and she could not speak, breathe, or cry out. She dropped the noodle bag. Without a thought, because she just knew, Tova ran down the steps to the lobby.

Yossi had been giving handlebar rides on Esther's bike when the bike rode itself over into the forest edge. They'd already pulled up the bike by the time Tova got down. The frame was bent in so that the bicycle wheel couldn't spin, but the tire was, amazingly, surprisingly, intact and plump.

Tova hugged Esther, Esther's face fresh and full in the cheeks, red and weepy. If only this were the single danger in the forest! At least there was a comfort against it.

Late afternoon Mike and Dave had not returned or called. Tova looked at the radio on the kitchen counter, stretched out her hand, pulled it back. She would keep the radio off. And even though she had call waiting, she'd stay off the phone.

"Where are our heroes? Our gunrunners?" Debra came through Tova's door into the kitchen.

"Are you worried?" Tova asked.

"I'm more worried that I forgot to think about dinner." True, Debra looked entirely relaxed, not a whit different from any other day. Though—was that eye makeup she had on? And lipstick? Debra never wore eye makeup and lipstick.

"What are you staring at?" she asked Tova. "Can you—" She came closer. She *was* wearing makeup. Maybe she had the thought, too, that if Dave didn't come back, and people would come over to the house . . . A woman had to look good. "Can you stretch your noodles?" Debra asked. "I have cucumbers and cheese."

Tova carried her large pot of noodles down to Debra's, tucking her portable phone under her arm. Debra pulled ketchup and cheese out of the refrigerator. She cut a bagful of cucumbers into half-moons and fanned them on a large plate.

As the children ate Tova sat with Debra on the balcony next to a small tent of hanging laundry. They shared a can of Budweiser beer, at twelve shekels a can like sharing five loaves of bread or a can of gold. The tanks and armored cars covered the main road below, moving out nose to tail, like a child's train set. "Do we have these situations often?" Tova asked.

"More than we should." Debra leaned over the balcony rail, posed her head, and made purring noises as if she had found something. "Finish the beer if you want."

Tova drank. "You know," she said, "I still feel Esther's screams from an hour ago. Like my insides dropped through my body. Until she got it out that it was her bicycle—I thought it was something else."

Debra leaned over the balcony again. Maybe she hadn't heard this confession. She looked out, far and beyond. Days like this the thin air created a pinpoint focus. They could see a hundred miles past the mountain range, if it weren't for the mountain range. "Well," she said finally, "it opens up this fear. You just have to close it up again."

"Doesn't everyone think the . . ."—Tova didn't want to be so explicit—". . . the same thing? The same terrible thing? You know that one reserve soldier was just married. The other became a father two days ago. The first one was able to call his wife . . . they'd made a wrong turn."

"I wonder why sometimes I feel different when it's soldiers. Military people and not civilians," Debra said.

"Yeah—I know—I can't figure it out either but it doesn't feel as bad . . . when you're a soldier there's an expectation . . . But the brutality. The chopping the bodies."

"With heaven's help," said Debra.

Tova waited for Debra to finish her sentence. "Yes? . . ." she pushed, a little.

But Debra didn't answer that. She was all leaping ahead, like to a war at the End of Days. "You know in the Talmud it says that for every evil, for all the power of evil, there's five hundred times the amount of good in the world. We have to find it—we have to use it to fight the evil." Then Debra stopped, closed the conversation right there.

After the children finished the noodles they put the empty pot on the floor. They decided to carve potato pictures with iced tea spoons. Then Shira suggested they could print the designs with pomegranate juice.

Out on the highway the tank movement stopped. Was it a good sign? A bad sign? The atmosphere had knocked all that year-round thrumming off the mountaintop. Debra's laundry hung, board stiff and still. Tova felt her pulse so clearly she thought she'd been turned inside out.

Esther came out with red, spread hands, looked like blood smeared all over her face. Debra jumped up and body-blocked her clean laundry. Esther was just playing; she'd wanted to raise the tension.

Was Tova the only one with the lead in her chest, weighing her down? Shira ran out, grabbed Esther at the shoulders, and the two of them leaned over the balcony rail at their waists. Debra pulled them back by their blouses.

A single civilian car finally turned up the highway. Tova knew at a glance, a bitter glance, it wasn't hers.

Debra saw the car too. "They'll be back soon. Twenty minutes."

"How do you know?" Tova asked. The beer had relaxed her and she heard a small sarcastic slip in her own voice. "Sorry," she said. For what, she thought: her tone? her intransigence? her cobweb of conclusions? "What are we doing here, anyhow?"

"We're the settlers. The obstacles to peace. This is our home." Debra was irritated too.

"I know. That." And that giving in to, well, *tactics* was letting the other side win.

A spate of civilian cars burst on the main road. The tanks and army cars stopped and the civilians broke out of the starting gate. They filled both lanes, into town and out. Tova was suddenly, utterly, despairing.

Debra looked over at her, out at the cars again. "You want to know what I'm doing here?" Debra said, as if she'd just thought of it, as if this were just a conversation. "Did you ever notice at weddings how many times we talk and sing about Jerusalem?" Debra said.

"I guess I take it for granted. We just do." How could Debra be talking about weddings at a time like this?

"See, you do take it all for granted. At a wedding you'll hear Jerusalem fifty times. A hundred times. Walking away from the *chuppa* everyone sings about Jerusalem. All the wedding songs are about Jerusalem, it's like a metaphor. But I didn't realize until my own wedding, when they kept putting us up on chairs, brought us together to dance, pulled us apart, singing Jerusalem, Jerusalem." She lowered her voice. "Back and forth. They brought us together and pulled us apart singing Jerusalem, Jerusalem. Us and Jerusalem. It's like when you want to be with someone and you belong together. It's the same kind of power. You know what I mean . . . ?"

Was Debra trying to say what Tova thought she was trying to say? Tova looked behind her to check that the children were back in the kitchen. Indeed, they circled Debra's kitchen table, red cheeks, hands, forearms, elbows. Tova pulled herself to the edge of the porch chair and leaned closer to Debra. "You mean like getting married?" *Getting married* was the most comfortable phrase she could muster, a euphemism to Debra's metaphor.

"Yeah—something like that," Debra said.

But Debra's enunciation was spiny and if her voice were graphed it would have looked like pine trees. She knew better than to broach the topic of a woman's intimate life with her husband, a conversation saved for therapy or need. But the tension had peeled them back to some essential elements and no one's patience was working today, not Debra's for the demure, not Tova's for a diamond-in-the-rough. Nevertheless, Debra persisted, "You know how on wedding invitations we write across the top 'We will raise Jerusalem above our chiefest joy'? You know it's talking about every joy in the world. Like a bride and bridegroom rejoicing."

"I got your point," Tova said. Was she so dense Debra thought she needed a lecture? But the effect was the one that Tova had been trying to avoid, that Tova conjured Dave as someone's joy. Dave, and his full course of nervous gestures: tucking his shirt, pulling his belt, stretching his neck, popping his eyes.

"And we're supposed to love Jerusalem more than that," Debra said.

Tova felt her face redden, neck to ears to forehead.

"Don't quote me, anyhow," Debra said. Her face turned red too, though it didn't have to because in the end what Debra really said had more to do with what she hadn't said. She rubbed her eyes with the back of her hand, smudging her makeup to blue crescents, fine as thumbprints.

Below, the main road was entirely empty.

The children were quiet. The thunder stalled, did not start again. Light broke into the farthest sky—rolling them in the shape of a bowl.

Debra had made the awkward silence and she was the one who broke it. "Speaking of weddings," Debra said, "did I tell you my Channie is starting to date? The matchmakers have been calling."

"You're kidding! What's that like?"

"Just the next stage. Like Dave says, we've spoken of it so much already. We've got the girl, the hall, the sisters-in-law. The rest is like filling in the blanks."

"Did she go out with someone yet?"

Debra looked at her strangely.

Tova froze. Maybe she wasn't supposed to ask, but Debra was the one who brought it up.

"She did," Debra said, quietly. "She will again this week—a second date. Only if things calm down though because he is from Gaza. Neve Dekalim. And they keep getting blasted there so it's actually hard to drive out of there. Look." She pointed down the main road.

A single armored tank wove between the civilian cars, making wild speed.

"The little engine that could. 'I think I can . . . I think I can . . . ' "

They laughed. They waited. Tova wanted to talk about love but it might provoke Debra to clarify her point about Jerusalem and weddings, anyhow, and more specifics on what exactly *chiefest joys* were.

If Tova had a name for everything she was thinking about and feeling she would make a list, all categories of emotion: love, fear, anger, awe. Like Mike, defiance, bravery. Above them, every color swirled into the sky as if someone were turning it up with a celestial spoon. Tova looked at her watch. She looked at Debra. She hunkered down to count the minutes.

# ONE LAST GIFT

THE SMELL HUNG LIKE INCENSE AT THE BOTTOM OF THE STAIRWELL: old fruit, new fruit, sachet, must, syrup, brine. Tova clutched Mr. S's ledger book and his clipboard against her chest. The smells set her stomach on edge, like sabotage. Past the steps and the security door to the storage rooms the smell shifted, condensed into one: boiled cabbage and bay leaf. She tiptoed to the rear emergency door and opened it. At her feet lay rubble and a mound of Twizzler wrappers, and the smell, as if it couldn't stand itself either, immediately fled.

Above the door the security light, perpetual as in shul, was burned out and on Tova's list of instructions was an explicit how-to on untwisting the cage and installing a new bulb. Looking at Mr. S's crude drawing it was hard to picture him today, this week, addressing the American Congress, flanked by his business manager, his American lawyer, and his Israeli lawyer (all women, she'd noted). She promised she'd do his collecting job this month—or however long it took him Stateside to defend his one-man mission. What she had discovered, scanning the ledger last night, was that the checks recorded in, for Mr. S and for Debra, one month for Ahuva too, had consecutive bank numbers and that the checks already clipped into this month's folder were all from the same bank account in Jersualem. His. Mike figured it out right away—didn't Mr. S quote the rabbis on taking care of basic needs? "If there's no flour, there's no bread."

The Gernokovskys' door was decorated with a *"Beruchim habaim."* Welcome. The sign was handmade and crude, like something the girls made in an after-school art class. The Gernokovskys did not have school-age children themselves, rather an extended family—wide-legged women who replicated, triplicated themselves till Tova couldn't figure how many of them there really were. Mr. Gernokovsky let her in. Home in the middle of the day. He worked part-time cleaning the boys' school and the little shul next door. In Russia he had been a chairman of a math department. From her former students Tova knew the distance between everyday language and professional language. She bet he could lecture in English in mathematical theory but couldn't ride a subway in the States.

Inside the apartment the cabbage smell had its origin, but diluted and ventilated, as if he too had found it odd and sent it outside. Someone—or a couple of someones—chattered in the kitchen. His salon windows were open, blinds drawn back and trembling with the slight breeze against the window frame. From this, the ground floor, the back view of the mountain was eye level, the tops of the trees like his personal flora, his balcony set out with the white plastic furniture everyone else had but— without being especially dusty—giving a squashed impression, depression. Poor—Tova mouthed to herself.

She snapped the clip on her clipboard and found his name with her finger.

"*Aht rozah cama tee?*" Mr. Gernokovsky was ready to treat her like a guest. "*Diet cola?*" The universal nouns. Tova smiled. "*Lo. Lo rozah.*" No.

He motioned her to sit down at the table in the salon. The apartment was more Israeli than Israeli, the furniture a gift from the government for those who had to or wanted to take: a thin-cushioned sofa, orange and red, two chairs, a wooden table. On three walls hung crocheted handiwork—more orange and red, the sunshine colors, and a Jerusalem print, the *Kosel* floating in a golden beam of light. Underneath, the quote from Psalms, "If I forget you let my tongue cleave to my cheek . . ."

When Mr. Gernokovsky spoke he didn't have an ironic edge, so Tova didn't get his humor at first. That, plus the fact that his Hebrew was better than hers and he slowed down as he looked at her face. He said, "Here in *Eretz Yisrael* we spend our time hugging each other and dancing round in circles. No?"

Mr. Gernokovsky was addressing her adjustment—their adjustment—the thing they had in common, the images they were working out of their heads. Tova's Hebrew froze. Underneath her head scarf she began to sweat at the hair roots, just like the last time she spoke to Esther's homeroom teacher. Mr. Gernokovsky spoke more slowly and began to use his hands. Tova noticed a metal folding table against the wall where they'd arranged blue and white cups and saucers and a blue and white cake plate on a stem. In a glass circle stood two bottles of Israeli liquor and small schnapps cups. Tova could picture this large family eating *Shabbos* dinner—Shabbat—to them, no doubt—of one chicken and pushing away the last piece, not out of politeness but because they were satisfied with little, with the life they had.

The rabbis say you really learn a person through his *ka'as*, *koce*, and *keece*—his anger, his drink, and his pocket. When Mr.

Gernokovsky handed her his check, he handed it over with joy on his face. She clipped the check under the small pile and didn't have to examine the ledger to know that he was paid up for every month.

Across the hall, Yossi Hacker's skateboard leaned against the wall, next to a folded Ping-Pong table. Tova knew that Mr. S had spoken to Sandy and Nathan about both those things. They had not received permission, yet, to open the Ping-Pong table out in the common area and Yossi still skateboarded in the hallways. The Hackers were like blisters on the process. The several times Tova had tried to speak to Sandy about Yossi's ball play with the girls she dead-ended.

Tova rang the doorbell and it repeated through the other side of the door as if the apartment were empty. She'd seen Sandy's car outside though—and Yossi riding around on a new bike. She ran her finger down the ledger book. There was a month here and there with question marks, obviously negotiated, all eventually paid, except for a month last summer that the Hackers had just skipped. Tova stood at the door. She rang again. She knew Sandy was home, and Sandy's sister too, unmistakably her sister, who had visited for Passover. Finally, Tova heard footsteps and saw a shadow loom over the peephole. She heard the chain lock fall. When the door opened she saw a Sandy, not Sandy but a version of her: a gargoyle, energy in sluice, welcome-out-not-welcome-in.


One afternoon when Sandy was ten years old Mother had glided into the house wearing a powder-blue three-piece suit, black hair bouffant against her pillbox hat; her looks a *confection,* Sandy had said. She'd meant to say a *perfection.* Then Mother had upturned her entire purse in the middle of the Formica kitchen table and topped off the pile with a confetti of torn dollar bills, ladies-luncheon raffle tickets, S&H green stamps. Still wearing her matching blue cloth pumps, Mother had changed into her tulip print wrapper, tying it together at the waist with the tulip print belt, and swooshed around like that for days, the wrapper breaking open at her thighs, higher. Sandy had been afraid to move the open purse off the table. Her sister Ceil came home from college and, with slight hesitation concerning the green stamps, knocked the whole pile with a disgusted sweep into a paper grocery bag.

That same year, Mother began to leave dirty tissues on the bathroom floor. First, Sandy'd thought she'd missed the toilet. But then Mother began to leave her underwear, stained and rolled into little balls, on the floor outside the hamper. Sandy decided, on weekdays at least, she'd only go to the bathroom when she was at school. But there, it turned out, she faced the other girls. Plastic barrettes pinched in their mouths, the other girls adjusted and readjusted—over and over and over—their half-ponies and back-sweeps, this being the first year they reached the mirrors over the bathroom sinks. The tallest girl could study the whole room behind her by looking straight ahead in the mirror and moving side to side. Three days she watched Sandy run in and run out. On the fourth morning, the tallest girl stared behind in the mirror and said straight to Sandy, "What's the matter with *you*?" As if she were the one with the problem.

Ceil's solution made Sandy think of the drawstring that pulled in the hood of her winter coat. Tighter and tighter, Ceil pulled the circle around them. Their father had been sickly all along, a vague man, although he had provided the structure of a parent in, a parent out. Ceil's instinct was to make things better on the surface. When she came home from school she made a point of showering Sandy with little *tchotchkelas*, gifts: hair bands, a silver-backed brush and comb set, a manicure kit. Ceil condensed the whole thing to one word and then never felt the need to discuss it further. "It was a five-star miracle we ever got married and had families, considering all the *garbage* we went through," Ceil said.

It was a bigger miracle they didn't fly, Sandy thought. She'd never understood how for ten dumb years Ceil's Mordy waited patiently on the side, like a trained animal. Ceil, forbearing as a mother, watched Sandy betray their circle first. The entire week before Sandy's wedding Ceil squawked at her, as if loosening the drawstring was a kind of cranking down. Then walking Sandy down to the *chuppa*, Ceil bawled—past the curl of a joke—"It is not done in this place that the younger sister gets married before the older sister."

Later, sixteen years to the month of Sandy's wedding, six thousand miles across the Atlantic Ocean, in a concrete stack outside of Jerusalem, in an excuse for a building in an excuse for a suburb, Sandy leaned back against the kitchen window, letting Ceil preside over the fourteenth of fourteen mornings. In ten hours she would be driving Ceil back to Ben Gurion airport.

All the night before, both dreaming and awake, Sandy had remembered saying good-bye to Mother; being locked into position at Mother's side by some kind of gravity. She'd held Mother's small dry hand, grainy and smooth at once like a bare bone. Mother had drawn her closer until Sandy practically fell on top of her. They'd never been a touching family, but these years later Sandy understood the power of Mother's pull. Against all restraint, didn't Sandy just plain want Yossi that way?

Sandy watched Ceil. Ceil shuffled a triangle from the refrigerator, to the dairy-silver drawer and then halfway to the sink where she stopped to press her pleated blouse back into the waist of her skirt. She stretched to the cabinet for a clean plate, and the blouse rebelled again, a fat gray mushroom cloud.

The morning would not end until Ceil decreed it, even though outside on the main road, the buses had been running for hours. Sandy watched her neighbors climb on the number fifteen. The bus revved forward, routing uphill before it would turn out of the neighborhood on the way into town. Black smoke hung in the bus stop like a storm cloud and old Mr. Stanetsky and Debra's Dave from upstairs stood, heads together, as if measuring the wind. They had no choice but to step forward into the rising black blotch. Tomorrow Sandy would be a bus person too, back to The Book Mart selling day-old *O Globo* to the Brazilian pilgrims, watching their gratefulness as they folded back the paper to read before they even walked out the door.

Still without a word, Ceil sat down at the table and helped herself to a generous piece of hand-baked matzo, left over from the seder. Ceil dug the tip of her butter knife into a jar of cherry preserves, and spread fruit on the matzo a good finger thick. Laying another flat piece of matzo on top of the spread Ceil made an awkward sandwich that she clearly intended to fit her mouth around. Sandy watched her with mild suspense. All these years and all the grown-up visits, they still aligned themselves like constellations.

Ceil cleared her throat. "You have to get me to one more place. I still have to get Mordy's gift," she announced. She took a giant bite of her sandwich and half the matzo fell back on her plate. "I decided, something for Mordy's office." Ceil chewed as she spoke. Sandy pictured Mordy, not hard to please. Mordy was the kind of person who smiled all the time, his features disappearing into folds in his face, his eyes like black-drilled holes. The agony and ecstasy of this purchase belonged entirely to Ceil.

Sandy pulled a chair out across from Ceil and slowly distributed her weight across the rattan weave. Yossi had managed to pop the bottom on every single seat by landing square onto the chairs from a running jump. One by one they had to stack the sickly chairs down in the storage room. And just this week, they'd chosen: new chairs or Yossi's new bike. He was outside riding right now, not—she hoped—giving handlebar rides. Last week he'd practically taken off Binny Altman's nose by ejecting him into an olive tree—and he wasn't even supposed to be playing with Binny anymore.

Sandy looked up at Ceil. "I think we've seen all the artwork there is in this country," Sandy said, as gently as she could. She knew that any word or inflection could inspire Ceil to something Sandy didn't want to hear. "But I'm ready to go when you are."

"You think you can leave Yossi?" Ceil said, chewing.

"Oh, stop it. You're embarrassing me." She'd told herself last night that saying good-bye to Ceil would be the equivalent of "backing down."

"I'm just teasing you. I can tell you've been dying to get at the window to look for him. You're always so worried about him," Ceil said. She wiped her mouth.

"Why not? It's part of my job description."

"You're like a mama bear," Ceil said.

"I used to call you that," Sandy said. "Behind your back, of course."

"I bet if you didn't tell Yossi, he wouldn't even notice you were gone," Ceil said.

Ceil finished eating. Sandy watched the matzo crumbs make a gritty pyramid on the plate. Sandy felt her chest flicker with anger. All those years and all those grown-up visits, the feelings never changed.

As soon as she was ready to go Ceil slid the strap of her purse over her shoulder and stood up. "My blouse is driving me crazy. I'm going to put on a dress." She straightened herself and walked to the back hallway. From behind, Sandy noticed, hardening her eyes and her forehead to keep Ceil in focus, Ceil looked off balance, like a stack of blocks the last second before it falls over.

Sandy and Ceil walked out into the dark hallway, dark as if light from the skylight refused to meet them down there. The elevator shone. A lighthouse, Yossi called it yesterday. When Sandy saw Yossi outside she would tell him how right he was about how it looked like a lighthouse and that she'd left a sandwich for him in the refrigerator. With garlic pickles, sliced. She conjured grown-up Yossi, walking into his own married home, family flocking to him, the family diet all Yossi's favorite things. Sandy'd already spent years squaring accounts with her daughter-in-law to be.

Ceil reached for the elevator door. As she grabbed the knob the elevator clicked, flashed the LOCKED light, then tunneled up the shaft. Ceil jammed the call button violently.

"Stop!" Sandy said. "Someone else must have called it a second before we did. Let's just walk. It's only two flights up to the lobby."

Ceil rooted herself in the darkest spot as if to emphasize her misery. Sandy wondered if she should repeat Nathan's joke comparing angels and elevators. What did he say? Something about the elevators only being able to do one job on each holy mission. She pulled Ceil's arm and led her toward the stairs.

They huffed up the steps single file, pushing their weight off the iron banister, and Ceil's blocked-out body eclipsed the faint beam of light even as it grew when they approached the ground floor. Where did they both get this squareness? Sandy wondered. Neither of them looked anything like their mother, who'd been so light, almost transparent. You saw the curves in her body from all angles.

At the last landing before the lobby Sandy noticed Ceil's dress, which Ceil had changed into, was unzipped in back.

"I can never see the top of my zipper in the mirror. I called you from the guest room but you didn't hear me," Ceil said.

As if somehow it had been *her* fault. Sandy stopped on the dark steps, annoyed. Her hands grazed for a second at the hair on the back of Ceil's neck, until she found the top of the dress. The physicalness of Ceil had always made a contest for her, she thought, breathing the clash of warm skin on rayon. Sometimes, depending on Ceil's mood, if Sandy had cried too much, Ceil had threatened to slap her face. And sometimes she had. Sandy found the zipper and held her breath on the inhale. The band of the cloth was stuck in the teeth. No wonder Ceil couldn't get it.

Repent! She's almost out of here. Ceil had never meant a bad thing for her. Sandy exhaled as she hooked the eyelet and loop on top of the collar.

Up in the lobby they discovered that the Gernokovskys, the Russian family from Basement One, had stopped up the elevator in-service, propping the door back with a case of one-liter soda pop. Mr. Gernokovsky slid a plastic picnic *sal* across the floor. The oldest son carried a small hibachi and another *sal* poking full of skewers and coals. They were loading the car, going on another outing.

"What right do they have to stop up the elevator at the lobby like that?" Ceil said, not bothering to whisper. Fortunately, the

Gernokovskys—at best—understood a slow, shop-talk English and they smiled at both Ceil and Sandy as they loaded the soda pop into their open trunk, already spread with mud-colored blankets and embroidered pillows.

"What can I say . . . they're my neighbors," whispered Sandy, nodding regards to the Gernokovsky babushka. She would try to be more calm with Ceil, superficially at least.

"Well, it's my last day," Ceil said.

"What?" Sandy asked. "But it doesn't mean you can insult them." The Gernokovskys distracted her too, but for a different reason. The Gernokovsky women were thick women like Ceil and her. But, except for the age differences, they were exactly alike as if one generation predicted the other. Even the babies had big, square hands and feet.

As they stepped out to the curb, Sandy spotted Yossi's new bike in the road. Where was Yossi? Where had he gone? She shook her head and stretched her arm, wishing she could will him back in place. Instead she beeped off her car alarm.

The next instant, the children braked their bikes and the handlebar riders slid to their feet, as if indeed Sandy had caused something to happen. Sandy and Ceil both turned. There was the ice cream truck swerving in wildly from the main road, around the curves at full speed, ringing just as it came to the first building in the block and shutting down silently as it came to a complete stop in front of their building. Sandy ran to move Yossi's bike to the curb.

Sandy smiled. She had a weakness for scenes of basic childhood pleasures. She liked to watch the children line up. In just a few seconds the children were snaked in two queues that curled out on either side of the front door of her building, behind her parked car. This ice cream man was the best; he could hand a cone to one child with his right hand as he took an order and money from another child with his left.

"You'll never get the car out now," Ceil said, tapping her foot on the curb. "The darn truck and those darn kids have you blocked."

"We can wait. This guy is quick," Sandy said, still smiling. In season she watched him twice a day. "He'll be out of here in five minutes."

"Look, we've got to go. I want to get this present," Ceil said.

"We waited all morning, we can wait five minutes more," Sandy said.

"Just because you want to put up with it doesn't mean that *I* have to. Just watch."

Ceil walked up to the front of the line of children and they moved back for her with an animal instinct. Ceil pulled a stack of shekels from her purse and waved her hands to the man— toward the car that was blocked, toward the curb, and toward the line of children.

The ice cream man grabbed the shekels and slid his window shut. In one quick roar he started up his truck and circled out of the dead end. One little girl holding the hand of her brother started to cry. Little sobs and *huh-huh-huh* sounds piped up like organ music.

Sandy watched helplessly as Ceil stalked back to her. Next to their car the Gernokovsky babushka grabbed a Gernokovsky toddler and clutched her tightly to her chest.

"Now why'd you *do* such a thing," Sandy yelled, grabbing Ceil by the elbow and pushing her toward the car roughly.

"We have to get Mordy's present." Ceil humped her shoulders in a show of logic. Then, she swung herself into the car, bottom first. Sandy squeezed past the Gernokovskys, avoiding their faces, and slid into the driver's side.

"You can't do things like that," Sandy yelled as she turned the ignition. "You're not supposed to do things like that to other people." She felt her face turn red and hot. She was not used to raising her voice to Ceil. She backed the car out of the lot, driving out of the dead end in two motions on the gearshift. Looking back in the rearview mirror she saw that the children still hadn't broken the queue, as if a phantom truck still stood at the curb. Then Yossi appeared, climbing over the forest fence. He jumped two meters off the top of the fence and landed on his feet. He'd heard the truck too and stepped into the road looking for it. Then he started to yell. The little kids finally broke the line and crowded around him, pointing to Sandy's car and yelling back.

How could this be? thought Sandy, so angry her eyes filmed over. She could barely see as she wiggled the car out to the main road. Her heart popped in her chest. The way the children looked at Sandy as if she were crazy too! This was precisely the kind of thing that she'd wanted to spare Yossi. Yossi was *Future*.


Fifteen minutes later, Sandy turned the car into Bar Ilan Street, telling herself she must stop grinding the accelerator. At the stoplight she nearly stalled as she shifted into neutral. She must will herself to calm down. Ceil, on the other hand, sat with a spent look on her face, her purse and her hands in her lap. Sandy pumped the car engine and leaned into a warm spot of sunlight on the windshield.

Diagonally across the intersection the bus stop was swarming with kids, five or six years older than Yossi. These were the soldiers who'd gotten to go home for the last days of Passover. Now they were going back to base and they wore their guns slung on their backs with the firing end to the ground. A girl soldier, tough-looking and brown, was kissing her father good-bye. He tried to carry her large khaki duffel bag up on the bus but her commander, a tall boy with yellow-streaked hair, held him back. Yossi would be that tall, that handsome, that straight.

Ceil followed her line of vision and broke the silence. "They're so good-looking, now that's like more sight-seeing. Maybe I can bring one of them back."

The comment struck Sandy as ridiculous.

"I don't think I would try it. Ever try to talk to one?"

"Not in their language."

"Did I ever tell you what Yossi did—said—when he was little?" Sandy said, suddenly feeling very light. Yossi would be taller, handsomer. He had that slimness, the long torso of Mother's. The signal turned yellow, then green, and the car shimmied in the daytime wind as they crossed through the intersection. "He was five—almost five, and we were at the *Kosel*—the wall. He walked up to one of the soldiers guarding there and said to him, 'You're just a baby.'"

"Why'd he do that?" asked Ceil.

"I don't know. He was real cute then," Sandy said, smiling, remembering. The car choked as she drove in full throttle, just past a hotel driveway, where the grounds workers busied themselves in the flowered bushes like scavenging birds. Sandy leaned forward again, as if to propel the car forward with her body weight.

"It's not so cute," said Ceil. "It's kind of fresh—obnoxious. I hope you said something to him."

What? Sandy thought. It was just cute. "We did say something—I'm sure," Sandy said. She hadn't wanted to start up again.

"You're afraid of it. You always were with Yossi. Funny, and you were the one who always wanted to be told what to do."

"No, I didn't always want to be told what to do," Sandy said. The tires crinkled, made little snapping noises. She slowed down and looked. There was loose gravel thrown across the road.

"You wanted it," said Ceil.

When Ceil had one of these ideas, she could direct her comments as precisely as a missile.

"Well, maybe I missed it. Missed something, anyhow," Sandy said, looking over at Ceil with a quick side glance.

"I don't think so—you were always . . ."

"Always what? I'm afraid to ask," Sandy asked, without meaning to ask, really.

"Always wanting things that no one could give you. And you were always getting angry about it. Just sharp and irritable. You always drew the wrong conclusions—I can't explain it. Like I'd come home from school and I'd have to pull you out of your bed. Your age—you could have made your own dinner or something. But you would be angry at me when I had to get you going again."

Yeah, you got me going with your *hands,* Sandy answered to herself, something she never liked to think about. In an instant the side of her face burned; nerves deadened thirty years earlier sprang to life.

Sandy decided she would not even look over at Ceil. Anyhow she had to concentrate harder on the driving because in town the traffic became the terrain of an expert. She drove across King George Street, past the Supersol Market where the tourists from the expensive hotels bought their orange juice and Waters of Eden. Two policemen rerouted traffic at the scant remains of no-man's-land, the '48 cease-fire line. Instead, there was a new luxury hotel and the more luxurious Village of David condominium complex. If she had it she would also pay a million dollars to drink her morning coffee in full view of the Old City walls. She swayed the car right, left, right.

She wasn't planning to say a word except about neutral things like the new construction in town. But it popped out. "Made my own dinner?!" Sandy drove up the ramp to Jaffa Gate.

"*Boobela*—I didn't mean to insult you. You were just a kid. But so was I. I just want you to know that I'm always here for you now too," Ceil said. She put her hand on Sandy's elbow. Sandy jerked her arm away. Ceil's comfort was a string pulling her back across time, back to a space where she waited for someone else's light. No more, she'd told herself for years now. Sandy had Yossi. Sandy was a light giver, now.


Once through Jaffa Gate, Sandy steered the car between a group of Armenian monks sweeping the road with their creased black gowns. Used to the cars in their alleys, they adjusted their stride to single file without looking behind them. Stone walls lined the alleys and bent trees growing from inside the walls twined together in the air, making a tunnel. Out in the sunlight again, Sandy drove the car past the pay-lot and spotted a prize, one bare parking wedge, pushed up against the back wall of Batei Machse, an old neighborhood. Sandy eased into the spot, tapping her left taillight on the stone holding wall, and tapping her right bumper on a Renault sedan squeezed behind her. The correct thing, it occurred to Sandy, was not to think a thing until Ceil left and she could right herself.

Side by side they walked to the guard station and opened their purses for a security check. Beyond their heads Sandy saw the *Kosel*, the plaza in front swarming with families.

"You want to go there for a minute?" Sandy asked. Even

though she'd promised herself not to react, a pressure moved down from the back of her eyes and her chest felt electric again. She had the urge to join one of those families down there.

"What do we need to go there for now?" Ceil said. "I have to get Mordy his present."

Typical, Sandy thought. With one stroke Ceil would determine what would be background, what would be foreground. They turned their backs on the *Kosel* and walked up the stairs to the Old City.


Young Mr. Stanetsky, her neighbor's son, stood behind the counter with a portable phone in his hand, the antenna held high in the hanging art. A cell phone was clipped to his belt. A pager hung from his buckle. His face had none of the energy of a proprietor; his father had bought the store as a present for him a year ago. He pushed the antenna down and clicked the phone off. The store was no bigger than Sandy's kitchen and the clutter reminded her of the Arab *shuk*. Every wall and ceiling spot hung with lithographs, silver work in frames, and fabric. Olive wood challah boards were stacked on the floor in one corner and pink and white havdalah candles pinwheeled in a canister on one side of the register. On the other side a placard announced: "Only official agent of internationally renowned Dan'il Bezalel."

"This," young Mr. Stanetsky said, tapping the card, "is my breakfast, lunch, and dinner."

They were the only customers. Young Mr. Stanetsky recognized Sandy, of course. "This is my big sister," she said, lightening herself, at least for the moment.

"I want that one," Ceil said. She pointed behind the register to a Scripture drawing of two hands clasped in prayer. It was beautiful.

"That one is not for sale," said young Mr. Stanetsky. He had the same face as his father, but more padded. Sandy had the feeling that if she touched his cheek her finger would make a permanent dimple. "That was a gift—to me."

"But that's the one I want," Ceil said, pushing, looking into young Mr. Stanetsky's face.

"It's not for sale," he said, firmly. "My father bought that for me from Rabbi Altman—you know, the school principal. Our neighbor."

"Of course we know . . ." Sandy began.

"I'll give you four hundred shekels," Ceil said. She opened her purse.

"It's not for sale for any money," he repeated. "I can't sell a gift. I have lots of other things. Paper cuts—how do you like the paper cuts? Geometric art. Photos. This is exquisite." He pointed to an old photo in a glass frame: "Maison Bonfils's 'Jerusalem from the Southeast.'"

Ceil shook her head.

Young Mr. Stanetsky lifted the portable phone off its cradle.

Sandy took his withdrawal as a mild threat. Ceil didn't seem to understand.

"What about this one?" He yanked up the antenna of the phone and used it to point to a photo of the soldiers in '67, breaking the nineteen-year blockade to the *Kosel* and crying. Jerusalem was reunited.

"Every Sunday school in America had that one on the bulletin board," said Ceil.

Sandy wondered when his patience would give out.

He came around from behind his register, still pleasant, and indicated a silver-on-silver etching locked in the glass case. Then he used the antenna to point to a paper cut on a purple backing. "This work is also very special." Wine cups and challah loaves.

"How can you call yourself a store if you don't want to sell?" Ceil asked.

"As you wish, ma'am," he said, turning away from them, finally, jiggling his shoulders as he tapped out a phone number. Sandy pulled Ceil toward the door.

"What a guy," Ceil said.

"I don't know . . ." Sandy said. "You just have to know how to talk to people."

"Look, you just take me somewhere else and I'll get what I need."

Sandy held the front door open for Ceil and looked behind her.

Young Mr. Stanetsky cupped his hand on the receiver and called after them, "There's a dozen stores like this one. Go to one of them. It won't be any different."

The idea of losing a customer didn't seem to bother him. When you are floated out of a good family, you don't have to worry about things that much. The thought depressed Sandy, suddenly.

Just outside young Mr. Stanetsky's door, Sandy and Ceil found themselves at a small plaza next to a roped excavation. The most recent archaeologists had found the richest lode and they had erected a new plaque, in Hebrew, English, and Arabic, listing their achievements and thanking their benefactors. Across from the excavation stood another little store with a revolving post-card rack in front and T-shirts in the window.

Sandy guided Ceil around the excavation. The other store could have been the twin of young Mr. Stanetsky's, except that in this store, one entire wall was hung with silver-on-gold city-scapes. Ceil decided quickly and bought Mordy three of them.

As they walked back out to the excavation the white sunlight suddenly appeared to come from straight above. The midday sun reflected off the stone formations without making shadows, making one place hard to distinguish from the other. Which way the car? Which way Batei Machse? Sandy was disoriented for a moment. Then she found the steps she thought were right. The car, of course, was in the direction of the *Kosel*. She took Ceil's arm. "I'm worried about you," she said to Ceil, choosing her words carefully.

"I'm worried about you too," Ceil said.

"Me?" Ceil's words broke in Sandy like an open blister.

"Don't think I can't see the kind of pressure you and Nathan are under."

Ceil was silent as they walked down the stairs, side by side, pressing their weight lightly, off the balls of their feet. Absurd, Sandy thought: the way they walked as if after three thousand years theirs would be the weight to crack the stones. Ceil wasn't finished. "Yossi—so hard. And the place you live in—don't be offended by my saying so . . . your neighbors. I want to give you something." Ceil opened up her purse and removed her remaining shekels, a stack as thick as a sandwich. Below them the *Kosel* and the plaza swarmed with families and a large group of boy soldiers in cardboard yarmulkes. They toured all the holy sites as part of their basic training.

"No, keep it," Sandy said. "You'll change it back to dollars." She shouldn't take it. She wouldn't take it.

"To tell you the truth," Ceil said, smiling for the first time in hours, "it hasn't seemed real to me anyhow. Looks more like Monopoly money."

The stack of shekels looked real enough to Sandy.

She stood and thought. Behind Ceil's head, all those swarming families and the soldiers became a blur, giving no particular inspiration. "Use it for Yossi for his bar mitzvah. Get him something from me but don't go back to these stores," Ceil urged. In one shrug she dismissed the whole retail world. "Find out where they make those silk tefillin bags."

She wouldn't tell Ceil she'd thought of it herself, already. She wanted to buy it for him herself. But Ceil still had the power of the big sister, confusing Sandy's logic, making her feel all second thought. Maybe she would take Yossi too, to one of those settlements, deep into the territories. She didn't know how to drive out there but the buses ran all day long. *A silk tefillin bag with his name embroidered on it in gold thread.* Sandy held her hand palm out in such a way so that when Ceil dropped the money in Sandy wouldn't feel her touch, her hand.

# TIRED

TOVA WAS TIRED OF THE PROMISE OF SPIRIT IN EVERY ADVENTURE; tired of driving north into the sun, north from Jerusalem on the way to celebrate *Lag Ba-Omer* in Mount Meron; tired of pulling the map open and trying to decipher the Hebrew transliterations as the car jiggled the words out of focus, and then tired of trying to figure out which crease to bend in, which crease out and over in order to fold the map back into a pamphlet or any shape she would recognize.

They were lost in Beit Shean just slightly, Mike said, after two circles around the plaza of one-story shops. Stubby olive trees breathed shadows onto the island strip, and they circled again, pelted by strong sunlight. Tova curled her hand over her eyes. When the Strauss ice cream billboard appeared out the right window for the fifth time, Tova insisted Mike stop at the next kiosk to check directions.

They parked under a swollen fig tree and bought Esther and Yoni—and themselves—a KanKal Kola. Avi slept through the heat, snoring lightly in his car seat. His fat knees printed rings of powder and baby sweat on the quilted plastic seat cushion.

Tova was tired. *She would have been tired, she was tired, had been tired.* Ten months an Israeli immigrant, nine months in Hebrew class, the finer conjugations pursued her. She had even started to dream in Hebrew, which she'd mentioned to Ilanna, yesterday at class break, when the teachers and students lined up at the coffee table, filling their cups-brought-from-home. But Ilanna, tucking her short blond hair behind her ear, responded from the other side of the water urn with a nod and arched eyebrows. Her hair broke back over her eye. Not a word; Tova of all people knew the old trick of the second-language teacher, making the student answer her own questions.

Okay. So all she really wanted was approval. Tova had also rebuffed the puppy-dog looks; neediness wasn't healthy. She'd even turned down a response to her hanging ad for English lessons—the man's voice so downcast and brave, but she of all people couldn't hold someone's hand. Tova walked over to the sofa in the lounge. Maybe the *tired* was normal, also. Outside on the window, corkscrews of old barbed wire weighing down in the honeysuckle bush tapped like someone's nervous fingers. Ilanna was a language teacher, Tova conceded, and even if she was a culture guru she was by no means a spiritual guide.

"Kids. Who needs to go?" Mike's voice came from the other side of the kiosk. He'd already been to the bathroom and back. "One last chance." Esther swung her head widely, and Yoni, watching her, did the same. Tough soldiers, tough travelers. "So let's get back on the road."

It was more instinctive to Mike from the very beginning how they just had to push forward. Adventure, he kept saying, adventure. Ten months now, yet that word never once occurred to Tova naturally. But as he spoke, his face—bright red from the heat—broke into peaks and points, as if it were reduced to essential parts. He'd gotten so thin this year, so wired-looking, in spite of the fact that his project finally stabilized and kept him busy enough.

"We're off," he said, nevertheless, the cheery cheerleader.

Climbing into the car, Yoni bumped Esther's arm and spilled orange soda on the front of his white dress shirt. A vulpine look crossed his face. Just six months before his face had been round and he'd worn diapers, and now he had this edge.

Esther, who loved her anger, even as a baby, wouldn't suffer an accidental bump. She smacked Yoni's arm and he spilled the orange soda a second time. Even Yoni saw how his shirt was a mess and his bravado crumbled. After all, he was the star of the day. Today, on *Lag Ba-Omer,* in the religious community in Israel, it was a custom to bring three-year-old boys to get their first haircut on Mount Meron. Another seventy, maybe eighty kilometers to drive. Meron was a holy site, the grave site of Rabbi Shimon Bar Yochai, author of the *Zohar,* primo teacher of Kabbala, and today was his *yortzeit,* the anniversary of his death. In his lifetime Bar Yochai transformed the celestial spheres; with a haircut the boys were initiated into, well, boyhood. Tova heard the explanations that padded out the connections between the spirit, the place, and the day, but she was tired and she'd come as much because Mike insisted as anything. What Mike didn't add—Tova didn't invade his privacy, but she knew it—was that part of the kick for him was meeting Rabbi Shapiro in Meron. He had become closer and closer to Rabbi Shapiro and if she pushed him, Mike would snap—as if it should have been obvious—that the first haircut was an honor he would have offered his own father, if Mike hadn't abandoned him in Florida, six thousand miles away. Sometimes Tova felt as if she were on a swing and Mike were pushing her from behind. Today was another swing day.

Mike held the car door open for Tova. The electronic beep on the dashboard signaled one of its stress combinations—ignition on, door open, belts off. Tova watched them buckle in, then looked out into the direction they were heading. Could be the conifer peaks were it, maybe they were that close. Out in the grass was a hand's toss of Jujubes, which, in short focus at the curbside, turned out to be small dots of colored flowers.

Back in the car, moving north up Route 90, Tova checked her watch. Because she'd been tired they'd left Jerusalem two hours later than they'd planned and driven this road that was the fastest but not the safest according to some opinions, and after this stop they were now two and a half hours late.

"Go to sleep," Mike ordered. She knew he could accept their being late if he thought that her tiredness was really lack of sleep and that he was helping her.

Five minutes later, Mike rolled down his window. A wave of heat hit her face and woke her. Her first thought was defensive: okay, so she had been physically tired too. Mike had to bring the car to a complete stop. The engine pitched and sang as he cut down the air-conditioning. A herd of cattle and two cowboys were crossing the road, blocking traffic in both directions.

The first cowboy led the herd into the pasture across the road. The second cowboy, with a green knit yarmulke and sandaled feet, stopped in the middle of the road in order to direct the traffic in both directions. He dismounted. His sandaled feet hit the road. He chucked his horse on the jaw and they heard him say, *"Tafsiki, Mammela."* The horse turned its suede nose, small and fine as a china teacup, and bussed her cowboy on the rear. *"Mammela, boobela. T'haki,"* the cowboy said. *Wait.* The horse nibbled the *tzitzis*, the ritual fringes, hanging out the back of his T-shirt. *"Mah eetach? Aht mishoogat?"* *Are you crazy?*

"*Mishoogat?*" Mike said. "What happened to 'Hi-ho Silver'?"

"Or *Kee-mo-sabee,*" Tova said. "Did you check out his sandals? Not exactly the Marlboro Man." She started to laugh and laugh. Mike's face broke out in points again, and he started to laugh also. Looking at him made Tova laugh even harder, until she was coughing. From the backseat Esther echoed with a giggle, so it must have been funny. Yoni stretched against the window, all wide-eyed. Tova could only guess which would make the better telephone story for his grandparents, when they spoke their thrice-a-week call, the cowboy or the haircut.

Finally, when the herd was through, the cowboy closed the gate on the empty side. He walked his horse onto the new field, shut the metal gate behind him, and mounted, *tzitzis* flying back, straight as the horse's tail. Tova could not go back to sleep.

Forty minutes later, Mount Meron appeared straight ahead, at the same time crowning the road and curiously shrunken from the Meron of Tova's imagination: an ordinary knob of a hill, green and brown. No sight of the grave site.

A kilometer closer, motorcycle police diverted them off the main road. Slowly, they rolled the car down into a bare field turned parking lot. They would have to walk the rest of the way to the knob, hardly appearing worth all the fuss, and considering the distance Tova became more tired, again.

Mike still had the capacity to renew his energy with optimism. "I hope we can still catch Rabbi Shapiro," Mike said. "Let's just bring up a few things. No need to schlepp half the car up the mountain anyhow."

"I would never have brought what I didn't think was necessary to begin with," Tova said. Esther and Yoni looked up at her so sharply she knew she had yelled.

She dumped two plastic shopping bags onto the car seat,

picked and consolidated. She chose Wild Turkey for a toast, more soda for the children, and chocolate *rugelach* whose tops had melted together in the heat. Napkins. A diaper for the baby, and—just in case—an extra pair of underwear for Yoni.

She unfolded the stroller for the baby and locked the wheels with her toe as she swung the baby's compact ball of a body into the stroller seat. Barely awake, he leaned forward and grabbed his bare feet. He could be happy grabbing anything. The parking field was bone dry, the ground stippled with cracks—runoffs from the winter rain. The stroller wheels didn't have a chance, spinning in place instead of moving forward. Mike took the stroller handles from Tova. They were supposed to have met Rabbi Shapiro outside the tomb site hours ago. Surely he would have given up on them by now, thought Tova, watching Mike's panic. Could it matter to him anyhow? One more little boy, one less little boy.

As they forced ahead, the thickness of the crowd doubled by the minute. Mike half pushed and half lifted the stroller from behind, running it on the two front wheels. They approached a blacktop sidewalk and Mike lifted the stroller over the curb. Then he ended up carrying the stroller through parked cars that had installed themselves tip to tip in a rude caravan, blocking the sidewalk.

After half a block, Mike put the stroller back down onto the blacktop and they looped around a Sephardi family who must have staked the space a week earlier. They'd practically set up house, hanging patterned cloth off their automobile to make a tent, and relaxing in rubber slippers, they grilled their *shishlik* and kebab and kidneys over a pile of smoking rocks as high as Yoni. Yoni threw his hands up to cover his eyes as Tova steered him out of the smoke by the shoulders. Esther coughed behind them.

The blacktop stopped suddenly at the edge of a gravel road, the point of entry to the grave site. Tova could barely move through the crowd. She had heard descriptions of Meron on *Lag Ba-Omer*: like a Woodstock, a bazaar, a celebration. A real carnival. And who knew how many people. Maybe a hundred thousand. They would hear the real number tonight on the English news at seven.

As they walked uphill, all Tova could see was the backs of her family. Yoni's shoulders bent him into a hump, a little ball rolling uphill.

Outside the tomb site, a crowd looped and swirled so tightly that even if Rabbi Shapiro was still there, they would never be able to find him. It was Tova's fault, she thought. From being *tired*. Then she discovered she had a second anxiety. She'd been so very tired from the car trip to Meron that she had left the scissors for Yoni's haircut in the car.

Tova squinted into the sun as if she'd find a heavenly response. How could she tell Mike? She pushed her hands down in her skirt pocket to check for the scissors there. Her forehead broke out in prickles of sweat. She wished she'd brought the bottled water out of the car too. Yoni pulled on her skirt, held it to his cheek, and pushed his first two fingers in his mouth. He'd been tired, *Hoo-ayafe, hoo-haya ayefe*. She patted his head, crimping the ends of the hair sealed with sweat on the back of his neck.

"I've got to find Rabbi Shapiro," Mike said. "You stay here with the kids, I'll start looking."

"No," yelled Tova, "you'll get lost and then what do we do?" Mike didn't hear her and he disappeared, getting sucked into the crowd agitating around the entrance and exit to the vault. Now she was tired and abandoned. She wondered if she'd paid enough attention to make it back to the car herself.

Esther stood next to Tova, still as a statue. She had recomposed her face into the hard lines of the morning. Any minute, Tova knew, Esther would let loose a litany of truths disguised as complaints. A man knocked the stroller. Tova pulled it in between Esther, Yoni, and herself and hooked the wheel with her foot. Yes, that was impossibly rude, she said to herself, but really to Esther. As Yoni held her skirt, she fished down in her pocketbook for anything, maybe a nail clipper. She moved around a comb, her shekel checkbook, her dollar checkbook, her notepad of Hebrew verbs. No scissors. No rabbi, nothing. Out of the corner of her eye Tova saw Esther open her mouth to speak but held it back. Yes, this trip was for nothing.

Tova looked down for a minute, concentrating her inner eye back on the car seat, scanning for the scissors. She'd put them in a Ziploc bag. Maybe they'd fallen out. Maybe she'd left them on purpose, a sick concession to her mood. She would never tell Mike half of this, she thought, straightening the front of her skirt where Yoni was twisting it, back seam to her side. She looked up to see if Mike had found his way back to them yet.

*And then Tova saw. And then she did see, she had seen*—she told herself afterward.

"He's here out of nowhere," Esther said, conjugating the present tense, out loud. Because suddenly in the space where there was no one Rabbi Shapiro appeared before them, and Tova had never noticed before how much of Rabbi Shapiro's face she could see under the beard (a beard that on men like him was usually as dense as a mask): perfect symmetry—and wasn't symmetry beauty?—blue eyes trimmed with thick black lashes. He couldn't be any older than her—or Mike.

Then Mike came up behind them. He had expected nothing

less than a miraculous find here, he announced to Rabbi Shapiro. Tova felt like grabbing Mike by the face and telling him to be quiet, because if Mike was implying that he had found Rabbi Shapiro and brought him here he was wrong; this wasn't good old cause and effect. Tova wanted a chance; it was *her* miraculous find.

Rabbi Shapiro's assistant wore a short blond beard that sprouted out and spread from the top of his cheeks. Carroty and pleasant, he carried a metal folding chair. He must have been carrying it around all day. The chair crackled as he spread the back and the seat to open it. Mike swung Yoni up on the chair and Yoni's feet scrambled for a second, buckling the seat. Rabbi Shapiro righted him with a laugh and leaned into him, whispering some endearment. From the smile on Yoni's face it looked as if Rabbi Shapiro had given Yoni candy, not words.

Rabbi Shapiro held his hand out palm side up, as if he were a surgeon. The assistant laid a scissors in his palm. Mike propped Yoni under the arms to steady him and changed Yoni's elbows into wings. Rabbi Shapiro pinched a handful of hair around each of Yoni's ears and pushed those sections forward across his cheeks. Then, as he cut the hair around the back of Yoni's head, instead of the fall away of cut hair, there was an appearance, a becoming: the hair on his cheeks turned into *payos*, side locks. As Tova watched, the baby Yoni turned into a little boy.

While Rabbi Shapiro folded up the chair Tova practically abacussed her fingers. There was a lesson to parse out from *cutting away* and *becoming*, like a recipe for life. Meanwhile, Mike opened the shopping bag and poured paper cups of Wild Turkey for all the grown-ups. Each of the children took two *rugelach* and then Esther snuck a third. She licked the melted chocolate off her fingers, and between exaggerated, extravagant strokes Esther smiled up at Tova and said, "How did Rabbi Shapiro just get here, like 'poof'?"

Mike froze his *l'chayim* midair and toasted Esther theatrically. Esther smiled back, chocolate cobbled across her front teeth, and Rabbi Shapiro beamed through his beard.

Maybe Rabbi Shapiro's appearance wasn't the strangest thing. Could Mike have, after all, found Rabbi Shapiro in this? Tova looked around her at the swarm, the frenzied swarm—like bees.

Tomorrow, in Hebrew class, when Ilanna would say, "*Mah hadash,* what's new?" Tova would have to decide. Was it *becoming* or *being*? Either way she'd begin with: suddenly, like that, when . . .

Ilanna would tell her slow down, don't rush so that you miss half of it, the whole story please. Tova would use her hands to fill in. Up to a certain point she could for sure get it right: outside the tomb site the people pushed.

Ilanna would dip her eyes, blond bangs pendant. "Go on."

Tova would hesitate like a Yvegenia. Childish. Abandoned onstage.

And either way, *poof!* A trickle of current exploded into a bolt of lightning.

Tova fished around in her brain, filed back, stirred up the neurons. She of all people knew better than to expose her innards in a classroom. Better to make a flamboyant and public display of fishing for the perfect word. What she came up with was *hashra'a,* the Hebrew for inspiration.

# THE PUNCH LINE

WHEN MR. S ARRANGED THE *SHABBOS* IN HEBRON HE FINESSED THE conundrum of danger and sanity and lobbied each head-of-a-household with a joke about perspective. The people of Tel Aviv sip their Wissotzky tea, snug in their seaside cafés, and say, incredulous, "What, you're going to Jerusalem?" The citizens of Jerusalem, as their bags are being inspected for explosives at the doorway of the Super Cheap Market, say, "What? You're going to the Old City?" The people of the Old City, who send their toddlers to *gan* flanked by armed guards, say, "What? You're going to Hebron?"

When Mike came home from shul he repeated the joke.

"The joke is a little outdated," Tova sparked. "Tel Avivans aren't so safe and snug anymore either. What about that sniper on the family beach? And the father who took a shot for his baby? He's been in the hospital two months."

"You're right," Mike said. And she was. Who knew where it was best to take care of your family in a land where a man could even wonder if he was able to. But his instinct snapped up her reticence. If he didn't flinch a muscle, if he stayed on the narrow topic and avoided the big questions she'd relax. "It's just that the joke isn't finished."

And Tova picked up on it cheerily. "It's like a seesaw stuck in the air. The punch line dangles," Tova said.

So what *did* the people of Hebron say? And what did it say about them? They suffered mightily for their ideals, for everyone's ideals, living in what amounted to armed compounds. Were they heroes or just plain crazy?

If it didn't sound so soupy or self-serving they were heroes too, and tired but not crazy yet. He had the same thought every night watching Tova climb up on the kids' beds when they were asleep, in one hand a hundred-watt penlight from his tire changing kit, in the other hand a metal lice comb, and she hacked, picked, flicked out head lice, working without a backward look at the clock, like a nurse on the night shift.


Thirty-five men, women, and children from Heavenly Heights drove out to Hebron in an armored bus. A pair of army Jeeps racked around with metal grate shields rode fore and aft, making their convoy official. They hadn't traveled twenty minutes when Rabbi Altman, perched in the front of the bus with his wife and her wheelchair, rose to pull his prayer hat from the metal racks and said the Wayfarer's Prayer out loud. The prayer jolted Mike. They'd just passed Gilo, another turn right they'd drive through Bethlehem with the tomb of Rachel who wept for the return of her children to their borders. You said the Wayfarer's Prayer when you went from place to place. Funny, he'd fathomed the whole trip figuratively and literally as a continuum. Wasn't that what it was all about? Supporting Hebron, which had the oldest Jewish community in the world, was asserting the ligature of the whole enterprise of *Eretz Yisrael*, like saying yes, the hipbone is connected to the thighbone, the thighbone is connected to all that body, all that past. Here, Abraham bought the Cave of Patriarchs to bury his wife Sara, and Hebron was King David's first home of the reign. Then the Romans, the Byzantines, the Crusades, the Mamluks, the Turks, the British, until the Jews were sliced and diced out of there in 1929.

Then, in all the excitement of getting there, they got to their room and realized the trip was BYOT, bring-your-own-towels. They realized the mistake when Tova and the kids used the bathroom one by one and everyone had no choice but to wipe their hands on toilet tissue, the crackly blue kind you were lucky to get when Mike was studying here in yeshiva, before college, but they hadn't bothered to sell for years in the neighborhoods with American immigrants.

"You were the one packing," Mike asked Tova. "How could you forget?"

"You never told me," Tova said.

"Mr. S told me. And I told you," Mike said. He remembered hearing it from Mr. S but maybe he had forgotten to pass it on. He didn't want to whine at Tova. He'd caught himself a dozen times since the rafting trip north. And he didn't want to argue; the flip side of his confidence and resolve was intransigence. He would find a way to take care of it, he said, going into the bathroom himself.

He couldn't believe they hadn't said a word: the floor was wet from an open leak behind the toilet. He called out, "Hey," to no one. The buck stopped with him.

The group had booked this large pension in Kiryat Arba, the

ancient City of the Four, the settlement next to Hebron proper. Their room was small as a jail cell—that was the first thing that came to mind when he entered—and Mike's eyes flew to the single barred and barricaded window. Just outside, posts from a balcony above rested against a row of low pine trees. He walked over and peered out across the thick transom; on a small grassless playground, a dozen toddlers were plugged in to what they did best. Play. Likely some were from Heavenly Heights, mixing in with the townies. For all the focus on their own families the men hardly recognized each other's kids the way the women did; whole families could look so much the same, like cookie cutter people, with the few exceptions of the older boys who made themselves conspicuous by growing a foot in two months, or the bad boys by getting drunk on Purim and getting found in their excreta a day later.

The children bounced and arced wildly on colored horses hitched to the concrete by steel springs—springs wide as a fist, short and strong as a man's forearm, a strong man's forearm. They were, he recognized those same horses in Heavenly Heights and the same horses Tova made a big deal out of seeing in the Old City of Jerusalem. Next to them, Rabbi Altman settled his wife in her wheelchair, fussing with the possibilities: under the tree? next to the bench? facing the sunset? facing the children?

When he decided on the sunset view he bent down to work the brakes by hand. He straightened up and tested the hand release, pointing forward and telling his wife something. But she didn't look as if she were going anywhere on her own. Then Rabbi Altman stepped away and stepped forward again to straighten her white beret around her face. At that gesture Mike reflexed back from the window, because of the power of the thought that hit him, how each man took care of his family and for some men the care became literal and concrete, not abstract or ideal or something the generations will idealize.

In the meantime, Tova unpacked their overnight bags and hung up the *Shabbos* clothes. The stone floor was hot, conducting heat up the walls and blowing it back at them like someone's hot breath. Mike had an insight into their immediate situation. He walked into the bathroom and he figured it out. No one should jiggle the flushers, he announced. It was one of those old-fashioned pull tops. It would take fifteen minutes to refill the tank, and jiggling at it just overpressured the tank and the pipes.


Little problems, little missions. Mike went down to the lobby to find Mr. S and came back a few minutes later. Mr. S said he had a friend in Hebron who could lend them some towels.

Ten minutes later he joined Mr. S outside the pension, where Esther was the only girl playing war games with the locals—the local girls, since she'd stopped playing street games with the boys—ambushing in the small shrubbery next to the playground. Shaindy Altman held a book in her lap, too low down to read, Mike suspected, but Shaindy concentrated hard.

Once out of Kiryat Arba, past the Cave of the Patriarchs, Mike and Mr. S walked single file down a hilly path. Mike had been to Hebron before, but not inside the rough seams like this. Above them, late-afternoon clouds heckled the sun—off spires of ancient rooftops, off an orchard of TV antennas. Then Mr. S, then Mike ducked into a stone alley, edging the casbah, past a fat Arab woman balancing a covered basket on her head and a barefoot toddler mouthing an open can of Coca-Cola. Above, pacing the rooftops, were this month's reserve soldiers, and on the ground, soldiers paired off in boxes the size and shape of an

American telephone booth. Just beyond the second booth, in an open stone plaza, half a dozen children already in their *Shabbos* clothes, hair still wet and slick like hatched chicks, vroomed on plastic Big Wheels. No different scene, Mike thought, than the children in Heavenly Heights, or Baltimore for that matter.

Mr. S began to count out loud. He ran his finger along the seams in the barbed wire. When Mr. S reached "five" they stopped at a single metal door with a large fired-clay mezuzah restored to the ancient cleft in the stone door frame. Dan'il Beza-lel, Mr. S said, was a special friend.

Next to the door, really more of a gate, windows were grilled about with iron bars. But the gate was unlocked, as if to assert this Dan'il's right to a safe and free passage, to assert his right to security like a small town south of Paris. They walked in, directly into a small corridor that was open to the sky, but screened on top with heavy-duty chicken wire. On top of the wire, throwing eyelet shadows on their feet, were a scattering of rocks and sticks and a couple of crushed soda cans, as if the throwers were some days bent on harm, on other days just adolescents. The floor of the corridor was lined with small ocher pots. Were they the ancient dug-up kind, lifted from sites, or reproductions? The pots bubbled up with clay fruit: red pomegranates, yellow cit-rons, and—in what looked like a game of perspective in an already tumbled reality—what appeared to be real potatoes, hard green tomatoes, cucumbers. Inside a second door, on the floor, lay a rice cake carton with two handguns thrown in.

"His wife—my friend Merielle—doesn't allow the guns inside," Mr. S said.

Mr. S, then Mike, entered the living room looking heavenward. Their instinct to seize inspiration was correct: the ceiling hung decorated with mobiles, scraps of ceramic work. Mike recognized the colors—violets, plums, lilacs, gold, like *Eretz Yisrael* in a dream, in his dreams. "Who is this Dan'il?" he whispered to Mr. S.

"Actually, he's Rabbi Altman and Shaindy Altman's cousin. He's the one who introduced them."

Mr. S was so simple sometimes. What Mike was really asking was, Give me the category; he was trying to convert the strong impression to horsepower, wattage, photons, gigabytes, anything more familiar.

On the right of the entry hung a lithograph. Jerusalem. More purples, gold tips on the conifer, the Third Temple rebuilt and melting into a sunrise: this was the fantasia. Aah. Mike knew who this Dan'il Bezalel was. He'd seen his work. Not in the mainstream, of course, with the dancing or fiddling Hasidim, not in the Israel Museum—a little too subversive. Rather, on the SHABBOS FOR ONE AND ALL posters plastered all around the Old City by the outreach bunch bent on introducing traveling teenagers to their heritage.

On the far side of the living room, the louver door to Dan'il's studio paddled open to the sound of Mr. S's greeting. Dan'il appeared in the doorway, a square granite cut of a man, and piling behind in a cubist event was Rabbi Altman, who must have flown here after settling his wife in her wheelchair. The two of them stopped short in the living room and expanded the picture to a side-by-side, nearly identical in red beard, height, affect, fire-breathing voice. They boomed, "Shalom aleichem." Mike and Mr. S echoed the greeting. It turned out Dan'il Bezalel and Rabbi Altman weren't just cousins, they were first cousins, sons of twin sisters, and they could have been brothers—were probably, genetically, half brothers. They shook hands with Mike and Mr. S.

Dan'il led them all to the dining-room table, already set for the *Shabbos* meal with a grape-colored tablecloth. He'd set the table himself, he explained. His third daughter who lived in Katif just had her fourth baby and Merielle had gone to help her. Dan'il bowed to the *mazel tovs*. Then he pulled out a chair at the head of the table for Mr. S and pointed him to sit. Mike squeezed between the table and a small Scandinavian cabinet against the wall. The cabinet was the only wooden piece in the dining room. The table was metal. Even the chairs were folding metal, with plastic seat cushions shattered into a thousand soft creases, Mike couldn't help but notice, his attention to physical detail, his scientist self, as much a comfort reaction as anything.

They sat. Dan'il was in no hurry but Mr. S stated their mission for towels plainly. "But of course," Dan'il said. "Anything for the friends of my friend." Mr. S, obviously, was a special kind of friend.

Dan'il got up, walked into his kitchen. He returned with several towels decorated like mosaic windows and draped over his arm. He also balanced a pitcher of *petel* water and plastic cups. He handed the towels to Mr. S, who handed them to Mike and poured drinks for them deftly, without spilling a single drop on the *Shabbos* tablecloth. He didn't want to hear of them leaving before Mr. S reported his goings-on with the American Congress.

"Mike is part of the *YESHA* council," Mr. S said in response, making the group and their call to action inclusive. Dan'il nodded and smiled. Of course Mike was one of them, and he and Rabbi Altman leaned forward, across the table to insist Mr. S recount his last month. The victory in the Israeli Supreme Court. The attempt to defame him in certain American organizations. The upshot was that Mr. S was going to keep pushing forward—Jerusalem, everywhere, here. Apparently, Mr. S had financed the Big Wheel plaza they'd just walked through. Mike looked at the three men: Dan'il, Rabbi Altman, Mr. S. Every one of them had their plates full, even if it was from just living here, and they looked tired, their faces lined like sculpture that was too realistic, though Mr. S was the most supple even though he was the oldest of the three. No, not tired. Tired was the wrong word. It was just that the energy it took figuring out where you act and where you stop could age a man.

Mike and Mr. S got up to leave. Dan'il sighed to relinquish them. "It's not so often I have such an important visitor and his friends."

As Mr. S offered his *Shabbos* salutations, Rabbi Altman took the cue, a beat behind. He would walk back with them, he said. On the way out to the corridor he stopped and scooped up his handgun from the rice cake box and said in a bruised English, "I have to go back—anyhow—now. Shaindy needs to me." As did all their families, Mike thought.


Back in the pension, after services at the Cave of the Patriarchs, after the *Shabbos* meal, Mike lay down on the bed, his feet hanging across the metal frame. The beds were *Sachnut* beds, three quarters the size of an American twin, and he wasn't that tall but his feet had nowhere to go but out. Instead of regular mattress stuff, this one was full of pea-size nodules. Mike sucked in air and let it out, and let it out again, an exaggeration of a real exhale, and waited for Tova to start and finish her joke about the pea under the mattress and the *prince* and the pea.

Once the joke was over he described the soldiers who lined the mountain paths and made a soldier convoy for their walk down to the Cave.

He'd been trying to put it all together: how the Patriarch

Abraham bought the cave from Efron the Hittite to bury his wife Sara. It was the first recorded real estate purchase in the world. Efron the Hittite was by some accounts smarmy, by some accounts respectful, and Abraham made a point of purchasing the Cave and the field next to it in public, in front of all the Hittites. Then there was an idea that a standard of dwelling someplace is having a burial place there. Past present future. You never saw much of Abraham's inner life. When he was told not to be afraid, well, he was just not afraid.

If Mike let a mood like this slip—who knew?—it could be a crack in the wall of a dam. And Tova would grab a thing he said—a phrase, a word—and separate it from the larger meaning and run across the field with it. His bravery, his personality, his strength, was what he relied on and when he let go of it, or when it failed him, he peeled back his skin to a spiritual flaw.

"I know the punch line," Mike said to Tova to test if she were still awake. In response, she evened out her breathing. She was drifting off. Anyhow, he knew she'd rather make small talk about the towels, which she had used after candle lighting the *Shabbos* way, throwing water on her face and patting herself dry. The towels were line dried, rough as tree bark.

From their beds in the dark room, while Mike was formulating the punch line so they could both sleep better, or maybe it would make them sleep worse, they heard the toilet tank gurgle and the sucking noise the baby made in his sleep. Out in town, somewhere in the direction of the Cave where, like them, the Patriarchs and Matriarchs were resting and watching, there was a siren—probably a car alarm, Mike told himself—and small explosions—probably the backfire of a truck.

# CHIEFEST JOY

IT WAS ONE OF THOSE SUNDAYS IN EARLY JUNE AFTER *SHAVUOUS*, THE Holiday of Weeks. On Number Four the clotheslines stretched a banner from balcony to balcony, swinging bibs and undershirts and sun suits in the morning sun.

Tova crouched at her window like a nervous cat, trying to subdue the sight in bits and spurts between her cleaning, sorting, and packing. In five days, she and Mike and the kids were leaving this home, this home she'd bought and paid for with her year, taking their first trip back to America. Reentry was traumatic, Mike said—the buildings so big, the drugstores so vast and supplied. And no one looks over their shoulder as they walk around the city and no one flips out from a backpack forgotten at a bus stop. Mike badly wanted them to accompany him, support him on one of his work jaunts and then they'd visit her folks, then his. Mike's father, lately, had been missing them loudly and he said he would pay them back the airplane fare.

She taped the bottom of another cardboard box and turned it over. The box smelled like fish. She hesitated, then threw in a handful of mothballs, inhaled the naphthalene, and suddenly felt how foolish her desire to leave her home "in order." It would change nothing: no matter what she did, every day had a rhythm, regular as religious service. Noontime, the women took the laundry in and watched the three- and four-year-olds walk themselves home from *gan*. Then lunch, and a nap, and everyone trickled back to the park at the blacktop next door. The mothers sat rear to rear on the single-slat benches and retied hats under the babies' chins, holding plastic water bottles at ready. Later, after school, the big brothers and sisters took over the play space like an invading army, loud and confident; girls playing *Machanayim* with a soccer ball, the boys daring each other down the slide, backpacks and all, landing smack into the three-year-olds and their colored digging toys.

With a last spurt of inspired energy Tova unloaded the entire floor of her closet. It lay on piles on her bed.

The best find was a pack of Gold Toe Fluffies, men's socks, new—the first new piece of clothing she'd seen in months. The next best find was a small white trash bag with torn T-shirts and ripped flannel pajamas. A rag bag was the very definition of home. The worst find was the pair of patent leather, spike-heeled shoes, ruined the first *Shabbos* almost a year ago when she'd tripped on a concrete block on the sidewalk.

If deep cleaning wasn't a sign of rootedness, she didn't know what was.

The most surprising find was her camera inside the nylon case; the camera was not forgotten, just never thought of, not necessary; the whole emigration here so far a natural series of images and impressions, her adjusting eye a changing lens.

Finding the camera made the whole day's labor worthwhile, Tova considered. It could take the burden off the inner eye—

aside from all her domestic busyness there was a lot to remember in Number Four that week. Of all weeks for there to be two weddings.

The first wedding was Mr. S's, two nights ago, which he'd announced just a few weeks before that. But they should have known it was coming. In the spring, after Passover, right after Mr. S returned from the States, hadn't he started to sweep the stairwells three times a day? Then one morning Number Four had woken up and all of a sudden the mailboxes were tidied, back panels rebolted, and next to the buzzers, sprouting like tubers in fifteen-point italic-on-brass, were the family names: Richmon, Gernokovsky, Hacker, Hammer, Min-ha-har (newly Hebraized, formerly Bergmann), etc.

Rachel—the new Mrs. Stanetsky—was an Argentinian-Israeli, with round blue eyes and springy black hair. Talk was that for ten years Rachel had lived in a rented room in a rented apartment. Her face was pretty—all the features right and in right proportion—but bland. How old was she anyhow? What had Rachel Stanetsky done to deserve a man like Mr. S? If Tova asked Mike he would answer, with some remark that said as much about Mike as it did all men, "What do *you* think?"

Well, it wasn't Tova's business, and Mike's comment needn't cloud up her week, and Mr. Stanetsky's marriage wasn't, anyhow, one of the things she'd figured she'd be taking to America with her.

Tova unzipped the camera case and tugged the camera out of its Velcro clips. She pulled the window blinds, all the way up to the window frame, and brought the camera to her eye.

Through the box viewer she saw her neighbor Debra cut out across the park, and she heard her yelling. Debra's daughters climbed out of the ball game and held down their heads. Debra was crazy this week because the second wedding belonged to Debra. Her oldest daughter, Channie, would marry Nachson Chaim, a shaggy, serious boy who wore a large knit yarmulke, full as a helmet. Tova took a picture, anchoring her elbows against her chest, thinking to give Debra a copy. At the right time, of course.

Or maybe she wouldn't. Then the thought came to Tova, the exact thought she'd tried to avoid, busy organizing the whole day: she'd had this experience leaving home before. What if once she got to America she felt as if Heavenly Heights were as far away as it really was? What if she liked it better in America? Should they have waited another year to go back? Debra said it would be like visiting an old boyfriend, that she had to prepare herself. Oh, Debra. Tova remembered that her adjustment problems had something to do with Debra, but she was so used to her now, she could conjure up that there'd been issues without conjuring the issues themselves. Maybe the trip would be like the vacation it was meant to be. Succor and spoiling until she got back where she belonged.

Tuesday afternoon Tova finished unrolling a bolt of mandarin-colored brocade. She was helping Debra make the girls' dresses for the wedding. She needed five more inches of cloth and they didn't have five more inches. Without a word, Tova stretched the brocade across Debra's living-room floor and across the top and back of the sofa.

Debra stood at the sofa back, clipping the scissors in the air. It wouldn't surprise Tova if Debra whispered something to it and the cloth would extend by itself. It wouldn't surprise Tova if

Debra whispered something to the scissors and then they cut the cloth on their own.

"Don't say it," Debra said, holding the scissors still for a moment.

"Don't say what?" Tova asked, embarrassed. She bent over and pinched the ends of the brocade, remeasuring.

"Don't say half of what you're thinking about. Like Mr. Stanetsky, for example."

Debra walked to the balcony door.

Tova put her thumb and pressed down on the tape measure. She'd been wrong, they only needed three inches. About Mr. S, everyone was talking, or trying not to talk about it idly: just that morning, five days after his wedding, Mr. Stanetsky had suffered a stroke.

Tova pulled the tape measure across one more time. Wrong! They just needed two and a half inches.

The transformer on the Singer Classic sewing machine hummed against the wall, hummed like an insect.

She looked up. Debra stood next to the balcony door. Beyond Debra's head the laundry flapped on the clothesline, as if this were a regular week.

"I'm going to miss these conversations. Even when you're not talking," Tova said, finally, glad to hit on nothing explosive. "You know what I found yesterday when I was cleaning out my bedroom?"

"Your camera."

"How did you know?"

Debra shrugged.

"Would you mind if I took your picture?" Tova asked. Debra looked surprised.

"Okay. As you wish."

"I really want to get a picture of your laundry," Tova teased.

Before Debra could answer, she grabbed the scissors from Debra's hand and anchored the top of the brocade. Then she ran up to her own apartment and came back down, swinging her camera case.

Back in Debra's living room, she made Debra stand just outside the sliding balcony door. A plane—or planes—thundered behind the mountains and the clouds. She waited until the noise passed and in those seconds felt her pulse ticking at her temple.

Tova stood back and scanned Debra through the camera viewer. At her feet, dusty socks and apricot pits from some kids' discus-type game curled together at the porch drain. The black socks stirred like snakes, lifted by nothing apparent. Around Debra's head the laundry dipped and waved. Debra smiled, ready. "You know the laundry makes me feel normal," Debra said, her voice singing, floating—feathering. Tova jerked her eye back from the viewer. She saw something swirl above the laundry, blowy white puffs, lustrous on the underside.

Tova drew the camera up to her face. She was going to get the whole thing. Record it. But with the camera lens all she saw was Debra and the laundry. Debra smiled nervously, pulling her skirt around the calves of her legs, glancing behind her shoulder one time. Tova pulled the camera down. The slight sheen off the balcony floor would change the light meter. Tova held it up again and shut down the aperture one notch, nudged it more, down one and a half notches. The laundry on the line was the background. The moving sheen stuff didn't come up on the viewer. Reality didn't always live up to its name. In the end, in front, in focus, Tova concentrated on Debra's face, just her face.

---

Wednesday night, Tova walked into the wedding hall and slipped into the bridal room with a bag. Inside the bag, just in case, were iron-on hem tape and a portable iron, 220 voltage. Channie looked right at Tova, saw her put the bag on the makeup counter, but was concentrating on inner thoughts. She mouthed Psalms of David from a miniature book in her hands.

At the bride's reception before the ceremony, Channie sat on a high-backed wicker chair, flowers woven into the top frame: a real throne. Around her the courtiers, her sisters, stood in their mandarin brocade dresses. Not one of them looked good in the mandarin brocade, but their necks were so long, especially Shira's, and those girls posed so well—there was no denying— some grandmother had certainly been a queen. Tova swung her camera case vigorously under her right arm.

Tova heard two clarinets, a drum, and an electronic keyboard. The sound came from far away, as if it were someone else's music. It came from the groom's reception in a room down on the other side of the bride's reception room.

The musicians arrived first, in a cluster, then split to either side in front of Channie. The bride started to recite her Psalms with more intensity, rocking her head.

The groom approached, half pushed and half dragged by his father and father-in-law to be, a crowd of men behind him.

The music stopped. The men shoved Nachson Chaim directly in front of Channie, a look on his face as if he were being taken captive. The sisters held their breath. Like his forefather, thousands of years earlier, he checked his bride. It was she. He reached behind Channie for the bridal veil, and pulled the veil over her face.

Tova stood in back. The entire Number Four was there, even

Rachel Stanetsky, clapping her hands to the music, heavy gold jewelry swinging at her neck and both wrists.

Next, the families lined up to walk the couple to the *chuppa*. The fathers held the groom by either arm, and the mothers walked the bride, her face thickly swathed with her veil. She couldn't see, she needed the mothers' arms to guide her. Climbing up to the canopy, the women paused. Channie moved her lips, passionately, reciting Psalms by heart. Once Channie stepped up to the canopy she would cross into another dimension, another life zone. Then Tova heard a small sound, the ripping of cloth. Channie's foot had landed on the hem of her dress. Debra bent over and unpinned Channie's high heel. Tova exhaled, enjoyed a righteousness for having brought the hem tape. She pictured the spot where she'd set it, on Channie's makeup table.

Under the canopy, the rabbi read the wedding contract. More rabbis and teachers were called up to make the seven nuptial blessings. The couple drank the wine. Debra smoothed the front of her dress. Nachson Chaim's father wrapped up a glass in a napkin, and placed it under Nachson Chaim's foot. The groom stomped. He ground. His lips rippled and he looked at his father. They waited. The father stretched his neck and whispered something to the son who stomped again.

The glass broke, sounded like an explosion. Then the band started playing: songs of joy and gladness, bride and groom rejoicing. Songs of Jerusalem. The groom's friends began to clap and sing. Channie's sisters grabbed and kissed her. Tova held her camera over the heads of the dancing friends. She focused on the faces of the couple, then the families, then the friends and the dancing. The floor came up to meet the dancers. She clicked.

Tova steadied her camera back, pulling her elbows against her chest. Rachel Stanetsky crossed in front of her viewer, mouthing to a small knot of women, "He is okay." Tova noticed Rachel Stanetsky wore shiny silver high heels.

Later Tova saw something moving along the floor, between all the dancing feet. Something underneath them. Did no one else see? Like the stuff on the balcony, like the stuff from the singing and the notes, but this time with a flat geometrical look, and all over the floor like confetti. She looked for Debra. Debra stood in a circle of women holding Channie up on a chair, moving Channie toward her husband.

Tova ran behind the circle of women, her camera flapping against her rib cage. Next to her chair she took her camera case. Inside, she knew she had an empty, little black film canister. She ran back to the dance floor where the young couple, aloft in chairs, held a cloth napkin between them. The wedding guests were dancing them together, apart, together, apart, and the couple was laughing and laughing. Tova worked quickly between the backs and forths, scooping up some of the stuff, pushing it into the canister, and tamping it down with her fingers. Curiously it had no weight, and after she clipped on the lid of the canister, the trace left on her fingertips was at first opalescent, then entirely clear.

Thursday morning Tova handed the taxicab driver a fist-size ball of rope. "They call me Avi," the driver said, in response. His right arm was gnarled, his right fingers scarred and white, a peculiar houndstooth. Avi threw their suitcases on top of the cab, looped the string over the roof rack twice, then pocketed the rest of the ball.

Had Mike seen what Avi did? Tova couldn't get Mike's attention. She climbed into the cab, sat in the second seat. The children and Mike sat together in the third seat. The cab lurched out into the road, making more noise than necessary so early in the morning.

Tova checked the film canister in her purse. She shook it. The canister felt lighter than the night before. She pulled it out of her purse and uncapped the lid. Avi the driver swung the cab onto the main road and the cab listed, practically on two wheels. Tova dipped her forefinger in the canister and held her finger to the light. The stuff was dusty, unglamorous, even a little viscous, disappearing as she watched. Perhaps she'd handled it too much. She looked back behind her, as if expecting an explanation. The children lay on Mike, like dominoes; Mike's eyes were closed. Beyond his head the stones of Number Four grinned pink in the morning light, practically blushing.

Months later, after Tova and Mike and the kids got plain stuck in America, waiting by the bedside of Mike's father, Tova bought two picture albums at Target but could not bring herself to sort the distance between the heart and the eye. The albums lay in their cellophane seal; the pictures in stacks in their drugstore bags.

Tova sat down on the beige sleep sofa next to an open porch window in her parents-in-law's apartment. She arranged the pillows behind her, having to choose between sitting too forward— her feet crossed on the floor—or too back, the edge of the sofa cushion forcing her legs straight out from the back of her calves. Her mother-in-law had personalized this apartment the way any woman makes a home. Here in the middle of high-rise country she had a mantel built—no fireplace but a mantel to primp with shells, crustaceans, family pictures. Mike and the kids were at the hospital visiting Mike's father, talkative between his chemotherapy. The North Miami Beach, which she saw through the window and across the waterway, took in a steady knot of cars. Silently, the drawbridge on the waterway stopped the traffic. Tova watched the cars drive up blindly, like moles, and then have to stop in line. Two yachts, with high fly fishers, glided through and the drawbridge clamped down, big animal jaws.

In the den/guest room her mother-in-law sat with the TV on loudly. Every morning Esther watched her grandma fold back the talk-show list in *The Sun-Sentinel*, the titles a wild garden of confession, abuse, trauma. "Grandma goes through all that trouble and then falls asleep with the TV on," Esther complained yesterday. The guest-room shelves were stacked with picture albums of their own. Tova had seen enough of Esther as a baby to last them all a lifetime. Tova had seen, in that same room, enough CNN news to last her three lifetimes. Tova's heart listed toward the east: this was not a pain she'd desired or invented. The air was hot, and moist. Her mother-in-law's house plants were limp, pale green.

Eleven o'clock. Time for mail delivery. Tova decided to check the lobby.

Back upstairs Tova sat at her mother-in-law's brown Formica dinette table and slit open another letter from Debra. A little square of paper fluttered out and fell to the floor. Tova held her breath and picked it up. It was a picture of Shira, signed with love to Esther.

Her letters were old-fashioned, Debra said, but she hated e-mail, and Debra picked up the conversation with Tova as if there had been no interruption. In the first letter Debra had caught on right away:

> *If Tova wished to get back, she might as well wish for Mike's father to die.*
>
> *Channie and Nachson Chaim moved to Katif, in Gaza. They got jobs and a little one-room trailer on a hydroponic vegetable farm. They were happy but the younger girls were afraid to take the bus out to visit them, so Channie was annoyed with the family for not coming out to see her new home.*
>
> *She knew all along.*

Knew what all along? thought Tova, annoyed. She was not at Number Four. She heard a horn braying outside. A boat or a car? she wondered.

> *Apparently Rachel Stanetsky was 35, younger than they thought, and she spent these last several months after her wedding in the hospital with Mr. Stanetsky where it was clear that her marital relationship blossomed, as she did, fuller and fuller, the lines on her face filling out with water weight until the women of the building knew she interviewed contractors to turn part of the balcony into a nursery. She'd ordered teak built-ins for the master bedroom, installed an extra-wide tub and two double beds.*
>
> *And, anytime anyone stopped in to visit her she was standing at the ironing board, ironing Mr. Stanetsky's shirts.*
>
> *Rachel managed quite nicely on her own, friendly but didn't socialize with the other women on Friday nights except once when she told them a funny thing. After he got out of intensive care, the medical service placed Mr. Stanetsky in a small rehab unit at Misgav Ladach, the hospital where most of the patients are there having*

*babies. Rachel was with him every day. On the first Friday night,*
*when he could button himself up in one of the* Shabbos *shirts she'd*
*ironed for him, Mr. Stanetsky—all by himself—said* Shabbos *ser-*
*vices for 100 women, Rachel included.*

*She earned him.*


And how was that? Tova thought.

"Who are you talking to?" her mother-in-law asked. Tova
noticed the sound of the TV was off. Her mother-in-law's face
looked as limp as her house plants, sleep lines hatched across her
left cheek.

"I just got a letter," Tova answered, knowing she wasn't
answering the question. She hadn't realized she'd been talking
out loud, talking to herself.

# EPILOGUE

27 *AV*, AUGUST 9

DEAR TOVA,

I'm almost changing my mind about the idea of earning something by suffering for it.

You write that this is the anniversary of your aliyah, that you would have been here a year.

You write how miserable you are sitting there in Florida, listening to the yachts whistle past the drawbridge, a whole traffic pattern changed for someone else's leisure. And then you wish you were here because this is your home? At Number Four we have to listen to the sound that Sandy makes and think about Yossi and Binny all the time. I wouldn't wish this on anyone.

I feel terrible that every time you called I could not speak, or not for more than a minute—anyhow. I could risk your friendship by saying exactly what you don't want to hear, that this is an experience you experience just by being in this place. There is a feeling, the families rumbling out of control. Everyone has a different way of showing he's not sleeping. The pitch is raised. The babies kink up—don't eat. The big kids get louder; they throw harder in the ball games. Then the games are impossible, breaking up after ten minutes. You know me—I start to yell.

Sandy plopped herself down in my kitchen yesterday and said she'd been trying to decide if all that lingering in the hospital was good or bad. Maybe the Altmans were lucky, she said, that everything happened with them right away. They even put up Binny's stone already. Did she regret, Sandy wondered, that she'd left Yossi with Nathan? But at least she had a chance to make a point, call attention. All the boys were doing was picking up the silk tefillin bag they'd ordered for Yossi's bar mitzvah and then going out for pizza. The army kept saying it was a minor incendiary— two kilos. But it blew out the back of the bus and Yossi and Binny were thrown into a drainage ditch. What I can't get over is how the bomber's family celebrate.

You've never seen Sandy so obsessed. She had to be out there on the road where it happened. The first couple of days she fought with everyone. The police; the Zaka men who had come to clean up the spot where Binny died and where the *chayelet*, the girl soldier, died. I understand why Sandy fought with them so much—it's like direct confrontation; the Zaka men are like a club, an exclusive club, wearing yellow and climbing around. They're worse than the Angel of Death, because when they come it has already happened. The *chayelet*, turned out she was just a kid nineteen years old, got here with her family from Kishinev two years ago. Sandy said they roped off the intersection until they got the blood wiped up from the rocks, the bramble. Did you know this? Because there was the girl's blood all over it, the Burial Society had to bury the bus seat the girl died on.

Sandy would spend half a day with Yossi in the hospital, and half a day demonstrating—some days in front of the *Knesset,* some days out on the road there with signs, calling the reporters. Half a dozen soldiers of her own, protecting her there. Binny and Yossi, suddenly the symbol of suffering for the land. Can you picture it?

Yossi was doing better, really fine. You called last Friday and I told you everything was fine.

Then, apparently, Yossi just shuddered. And then he smiled. Nathan was with him. That was it, Nathan said.

In Number Four we were already counting down to *Shabbos*, the kids taking baths, some of the little ones running around in their good clothes already, with their hair wet. I remember: the building was reeking. Ahuva's parents had just brought her a new microwave and she'd had a tinfoil fire. The hallways smelled like a welding torch. I was grinding potatoes and frying onions. I was looking at my sack of salt, and made a whole song out of my thinking, like wondering if I had enough or should I send Shira to the store, if the stores were even still open, or who could I borrow from. Then it seemed as if we all found out the same moment. Nathan called Rabbi Altman, and their second son ran over to tell Shira, then the next thing we're all down in the lobby, the smell of the welding torch sour, the air at the ceiling black. A couple of people coughing. I remember hearing Ahuva tell her daughter, the right thing to say is "Blessed is the true Judge."

We left everything. The ironing boards open, the pots on the stove. You would have thought it a ghost building. I left the potatoes in the grinder and later when I came home where it wasn't green it was gray and I had to throw it out. Shira was crying to come but we had to arrange the little kids and she's one of the oldest of the youngest and we made her stay back to watch them.

Out in the parking lot, Ahuva, of all people, got real efficient and figured out who went in which car. When we got to Har Hamenuchot, Sandy and Nathan, and of course Yossi and the Burial Society, were already there. I'd spent the whole day inside and I was surprised how so late in the afternoon the sun was still baking—you know, one of those days when it finally goes down and you feel like you've gone down with it.

Up there at the cemetery the ground crunched when you walked—I think I was being extra sensitive. We just followed the Burial Society. We had to walk quite a bit, to the back side of the mountain. Just before we got to Yossi's place, there, lounging across a row of pink headstones, was a family of cream-colored cats. They were licking their faces, washing behind their ears, and staring at us. Granny used to say cleaning cats are expecting guests. We were their guests.

At the grave site, Rabbi Altman said something about Yossi being a gift, and about having to return him.

Rabbi Shapiro said something about *gilgulim,* how souls recycle and return.

Nathan was absolutely quiet and Rabbi Altman kept him next to him, whispering, showing him things in the prayer book.

By the time we were done it was close to candle-lighting time. We were walking on top of our shadows, what with the way the mountain blocked the light. The Burial Society turned on floodlights. We descended on Jerusalem in a beam, like we were the angels coming down to earth—instead of the opposite, instead of watching someone ascend. We walked down to the cars, our feet practically cut off at the ankles. I couldn't feel my body either. I looked for the cats, had a strong feeling to tell them to go be with Yossi, but on the way back the cats were not there anymore.

As she got in the car Sandy cried that cry I started to tell you about—and it's a sound I can't remember ever hearing, except maybe out in the woods when I was a kid, or a sound that I *thought* I heard out in the woods when I was a kid. Like a bear, maybe. But broken.

At the shiva one night, Rabbi Altman, who's got his hands full, said, it is the heavenly wheel, turning.

Nathan seems to hear those things, not Sandy.

Sandy always has an answer, like "turn it back."

I see Rabbi Altman come over every day now with a book under his arm and Nathan walks Rabbi Altman home with a lot of talking and hand gestures.

Mr. S bought three house trailers and a Torah scroll and settled a minyan of students out on that bald hill beyond the radar. That's where they said the kaddish for Binny too, and I think he's going to make a school there.

I feel as if I'm waiting for Sandy to disappear and join Yossi.

Then when I stop feeling I start thinking about how unhappy you are being stuck over there and—I'm not any great letter writer—but just so you'll know, there is some part of us that is not here either and we are *home*. We end up with the same questions: can we bear these distances?

> Your loving friend,
> Debra